Ascension

MORGEN RICH

and

BRIAN RATHBONE

ISBN: 1-945465-04-2
ISBN-13: 978-1-945465-04-8

DEDICATION

For our readers.

The Greatland
Northern Wastes
Sylva
Faulk
Adderhold
Lankland
Mundleboro
Astor
Endland
Westland
Vasterberg
Southland
N
W
E
S

ACKNOWLEDGMENTS

Special thanks to Andrea Howe for her editing.

ASCENSION

Chapter 1
A life well lived is a life well earned.
--Margaretta Ahlgren, mother

* * *

Gwendolin yanked the wash-worn coverlet up to meet the stuffed sackcloth that was little more than a lump she laid her head on when she slept. Stepping back, she assessed her work then smoothed the wrinkles in the coverlet. Her grandmother would never be satisfied with the way Gwen made her bed. "You're too careless, too hurried. You have no discipline, child," she would scold. Gwen knew her grandmother was right about always being in a rush and not caring about many of the things the old woman put so much stock in. What did it matter if her cot was untidy? Nobody would see it. Why shouldn't she rush through her chores? She had more important things to do than sweep away winter's cobwebs and air out stale feather beds. With winter ended, spring school sessions would be starting, and Gwen had finally reached the age of decision. She had reached her late teens, and that meant she could decide which type of education she would specialize in for the remaining two years of study.

She stepped onto her cot and stood on tiptoes, fingertips clinging to the rotted windowsill, and peered outside through the sheer curtains. Her grandmother, clothespins clamped between aged teeth, reached into a basket and shook out most of the wrinkles and excess water from Gwendolin's father's shirt before draping it over the rope strung between the tall pigpen gate and the top wire of the chicken coop.

Gwen ducked down before her grandmother could look toward the cottage and spot her. She sprang off the bed, which creaked in complaint. With her grandmother busy behind the cottage, Gwen escaped cleanly out the front door and avoided being assigned yet another chore.

Winter had crawled to an end, and Gwen was eager to see her friends in town and hear what choices they intended to make when the traveling schoolmistress pressed them for their decisions. Of course, Gwen would have to avoid the butcher shop, but she had become adept at slipping past while her father was rapt in service to the patrons. Jacob Ahlgren, Vasterberg's butcher, was nothing if not attentive to the people who visited his tiny shop. "Folks with means don't care 'bout nobody but themselves," he always said. "They want to feel like every piece of meat's been specially cut and cured for them." That was exactly how Jacob treated the Westlanders with enough money that they didn't have to hunt for their food or slaughter their own livestock--as if they, like the meat they bought from him, were special.

Today she didn't have to slink through town in the midst of a crowd to get to her best friend's house at the far end of the main road that ran through town, though. Gilly met her as she approached Vasterberg.

"Gwen! I was coming to get you. You have to see who's come to town. They're magnificent!" Gilly's grin spread wide, and so did her arms as she rushed toward Gwen.

The two girls clashed in a hug and spun 'round and 'round. When Gwen released her friend and stepped back, Gilly's exuberant proclamation continued as if it hadn't been interrupted by the warm hug of a friend she'd not seen for almost four months.

"You'll never guess. Not in a million years. Aren't you going to guess? Go on. Guess!"

Gwen laughed and shrugged. "Who has come to Vasterberg?"

"No! You have to guess."

"The crown prince of an exotic land?"

Gilly shook her head so hard Gwen thought her friend's fluttering locks would lift her off the ground and send her spinning back down like a whirling seed pod.

"I give up, Gilly. Who's come to town?"

Gilly reached into the purse on her belt and pulled out a folded parchment, handing it to Gwen, who examined it before unfolding it. It was poorly made, probably the off-cast of a crier's apprentice, too unevenly dipped to use for documents meant to last a long time but good enough to sell at a discount to pay for more supplies. As she unfolded it and held it out in front of her, light streamed through in spots where the cotton fibers were so sparse that even the slightest touch of a quill would have torn through.

Before Gwen could read the sloppy words scribbled inside the lines of a drawing, or even make out what the drawing was, Gilly started bouncing up and down, squealing and pointing to the writing, "They call themselves 'The Hermetic Circus, a Masquerade of Spectacle and Magic.'"

Gwen laughed. "That's a long name. Whatever does it mean?" She studied the drawing and saw it contained a roughly sketched cauldron, crude stars, and a stag. The stag was the only image with detail, its antlers majestic atop a proudly held head.

"Mother says they're just a troupe of actors and charlatans, that none of them know any *real* magic, but you know Mother. She's never liked it when someone thinks they know more about healing than she does." She pointed to a line that read, "Magical Health Elixir--See what it can do for you!"

What Gilly said about her mother was true. Mignon Bastwick was Vasterberg's hedge witch, and she guarded her role with as much diligence as she put into every concoction she made for coughs or smudge sticks she bundled for warding off evil spirits. Gwen had always liked her, in part because Mignon had been the best friend of her dead mother and had treated Gwen with utter kindness. It had been Mignon who had stood up to her grandmother and father when they'd forbidden Gwen to attend the lessons of the traveling schoolmistress. "Margaretta was well educated. She would rise from the grave if she knew you were trying to keep her daughter ignorant. Shame on you!" she'd scolded. And in the end, she'd won the argument and convinced them to allow Gwen to come to town three times each week from spring until winter. Gwen would be forever grateful to Mignon for that. But there was another reason she'd always liked Mignon. She was an adept herbalist, and she freely shared her knowledge with both Gilly and Gwen, though it became apparent early on that Gwen was the more gifted of the two girls when it came to identifying plants and memorizing their properties and uses. Mignon's generosity had, in fact, helped Gwen develop her ability to learn, and that had earned her a reputation as Vasterberg's most bright and talented student.

"There's only one way to find out if your mother is right," Gwen said. "Did she forbid you to go to a performance?"

"Not exactly," said Gilly. "She said it would be a waste of the money I've been saving and that I had to finish all my chores before the Day of Rest. She said if I decide to toss away my earnings to gawk at traveling swindlers, then it would have to be on the one day when I don't have chores. Oh, and I'm not allowed to go alone."

Gwen laughed. Mignon had never minced words. "Well, then, we'll just have to see that you get all your chores done. How much does it cost to see the performance?"

Gilly scrunched up her nose as if she'd just stepped on a stinkbug. "A bronze piece."

"Ohhh." Gwen's enthusiasm sank. "Maybe one of the other girls . . . I don't have a bronze piece. I can't go with you. I'm sorry." She handed the parchment back to Gilly, who stuffed it into her small leather purse.

"You don't have a bronze piece *yet*," she said, a mischievous grin stretching her lips. "As I was coming through town, I passed the stables. The widow Crookstaff was fussing at the stablemaster something awful. She said she needs chives for her venison and turnip pies, and she was all afluster because the stablemaster's barn cat dug up the bulbs in her garden sometime during the winter. It must have smelled a vole." Gilly shuddered and Gwen understood why. Neither of the two cared for vermin of any kind. "Anyway, she has no chives, and one of the councilman's wives is planning a party for some dear friend's relative who is coming to visit. She's ordered thirty whole pies! But the widow Crookstaff said her back is too stiff to go looking for chives in the meadows. I thought she was going to smack the stablemaster with her wooden spoon when he said, 'And what do you want me to do about that?' She saw me and said, 'Pay Gilly to find some. It was your cat!' The poor man agreed to do it. I think because he wanted her to just go away. People were starting to stop and stare." Gilly grinned, the pride in her solution to Gwen's finance shortage beaming. "A whole bronze piece if we bring back enough to replant her garden!"

Gwen threw her arms around Gilly and squeezed until her friend grunted. "You're the best friend ever, Gilly Bastwick, and I know just where to find chives!"

* * *

Gilly's plan gave Gwen a reason not to sneak through town. The pair walked hand in hand straight to Jacob's butcher shop, where he stood with a cleaver in hand and the leg of some unfortunate spring lamb splayed before him on his cutting table.

"Hello, Father," said Gwen, letting go of her friend's hand long enough to approach her father and kiss his cheek. She was careful not to brush against his bloody apron, a lesson she'd learned by ruining many a dress.

Jacob looked around Gwen and smiled at her friend, who was standing with hands folded in front of her own crisp and clean apron. "Well, if it isn't Gilly Bastwick. You've grown, lassie! You'll be as tall as your father if you don't stop soon."

"Hello, Master Ahlgren," Gilly said politely. "My mother says the same thing."

"And how is your mother?"

"Busy, as usual, sir. Mistress Coopersmith's twins have the croup, and old man Theron -- I mean, Farmer Theron -- has lumbago and gout. Mother is running about delivering medicinals and preparing new stock. She says this spring will be particularly difficult for those who wheeze and sniffle when the wind blows, but that the alfalfa crop will be abundant."

"That's good news for those of us with livestock to feed. The milk cows will be fat and happy, and we'll have butter to slather on our bread. A sneeze is a small price to pay for such a grand gift if you ask me." He laughed in the full-bellied way that embarrassed Gwen because it was the unreserved laugh of the lower classes. When he did it in the shop, it made her want to hide under his cutting table. "Please give your mother my best, and tell her I'll call on her soon to discuss our annual trade."

"Yes, sir. I will."

"Father, we've been asked to collect chives for the widow Crookstaff. Do you have a bucket we could borrow?" Though certain Mignon would have a bucket or gathering basket they could borrow, getting one from her father justified the unexpected visit into town with Gilly and might, just might, stave off a harsh scolding from her grandmother.

Jacob set down his meat cleaver and rummaged through the tins and pots on a shelf in the corner until he turned around, a bucket swinging from a rope handle in the three curled fingers and stub of his right hand. He'd lost a finger during his apprenticeship, but he hadn't let the missing digit dissuade him from learning the craft he'd chosen when he'd reached the age of decision. He'd learned to balance the nub against the meat he was slicing and use it to shove the uncut meat toward his knife.

Gwen hated seeing it. It, too, embarrassed her and reminded her of the shortcomings of the Ahlgren family's status. They were shopkeepers, tradespeople, and she was just the butcher's daughter. "Thank you," she said, retrieving the bucket from her father's grasp and pecking his cheek before she turned, grabbed Gilly by a hand she thought of as perfect and noble in its own way, and skipped out of the butcher's shop with her friend yelling over her shoulder, "Good day, Master Ahlgren!"

"Why didn't you tell him about the bronze coin and the Hermetic Circus?" Gilly asked when the pair reached Mignon's garden shed. They slipped inside to get a spade before running off toward the meadow at the edge of the woods, where Gwen remembered seeing the purple blossoms that topped chive plants.

"Because I'm not going to tell him I'm going," Gwen finally responded when they stopped to dig up a chive plant.

"But won't he be angry?"

Gwen shrugged. "Probably, but if I tell him, he'll want to discuss it with Grandmother, and she won't let me go. You know how she is, Gilly." Gwen viciously attacked the soft soil under the bulb of the chive plant.

"She worries about you . . . because of what happened to your mother. That's all."

Gwen looked up at Gilly, her cheeks flushed with the anger seething in her. "My mother died. It wasn't her fault. It wasn't anyone's fault. That wolf was sick with the foaming disease. It never would have attacked her if it had been well."

If Gilly was pained by Gwen's lashing out, she didn't show it. Instead, her expression was compassionate. "I know. Your mother was her child, though. And you're all she has left of her."

"I know." Gwen sighed and returned her gaze to the task that was going to net her some excitement other than a scolding. Carefully, she lifted the bulb of the chive plant out of the dirt and shook off its roots. "That's one. About fifty more, and we'll be done."

Gilly giggled and Gwen was grateful for the change of mood and topic.

The pair worked their way through a patch of chives at the edge of the meadow where the sun shone brightest and had melted the winter snow first. Their bucket almost full with enough plants to replenish the widow Crookstaff's cat-raided garden, they decided to hunt for plants as they made their way back to Gilly's house. Before they got to the spot where the woods ended, a sharp crack of a breaking branch stopped them.

All Gwen could think of was the wolf that had attacked her mother. Gilly's terrified expression said that she was thinking the same thing. Gwen froze in place and whispered, "Don't run and don't turn your back on it. If it comes toward us, wave your hands. On three, turn around and start yelling at it." She handed the spade to her friend. "Use this. I'll use the bucket." Gwen tightened her grip on the rope her father's deformed hand had held not two hours before. How she wished now that it were his hand holding it again.

Gilly nodded ever so slightly.

"One. Two. Three!" The girls spun around and started screaming, their arms flailing in the air.

Chapter 2
Few things are as deceptive as appearances.
--The Pauper King

* * *

Staring back at them was an unlikely pair--Thomlin Frank, the miller's son, and Rolf Rosenkranz, a rough-and-tumble son of a local hunter. Gwen hadn't seen either of the Rosenkranzes in years. Rolf had left lessons when he was ten, and like his father, he'd avoided Vasterberg and its citizens.

"Umm. We mean you no harm." Rolf was the one who spoke, his hands raised in the air. His bow, slung over a shoulder beside a quiver full of arrows, still rocked side to side from the rapid lifting of his arms.

"What are you doing in these woods? Why were you spying on us?" Gwen demanded, her heart still pounding hard from the startle she'd just had. She avoided eye contact with Rolf, but even his presence made her all the more nervous.

He slowly lowered his hands and flashed a broad smile. "We were just hunting."

"Hunting for what?" Gwen pressed.

"Food," said Rolf. "Squirrels, rabbits." He held up a rope, the end of which looped around the ankle of a wide-eyed hare.

"Eww," Gilly said. Gwen wanted to smack her for showing any weakness to these dullards.

"It won't hurt you. It's dead." Rolf gave a little laugh as he shook the rope and made the dead hare bounce. His other hand secured behind his ear wavy locks escaping the ponytail at the nape of his neck.

"Rolf!" Thomlin scolded. "Be nice."

"Do you have permission to hunt in these woods?" Gwen asked, one hand moving to her hip.

"Gwen! What's wrong with you? They haven't done anything wrong," Gilly squeaked.

Rolf gave a knowing nod and grinned, again his fingers taming stray locks. "Ah, so that's who you are. I wasn't sure. You've . . . changed."

An awkward silence followed, during which Gwen acknowledged the confusion this dark-haired boy made her feel. He was an arrogant little twit. At the same time, his grin was devastatingly cute, and his dimples made it impossible not to look at cheekbones chiseled by too few and lean meals, sun-darkened skin that she couldn't help but think would glisten after a much-needed steamy bath, and shoulder-length waves of hair the color of oak barrels. His hair betrayed a tendency toward orderliness every time he reached up and pushed an escaped lock behind an ear. It made Gwen want to smile. He'd definitely changed since she'd seen him last.

"And you, fair lady, by what name go you?" asked Rolf, sweeping his arm across his stomach and bending into an exaggerated, low bow.

"Her name is none of your business," Gwen replied. "Be on your way."

"Gilly! Short for Gillian, named after my great-great-great-great grandmother."

"It's a beautiful name," said Thomlin. He whispered to Rolf, but the breeze caught it. He may as well have said the words aloud. "She's the Gilly I was telling you about."

Gilly giggled and Gwen wanted to smack her atop her curly hair. "Come on, Gilly. We have to go. We are *expected*."

"We are?"

The boys chuckled in unison.

"We *are*." She held up the bucket of chives. "My father will want his bucket back before he closes the shop for the day." She smirked at Rolf. "He knows where we are and what we're doing. He'll come looking for us if we don't return soon."

Rolf shrugged. "Like your friend said, we haven't done anything wrong."

Thomlin stretched out a hand in front of Rolf, as if he were holding him back from stepping forward. "You should get back before it gets much later. I'll see you again when Mistress Bourgogne returns, I hope." The way he smiled at Gilly made it apparent his kind words were meant for her and not for Gwen. "And I'm sorry if we frightened you."

Gwen grabbed Gilly's hand and turned back toward Vasterberg, her skirt flapping so hard from the abruptness of her movement that it snapped with a sting against her legs. She managed not to wince until her back was to the two boys. She fought the urge to turn around, in part because she didn't want them to know she cared if they followed and in part because she didn't want to be disappointed if they weren't behind her and Gilly. Instead, she listened for their footsteps, and when she was sure she'd heard none and they'd gone far enough to be out of earshot, she shook off Gilly's hand.

"What's the matter?"

"You shouldn't have told them my name or yours. We don't know anything about Rolf anymore. He's been gone from lessons a long time," Gwen said.

"But we know Thomlin, and we kind of know Rolf." Gilly giggled. "And aren't they handsome?"

Gwen rounded on her friend. "Gilly Bastwick. What would your mother say?"

"Since when do you care what any adult has to say? What's wrong with you? You were rude to those boys. They were just looking for food. Didn't you see how gaunt Rolf has become? He looks like he hasn't eaten in a week. You should be ashamed of yourself, Gwen."

Gilly's outburst came as a surprise. Her friend had never spoken a cross word to her in all the years they'd known each other, and now she had, and Gwen felt ashamed for scolding her and for not noticing the boys approaching. It was unlike her not to be observant. She took her best friend's hand in hers again. "I'm sorry. I don't know what got into me. I guess I'm angry with myself for not hearing them sooner. They surprised me. It's just . . ."

"Just what?"

"Just that it reminded me of what happened to my mother."

Compassion filled Gilly's tone when she spoke. "But that was a sick wolf, Gwen, not two hungry boys."

Gwen felt even more ashamed. She'd heard rumors that Rolf's father was cruel to him and that his withdrawal from lessons was because his father insisted he was needed to help with hunting. "I know. I'm sorry I yelled at you."

The two friends resumed the walk to Vasterberg hand in hand, Gilly's bubbling excitement about the circus infecting Gwen and taking her mind off what had just happened. In exchange for a bucket brimming with chive plants, the widow Crookstaff paid Gilly the bronze coin the stablemaster had given her. Once they'd left the baker's cottage, Gilly handed the coin to Gwen. "There. We can go to one of two performances. Noon or afternoon on Rest Day. Which shall it be?"

"Noon. Let's be the first to see it."

"Ooh. Good idea, Gwen. Tomorrow, I'll show you where they're camped. They're magnificent."

"You said that."

"Because they are! You'll see."

Gwen felt less upset about their earlier spat when Gilly smiled and shared her natural enthusiasm. That was the Gilly she'd come to think of as her only close friend, her best friend, a girl as close to her as any sister could have been. Gwen squeezed Gilly's hand. "Thank you for finding a way we can go together. It will be magnificent."

"It will!"

The two laughed as they wove through a thinning crowd to the market street. They finally reached the butcher shop, where they vigorously scrubbed the bucket and spade while Gwen's father put away his own tools. After he closed and locked the shop door, Gilly headed for home, and Gwen walked back to the farm with her father.

"Grandmother will probably be angry with me."

"Oh? Why?"

"I didn't tell her I was leaving."

Her father sighed. "Gwen. She worries about you because she loves you."

"I know, Father. It's just that she is so stern and never lets me have any fun or see or do anything new. Mother wasn't like her at all. She let me play with friends and took me with her everywhere." Gwen stopped speaking, overwhelmed by sadness as she remembered a time her mother *hadn't* taken her along--her mother's last day. Maybe she would be alive if Gwen had been with her that day. Guilt stabbed at her in the silence.

"Tell her you came to the shop . . . which is true." His tone and careful word selection Gwen knew to mean he was going to cover for her once again. "And don't mention trotting off with Gilly."

"Thank you, Father."

* * *

Suppertime went almost as Gwen had expected. Her grandmother scowled through the meal and glared at her every time she contributed to the conversation. After several attempts at idle chitchat, Gwen fell silent and listened as her father recounted the news his customers had shared with him. Master Narth had come in for pork and said he'd heard from a cousin in the east that the Zjhon were building their forces again, that they'd conscripted a few boys from the outskirts of the Lankland capital and moved them to the Southland coast to train on great ships. Mistress Theron, the wife of Farmer Theron, had reported that a troupe of wagons had set up camp on the western edge of Vasterberg. She was sure it was they who had stolen her chickens. After picking up her sausages, she headed straight to the constable's office to file a complaint. That tidbit knotted Gwen's stomach. She hoped the circus wouldn't be forced to leave before the Day of Rest performances.

"The widow Crookstaff came in and placed a large order for venison. Seems she's going to bake her famous meat pies for a welcoming party Councilman Grayston's wife will be holding for a visitor from Sutherhold, the daughter of a dear friend from her childhood. I told her I didn't have that much venison, and she was beside herself, I tell you, beside herself."

"That's a pity, Jacob. We could have used the gains from a sale that large. Why, the curtains in Gwen's room are threadbare." She shot a glare at Gwen, and it irked the girl that her grandmother had such an underhanded way of chiding her father for making a meager livelihood. Part of her wanted to smirk and say that the curtains had been thick enough to obscure her grandmother's view before she'd sneaked away.

"Not to worry, Mother. I calmed her down. Told her I could fill the order by the date she needs it."

"But how, Jacob? Who will run your shop while you're hunting?"

Her father grinned and winked at Gwen. "Early this morning, Thomlin

Frank came into the shop with another boy. Turns out he's the son of Rastof Rosenkranz. I think his name's Roland or Randall or something like that. The boy seems to be an excellent hunter."

Rolf, thought Gwen, as she choked on her food. Her father slapped her on the back, and she swallowed the piece of potato that had lodged in her throat. She took a drink of water to wash it down.

"He sold me a whole boar, and every bit of the meat was good. A single hole in the head, right above its snout." Her father placed his fingertip between his eyes then removed it and laughed. "Imagine that. A boy who can kill a boar with a single arrow. Well, don't you know I hired those two on the spot. Told them I needed some wild hare and squirrel. They'll be back tomorrow, and we'll see if Rosenkranz is as good as Thomlin says he is. If Thomlin's right, I'll send them out to bring down a buck or a couple of fawnless older does if the herd's too large. A single shot." He laughed again and dipped his spoon into the stew.

Gwen rose from the table and started clearing the dirty dishes. She didn't want any questions from her grandmother, who had seen her come home with her father and hadn't pressed either of them about Gwen's disappearance. She didn't want to have to lie. But most of all, she didn't want to tell her family about the scare they'd given her and Gilly. Any reminder of her mother's death usually resulted in a tighter rein for a while, and a tighter rein might stop her from being able to attend the circus with Gilly.

After she'd cleaned up the table and cooking utensils, Gwen's father called her to come sit beside him near the hearth. Her grandmother had already picked up her sewing basket and was busy darning one of Jacob's wool socks. Gwen settled onto a low stool and put her own sewing basket in her lap. It held an array of minor projects, none of which she'd completed--a handkerchief awaiting embroidery on one of its edges, a kitchen cloth with rough hem, a cotton shift with a sleeve that needed mending.

"Your grandmother and I want to talk with you about Mistress Bourgogne's visit. She'll be here in a few days if I remember correctly."

"Yes, Father. Soon after Rest Day."

"Someday, you may need to care for yourself. I won't live forever," her grandmother said.

As cross and coarse as her grandmother could be, Gwen did love her, and she didn't like to think about her dying.

"What your grandmother is saying is that we'd like you to choose one of two paths for your education moving forward, something that will give both of us peace of mind that no matter what happens to either of us, you'll get along well and want for nothing."

"Oh, spit it out, Jacob. You treat her like the tender shoot of a frail flower."

Her father frowned at his mother-in-law, but his look softened when he gazed back down at Gwen. "I've not done too badly as a butcher."

"But I don't want to be a butcher, Father."

Jacob let out an unreserved laugh. "Of course not, my sweet girl, but having a shop is a stable way to earn a living, whether it be butcher or baker. The widow Crookstaff won't live forever, and she has no children to keep her bakery once she's gone. Aged as she is, I'm sure she'd be happy for the help of an apprentice."

Gwen couldn't believe what she was hearing. Did her father really believe her talents would be best suited for baking? Hadn't he noticed that every meal she ever cooked ended up burned or raw, every loaf of bread hard and dry?

"That or the monastery," said her grandmother.

"What?! The monastery?" shrieked Gwen, jumping up off the stool in such a fluster that she dumped the contents of her sewing basket onto the aged wood-plank floor, sending her pin cushion rolling toward the fire.

Her grandmother stuck out a foot and stopped the hay-filled ball from certain destruction. "Yes, the monastery. You need discipline, child. You are lazy, disobedient, and keep the worst of company."

Gwen fumed at the slander of Gilly, who was sweet, kind, and polite to everyone she met, even Gwen's grandmother. "If you're talking about Gilly, you take that back. She's never done anything to you or anyone else."

"She's the daughter of a hedge witch. Nothing but a ragamuffin whose loathsome mother allows her to consort with--"

Jacob raised his voice to intervene. "That will be enough, Mother. You aren't helping."

But there was no consoling or quieting Gwen. Her grandmother had pushed her beyond the point of self-control. "Consort with whom, Grandmother? With me? The daughter of a poor butcher with worn-out socks and the grandchild of a bitter old hag?"

As soon as she'd spoken the words, Gwen regretted them, but it was too late to take them back.

Her father's voice boomed, "Go to your room at once, Gwendolin Ahlgren, and don't come out until you are prepared to apologize to your grandmother."

Her vision blurred, Gwen stumbled to her bed and threw herself onto it. She struggled to hold back the tears, intent on not crying, but the tears came of their own accord. She couldn't believe her father had conceded to her grandmother's wishes. Gilly's mother's talk with them so many years ago clearly hadn't been enough. Her grandmother controlled her life, and if she had her way, Gwen would be either a frumpy housewife who baked for people richer than she or an old maid nun who walked the grounds of a drafty monastery in silence. How could her father have wanted that for her? She would never forgive either of them. Through sheer will and one thought, she managed not to sob. *I will do what I want and have what I want, you hateful old woman and spineless man.*

Chapter 3

*Destiny is like smoke on the wind; the harder you try to chase it, the less likely you
are to enjoy it.*

--unknown philosopher

* * *

Before the speckled rooster crowed, Gwen rose from her bed and
dressed in a fresh shift and apron. Her sleep-filled eyes strained to see the
way to the hearth, but she managed the trek without stumbling over
anything or making any noise. She started a fire and went outside to draw
water from the well. After she'd set a kettle of water on the hook in the
fireplace, she went back outside and gathered wood to replenish the kitchen
stock. By the time the rooster sounded off and her father and grandmother
came out of their tiny rooms at the back of the cottage, she'd set the table
with sliced bread and goat cheese and fed the chickens.

"Good morning," she said in a solemn tone and kissed the cheeks of
both her father and grandmother. "I apologize for being disrespectful last
night. I'll try to be more mindful of my tongue and temper."

Her father smiled at her. "I know you're upset, Gwen. We just want
what's best for you."

Gwen nodded but said nothing in response. She had a few more days
before Mistress Bourgogne arrived in Vasterberg, and she hoped she'd be
able to reason with her father and convince him to let her choose her own
path before then. If not, perhaps Gilly's mother could reason with him.
He'd said he would be stopping in to see her, and Gwen had every
intention of recruiting Mignon's aid when she went to help Gilly with her
chores. This was a battle for the rest of her life, her very happiness, and she
was going to mount an attack on as many fronts as she could.

"Sit down and eat, Gwen. I'll be in as soon as I feed the chickens."

"I've already fed them, Father."

Jacob gave an approving nod. "And I see you've brought in more
firewood too."

She turned to her grandmother. "Are there any chores you need me to
take care of today, Grandmother? Please, let me make up for my outburst."

"Chores won't cure your willfulness."

Sleep and an apology hadn't softened her grandmother. Gwen gritted
her teeth until she knew she could speak respectfully and calmly. "You're
right, Grandmother, but at least let me make your workload easier today.
Let me make *some* amends. I truly regret speaking the way I did." What she
said was true. She did have regrets. Having been unkind to her mother's
mother, she'd made her cause more difficult in the process. She'd have to

work harder than ever to win over her father to her way of thinking.

"Air out your bed and sweep the floors."

"Yes, Grandmother."

She'd barely bitten into the sliced bread when her grandmother added, "And then you can slop the pigs."

Gwen stopped chewing her bread. Though she remained silent, her mind screamed out in protest at the cruelty of her grandmother's punishment. The old woman was well aware Gwen was deathly afraid of pigs and the way they rushed at her when they saw the slop bucket. This was beyond unfair. Gwen finished her meal in silence, kissed her father good-bye before he left the cottage, and started the chores she'd been assigned. Dread swelled in her when she swept the floors and opened the door to brush out the pile of dirt her broom had collected. It loomed over her as she opened the window to her room and stuffed half the lumpy feather bed through the opening, the pigpen in clear sight. Finally, she could delay the task no longer. She held her breath as she lifted the lid to the slop bucket. It was a wasted effort; the rancid smell of the previous night's meal, along with scraps of spoiled vegetables her father traded for bones and fat trimmings, rushed into her nostrils. She gagged and quickly tossed in the remnants of their breakfast before slamming the lid back down, sending a gush of the putrid odor into the room with such force that the whole kitchen reeked.

Grabbing the bucket handle, she rushed outside before the scent overwhelmed her. Every step was a trudge, as if the worn path were knee-deep mud. It wasn't, of course. There'd been no rain for a week, and the ground was still hard from winter's last freeze. Though she tried not to draw the pigs' attention, their snouts had caught the scent of the slop, and the entire passel raced for the gate.

"Get back!" she yelled as they stormed toward her. She threw the container's lid at them, but the stampede kept coming. Tilting the bucket, which was swinging wildly by now, she ran along the feed trough, spilling slop into it. As it hit the wooden feeder, it splashed and splattered, and some of it landed on her apron. Gwen didn't care. She just wanted out of the pigpen. With the swine distracted by crowding around the feeder and snarling at each other when one pushed its way into a space too narrow to fit into, Gwen ran out of the pen, picking up the tossed lid with a swoop on her way to the gate. Once safely outside, she secured the latch then turned around and leaned against the gatepost. She was out of breath, and her heart raced. A whiff of the slop on her clothing made her groan. She'd have to wash her apron before she left for Gilly's. Yet another chore.

Just then, one of the hogs attacked, or so it seemed to Gwen, who let out a screech. She spun around to see a small pig on the other side of the gate, snorting and snuffling the dirt where some of the slop had splashed out of the bucket when she'd removed the lid. It blew out another snort and sent a cloud of dirt flying between the gate's pickets and onto Gwen's bare legs. And then the sound of a low laugh wafted past her. She looked up to see her grandmother at the cottage door with a snaggle-toothed grin.

Humiliation flushed Gwen's cheeks as tears stung her eyes. She dropped the bucket and took off at a full run toward the road.

* * *

"You truly do smell awful," Gilly said as she helped Gwen remove the slop-stained apron. "We'll dip it in the wash bucket and let it sit there for a while. Besides, you look like you could use a warm mug of one of Mother's concoctions."

Gwen ran the sleeve of her shift across her cheeks, dabbing at tears still escaping her reddened eyes even though she fought to hold them back. Sniffling, she recounted her horrid encounter. "She knows I'm afraid. Father always slops the pigs. It wasn't a chore of hers." She broke down into sobs again. "Why did she laugh at me? Does she hate me that much?"

It was Mignon Bastwick who interrupted Gwen's rambling. "Make sure that apron is fully submerged, Gilly. Then come inside with us." She placed an arm around Gwen's shoulder and ushered her into the two-room cottage barely larger than her father's storefront butcher shop.

Guiding the sniffling girl to a rickety wooden chair in front of the fireplace, Mignon set to work mixing herbs in the methodical way Gwen had always admired. In a stone bowl, she crushed a pinch of chamomile flowers and tossed in a sprinkling of dried lavender. Next, she added blue-green leaves, the pungent scent of which Gwen recognized as lemon balm. Mignon stirred the mixture together and sniffed it before reaching for a tin on the top shelf of her sideboard. Out of it, she pulled a clump of chopped leaves and stems and dropped them into the bowl. Picking up and dropping the mixture from her fingers, she rubbed the components of her concoction together, bending over it and wafting the smell up to her nose several times before she seemed satisfied. There was nothing happenstance about Mignon when she worked with plants and oils.

"What are the stems and leaves you took from the tin?" asked Gwen.

"Skullcap."

"What are its properties?"

Gwen caught a partial smile in Mignon's expression as she dumped the mixture onto a cheesecloth square, which she tied into a bundle with a short length of twine, and dropped it into an empty mug.

"It relaxes."

"Like the chamomile, lemon balm, and lavender?" Gwen asked.

"Much stronger. It should never be mixed with valerian root, catnip, or kava."

"Why?"

"Too strong. The drinker of such a tea could fall asleep and never awaken."

Gwen nodded and made a mental note of the warning. She trusted the hedge witch's judgment without question when it came to knowing exactly which recipe to use for any condition or illness. She wished she had thought to bring the leather-bound record she kept of what she learned about medicinal plants. Rarely had she come to Gilly's house without bringing it. She'd have to remember to write this new knowledge down when she returned home.

As Mignon retrieved a kettle hanging over the edge of the fire, she spoke in a quiet and comforting tone. "She doesn't hate you. She's filled with fear and has been for a long while now." Steam rolled upward, and the woman leaned away from it when she tilted the kettle and poured the boiling water into the mug.

Gwen stretched forward to see if the bundle floated, and she caught the corners of Mignon's thin lips curling slightly upward.

"Let it sit a bit and infuse completely."

"Where do you find the plant, and what does it look like?"

Mignon chuckled. "A bit like other mints, but with spear-shaped leaves and blue or bluish-purple, long-throated flowers that cluster near the tips of a stalk much like foxglove. You'll find it on a sunny slope with moist soil but not too much sunlight. I'll show you the next time we forage."

The thought of gathering flowers and herbs and all manner of plants with Mignon made Gwen smile. She savored their time together.

Just then, Gilly came in. "I'm so glad we don't have pigs," she said, dunking her hands into the washbasin before drying them on a piece of what Gwen recognized as one of Gilly's old skirts recycled into a rag.

"You're fortunate you don't!" said Gwen, taking the mug of herb tea Mignon offered her.

"And if you didn't have pigs, then many of us wouldn't have sausage, would we?" the woman said. "There are many unpleasant things in nature we must endure if we are to reap their rewards."

"I could live without sausage," Gwen insisted.

"Perhaps," said Mignon, "but your father's trade would be diminished were that so."

Gwen thought about her father, and she felt pained at how he would react to her running away from her grandmother, but that feeling was squashed by another. "My father didn't stop her."

Mignon sighed and took a seat on the other hard wooden chair by the fire. She motioned for Gilly to sit on the stool near her, and when the girl had taken the spot, Mignon reached down and began to run her slender fingers through Gilly's hair, upsweeping it and separating it into strands. As her fingers manipulated the segments of hair into braids, she kept her gaze on the task she was performing. "Your grandmother is fearful because you remind her of herself."

"What do you mean? I am nothing like my grandmother."

"Drink the tea, and I'll tell you a story. Maybe it will help you to understand your grandmother."

Gwen complied, never thinking for a second not to, though she doubted there was anything about her that resembled her grandmother. Nonetheless, she was curious to hear what Mignon had to say, so she listened as she sipped her tea.

"When your grandmother was about your age and her eyesight was still keen, she had already become quite a talented seamstress. Did you know that?"

Gwen shrugged. She'd seen the beautiful dress that her grandmother had made for her parents' wedding celebration.

"At the beginning of the spring your grandmother was to reach the Age of Decision, she was offered an apprenticeship under the tutelage of a well-known and respected tailor in the east. It was quite the news in Vasterberg, according to my mother's account of it," she said.

"Why?"

"It was scandalous for womenfolk to fill the apprenticeships of menfolk, who would need the work to feed their families. Despite all her parents' efforts, she was willful and determined to have her way. When they outright forbade her to accept the apprenticeship, she fled to the east before they knew she was even gone."

Gwen wrinkled her brow. "I don't remember ever hearing that my grandmother went to the east. She's never mentioned it, and neither have my parents."

"That's because she didn't stay, Gwen, and I doubt it's something she's proud of. The parents of a boy who had expected to be placed in the apprenticeship made an awful fuss about the whole situation. Your great grandparents were derided for raising an unruly and disrespectful girl who had stolen the livelihood of a boy. Customers stopped bringing their horses into her father's blacksmith's shop to be shod.

"The family almost starved that winter. In the end, they couldn't bear being ostracized by the people of Vasterberg. They made an agreement with a farmer that he could marry your grandmother if he would pay someone to find her and bring her home. The farmer hired a bounty hunter who did find her, and the other boy was sent to take her place. The people of Vasterberg, satisfied the wrong had been righted, once again began to visit the blacksmith's shop, but they punished your grandmother in the way that would sting the most. Despite her marvelous talent at stitchery, they would buy nothing made by her hand. Her skill as a seamstress fell to waste."

Mignon tucked the end of Gilly's braid into the weave of the other braids and looked over at Gwen. "When your grandfather died, she was left without a means of providing for herself. Even if the people of Vasterberg had forgiven her for the choice she'd made, her eyesight had faded too much by then to sew for others, and she'd not trained an apprentice who could help her. The farm was sold to pay your grandfather's debts, and she moved into the cottage with your father and mother. She was left at the mercy of her daughter's husband when Margaretta died. She wants you to be able to provide for your needs if you are left alone in this world."

"But baking or living in cold silence as a pauper?" Gwen whispered as if she were asking for taboo knowledge.

"Can you say either is worse than being married off to someone not of your own choosing? And not having the chance to make your own way in the world with skills and talent?"

The compassion in Mignon's voice further relaxed Gwen, whose previously tense muscles had slackened from the tea. She thought about the options. "I suppose not," she finally conceded, but she fought for a shred of her own desires to be acknowledged as she added, "but what if neither makes me happy?"

Chapter 4

To build new worlds, we must shatter the old.
--Argus Kind, usurper king

* * *

Gwen awoke to calmness and the comforting scents of hot cinnamon and baking bread. She didn't remember having fallen asleep, but she knew she had because she felt rested. All the tension in her neck and shoulders when she'd arrived at the Bastwick cottage had melted away. She sat up and dangled her feet over the edge of Gilly's straw bed in the corner of the main room.

"It's about time," said Gilly, who was standing near the stone hearth. "The cinnamon sweet rolls are almost ready."

Gwen smiled at her nose's accuracy. "How long did I sleep?"

"Most of the morning. Now get up, sleepyhead, and help me finish my chores, or Mother won't let me go to the circus."

"What's left to do?"

Gilly picked up an iron rod and hooked the end of it onto the handle of an iron pan, which she pulled out of the brick oven above the fire. She set the pan on the hearth, well away from the fire, to cool. "Gather the eggs, snip some thyme and tarragon, and strip some herb stems Mother has been drying in the garden shed."

"That's all?" Gwen was amazed at such light duties. She'd expected to do much harder labor.

"Well, I've done everything else except . . ."

"Except what?"

Gilly turned around and flashed a mischievous grin. "Except slop the pigs." She broke into laughter.

Gwen snatched Gilly's pillow and threatened to toss it at her but didn't for fear she'd cause the cooling bread to fall. Nonetheless, she laughed along with her friend. Mignon's concoction, the revelation about Gwen's grandmother's past, and Gilly's infectious laughter had soothed Gwen's humiliation and pain.

"Where is your mother?"

"Gone to visit your father," Gilly said. "She took some herbs he uses when he's curing and smoking meat."

"Grateful" was the only word Gwen could think of for how she felt about Mignon talking with her father regarding her future, for she knew that was exactly why Gilly's mother had gone to the butcher shop. "All right, then. I'll get the thyme and tarragon." Gwen headed for the door.

"The shears are in the garden shed," Gilly called out to her, and Gwen turned around just in time to see her pinch off a piece of one of the rolls. That made her smile too.

By early afternoon when Mignon returned from her trip into the village, the two girls had finished all of the chores and were sitting at the table nibbling on a sweet roll they'd agreed to share. The scent of the fresh baking still lingered in the cottage.

"Hello, Mother."

"Hello, dears," she said, offloading onto the table a basket teeming with dry goods and meat.

Gwen wasted no time in discovering her fate, for as the day had worn on, she'd decided there was little hope of changing her father's mind. "Gilly said you were going to visit Father." After she'd spoken, she was disappointed in herself for not having the courage to ask a direct question.

Mignon took a seat at the table and began to lift the contents out of the basket one item at a time. A burlap bag of cracked wheat came out first. "I did . . . and I'm sorry to say I could not change his mind."

Confirming her suspicions was more disheartening than Gwen had expected. She found herself wanting to cry but swallowed hard instead and just nodded, tightening her lips to hold back any sound for fear it would erupt into a full-fledged wail.

The hedge witch pulled out a hunk of cheesecloth and unwrapped it, revealing a thick, marbled chunk of beef. Gwen knew it was part of the trade her father had made with Mignon.

"I *was* able to convince him, however, that he should reconsider and speak with your grandmother about a compromise."

Gwen, who had been staring at the hunk of beef, looked up at Mignon, whose face wore the same mischievous grin Gilly had used earlier that day.

"Truly? He's going to reconsider?" Gwen asked, hardly believing that even Mignon could have swayed her father.

The woman's grin subsided into calm seriousness. "Yes, truly, Gwendolin. He understands you have no idea what you want to do for the rest of your life. He *does* want you to be happy, and he is willing to reconsider allowing you to continue your studies for a while longer so you can find a trade that will satisfy both you and your grandmother."

"But I *do* know what I want. I was going to tell them, but they didn't give me a chance."

Mignon's expression changed again. This time curiosity relaxed the seriousness and lifted her eyebrows as she tilted her head as if to hear better from the ear closest to Gwen.

"I want to be a hedge witch."

The woman blinked, surprise widening her eyes and lifting her eyebrows farther and farther up until they could go no higher and her forehead had become rows of wrinkles filling the space between eyebrows and hairline.

Gilly let out a whoop and clapped her hands. "You'll be so good at it!"

Gwen smiled at her friend but returned her gaze to Mignon, whose face now wore concern. "What?"

"He agreed to let you stay with us until after the Day of Rest, Gwen," said Mignon, "just to give him time to convince your grandmother to allow you to continue your studies for a while longer before you take an apprenticeship. But . . . but you know your grandmother will not consent to an apprenticeship with me."

"Why not? Everyone knows you're the best hedge witch in the Westland."

"Perhaps, but even were that true, your grandmother would not see it that way. Since I was a child, she has viewed me as flighty, and she believes I influenced your mother in ways that made her less cautious than she should have been."

"That's not true," Gwen said.

Mignon shrugged. "It matters not. Your grandmother will not consent to you studying herb lore with me." She placed a hand atop Gwen's. "Listen to me, Gwendolin Ahlgren. Take the compromise if your father can get your grandmother to agree to it. Continue your studies with the Mistress. Learn all you can from the books she brings to you."

Gwen interrupted. "And bide my time."

Mignon nodded, her eyes filled with warmth and understanding. "Prove to your father and grandmother that you are a serious student, that knowledge of herb lore will be your salvation, not your downfall. Then and only then might you be able to change your grandmother's mind by setting it at ease."

Gilly cleared her throat and picked up the chunk of beef. She looked at it almost adoringly, which made Gwen laugh. "You, my dear," she said to the hunk of meat, "are going to be a fine roast for tonight's celebration in honor of our guest, the lovely and talented hedge-witch-to-be, Gwendolin Ahlgren. And tomorrow, I shall bake your remains into scrumptious meat pies."

Mignon and Gwen laughed, and Gwen thought about how fortunate she was to have a good friend in Gilly and a wise supporter in Mignon. She was thankful her mother had chosen such a faithful and sensible friend.

* * *

The next couple of days passed with a mixture of speed and sluggishness. The days were filled with laughter and seeking plants, an activity Gwen relished. Each plant search Mignon assigned was like a quest in which Gwen could prove her mettle. Her memory for the location of even the most rare and tiniest flora gave her a sense of pride, and when

Mignon would later tell her how she planned to use the plant, Gwen would take down the particulars with precision on a piece of parchment Gilly had given her. Upon her return home, she planned to add the parchment to the book she had diligently filled over a number of years with the knowledge she'd gained about every plant she'd encountered in the Westland.

Finally, the Day of Rest came, and the two girls arose early that morning, both filled with anticipation and excitement over attending the first circus performance. By mid morning, they were restless.

"Go on, then, the both of you," Mignon said, clearly annoyed with their hovering.

Gilly bolted over to her mother and bent down, kissing her on the cheek. "Thank you, Mother!"

"Out! Out with you! Leave me to rest."

"We'll tell you everything we see, Madame Bastwick," said Gwen.

Mignon waved her hand in the air as if brushing away something. "Don't dally on the way home."

Gilly grabbed Gwen's hand and rushed for the door, yelling behind her as she pulled it to, "We won't. We'll come straight back when it's over and tell you all about it!"

The pair raced each other to the edge of town where the circus tent and wagons had been set up for the performance. As they approached the site, Gwen took in every detail of what looked as mysterious as the announcement's promises. A large blue- and gold-striped tent sat in the center of a circle of smaller tents, each a shimmery fabric in a jewel tone--emerald, sapphire, and ruby--or in gold, silver, or copper. Outside the circle of smaller tents, several wagons parked end to end formed a ring around the entire circus, save for one wide space framed by two posts with a sign above it, like a gateway. Like the announcement, it bore the name of the troupe: The Hermetic Circus.

"The portal to the mysterious," Gwen said as they approached the entrance.

Gilly giggled and squeezed Gwen's hand. Together, they walked under the sign.

They were met on the other side of the entrance by an imposing man with a coarse beard. "One bronze each."

The girls pulled out the coins they'd carried in their waist pockets and handed them to him. He flashed a smile and exposed a mouth full of gold teeth before he closed his fingers around the coins. In a flourish, he took a low bow and waved toward the inside of the compound. "Welcome to the great Hermetic Circus, where mysteries and peculiarities abound."

Gwen wanted to get away from the man. Something about him seemed dangerous. She gave him a quick smile and pulled on Gilly's hand. Once well away from him, she stopped and looked around. Between the wagons and small tents, tall, muscular horses grazed, but as far as Gwen could tell, none of their reins or leads were tied to anything. Though free to roam, they seemed uninterested in wandering beyond the imaginary boundary of the wagons.

"Look," said Gilly, pointing to one of the small tents. Outside the sapphire tent stood a woman in a multicolored skirt so full, it hung in folds. When she turned toward the pair, the heavy skirt rustled, and she motioned for the two to approach her.

"Stop pointing," whispered Gwen, suddenly conscious that the woman's gaze wasn't particularly friendly.

Gilly's hand flew down to her side.

The woman motioned again, this time with a kinder expression on her face.

"Let's see what she wants," said Gilly.

For a beat or two, Gwen's heart thumped harder and faster than normal, and she had a sense of dread. As the two got closer to the woman, Gwen saw that she looked kinder and much less intimidating than she had from a distance.

"The early birds have arrived," said the woman, who flashed a sweet smile at the girls.

"Oh, yes!" said Gilly, "We've been waiting for this all week. When does the performance begin?"

"In a bit," said the woman. "Your wait won't be long." She pointed toward the big tent in the center of the compound. "The barker will call out when it's time to take your seats."

"Thank you," said Gilly.

"Do come inside while you wait," said the woman, lifting the flap of the tent.

Gwen and Gilly peered into the darkness. In the center of the tent sat a small table draped in a dark blue silk cloth with pictures of stars and crescent moons on it. Two chairs flanked the table opposite each other. Atop the silk tablecloth sat a crystal globe on a copper base shaped like two claws resting back to back on each other, with three talons of one claw serving as the legs of the base and three cradling the globe. Hanging over the table was an ornate lantern with a single candle burning inside of it.

"We haven't any more coins."

"You paid the man at the gate?"

"Yes."

"Then come inside. All who have paid can see their destinies here. I am Madame Verona. Come."

Gilly looked at Gwen and grinned. "I want to know who I'll marry."

Gwen frowned. "I don't know. Maybe it's better not to know that."

The woman shrugged. "Or perhaps one can make wiser decisions if one knows one's destiny."

"Come on, Gwen. It won't hurt. It's just a game."

Gwen looked at the woman, who lifted a single eyebrow at Gilly's comment. Despite reservations, she followed her friend inside.

The woman entered behind them and closed the flap, pulling it tightly across the opening so not so much as a sliver of light penetrated. The room, lit by only the hanging lantern's candlelight, seemed to grow in size in its darkened state, as if it were larger on the inside than on the outside. The woman motioned toward a chair and looked at Gilly, who scrambled into the chair and settled on its plush cushion. The same heavy rustle of fabric followed the woman to the other chair, onto which she lowered herself so gracefully Gwen found the movement near mesmerizing.

"Tell me your name."

"Gilly."

"Your full name, my dear."

"Gillian Margaretta Bastwick."

The woman grasped the globe with both hands, running her palms over the smooth surface as if she were caressing it. "Ah, Margaretta. Such a sad name for such a perky young one. This is why they call you Gilly."

Gilly looked at Gwen, who frowned. Gilly returned the look with a compassionate smile. Gwen didn't feel comforted.

"Gillian, you have a talent with . . ."

"Not a single thing." Gilly laughed.

"Ah, but you are mistaken. Food. I see food and children, many children."

"Well, I do like to bake."

"And baking you shall do, Gillian Margaretta Bastwick. But that is not what you wish to know, is it?"

Gilly shook her head with vigor, and her braids danced in revolt. "I want to know who I'll marry."

The woman caressed the globe once more and stared into it. Then she removed her hands from it and looked at Gilly. "Thomlin Frank."

Gilly's mouth fell open. "Plump Thom Frank? You can't mean that."

The woman laughed, and again Gwen felt discomfort. "It is not my choice, Gillian Margaretta Bastwick. It is your destiny. You will marry Thomlin Frank, and you will bake for him and all your many children and live a happy, long life with him. That is in the stars."

"But, . . ." Gilly started in protest, but the woman interrupted.

She waved her hand. "It is done." Looking up at Gwen, she said, "And now it is your turn. The stars await your question."

Gilly, frowning and grumbling under her breath, tumbled out of the chair as if she'd been shoved off the cushion but recovered her balance and stood upright. She moved to a dark corner of the tent. "I did it. It's your turn."

Unsure she wanted to follow through after seeing her friend's predicted ill fate unfold, Gwen took her place on the chair, her thoughts swirling with images of the shy, plump miller's son gobbling up Gilly's delicious sweet rolls with no appreciation for how truly scrumptious they were. The cushion, which had appeared so plush before, revealed itself for what it was: a hard and lumpy reminder of the feeling of discomfort Gwen felt about the entire escapade.

Once again, the woman placed her palms on the globe and rubbed it, gazing at it the whole while. Gwen looked at it, too, but all she could see was the woman's fingers enlarged by the prism. And then, a light flashed inside the globe, and Gwen leaned in to get a closer look.

"Tell me your name."

"Gwendolin Ahlgren." Gwen couldn't take her gaze off of the light, which pulsed and grew larger as it changed from white to yellow to orange and then finally to red.

The woman pulled her hands away from the globe and stared at them with an expression of agony that contorted her face so much it was painful to witness. In a monotonous tone nothing like the one that had come out of her mouth when she had predicted Gilly's future, she said, "Ohmahold. The fate of the Greatland rests with you, Gwendolin Ahlgren, and only by love can you save her."

* * *

"I've been thinking about what the fortune-teller said. What do you suppose it means?" asked Gilly as they walked back to the cottage in the early afternoon sunlight.

"Nothing. It means nothing," replied Gwen, still miffed she'd worked so hard for a coin she'd wasted. The fortune-teller's vague prediction had set the tone for an afternoon less filled with wonder and excitement than Gwen had expected. The fire-breathers, stilt-walkers, and clownish acrobats had been underwhelming. Even worse, between each short act in the main tent, the barker had approached the audience, holding out the cure-all medicinal and extolling its virtues until at least one villager had succumbed to his sales spectacle.

"I don't know. She seemed certain. Did you see the look on her face?"

Gwen rounded on Gilly, grabbing her by the arm. "It's nonsense. Why would we believe it?"

"But what if it's not nonsense?" Gilly pulled her arm out of Gwen's grasp.

"I'm sorry," Gwen said, realizing she'd been physically rough with her friend. "I'm just angry that we wasted our time and coin."

"I admit the show wasn't as exciting as I thought it would be. But maybe the circus wasn't a complete waste. Maybe what the fortune-teller said is truly our fates."

"Do you believe you're going to marry and raise a brood of children with Thomlin Frank?"

Gilly scrunched up her face. "Well," she said, dragging out the syllable. "He did offer to share his tart with me after the show."

"And share he did, indeed!" A full laugh rolled out of Gwen at the memory of Thomlin's sticky fingers holding out the fruit tart to Gilly. He'd squeezed the tart, and syrupy fruit had oozed out of it and landed on Gilly's shoe with a plop. "I thought I would die on the spot when he bent over to brush off your shoe and came up with those sticky fingers all covered in dust and twigs."

"I felt sorry for him. He was just trying to be nice." Gilly's disapproval of Gwen's laughing at Thomlin was unmistakable.

Gwen took the hint. "I'm sure he was, and I'm sorry I laughed at him. I did apologize, though."

"After you hurt his feelings."

"I said I was sorry."

"Sometimes you don't think about anyone else's feelings but your own, Gwen. I was embarrassed for poor Thomlin, but I was more embarrassed at how you acted."

Gwen's mouth dropped open. She couldn't believe her best friend was speaking to her in such a way, taking the side of a boy against her. Not just any boy, but Thomlin Frank, a boy Gilly hadn't paid an iota of attention to before the fortune-teller's prediction! "Maybe I should just go home."

"Maybe you should," said Gilly, looking down.

Chapter 5
In the heart of a mother lies the purest love.
--The Lady Mangst

* * *

Gwen lumbered home along the worn road, feeling like she'd been abandoned by the only friend she had. Truth be told, Gilly *was* her only friend, and realizing her behavior had pushed Gilly away was painful. At the same time, Gwen couldn't dismiss the role the fortune-teller had played in it all. If she hadn't told Gilly that awful lie about Thomlin Frank, whom she'd quite obviously already spoken with before the two girls arrived at the tent, then maybe her friend wouldn't have defended his clumsiness with such fervor. Just before she entered the gate to the cottage's yard, Gwen kicked at a pebble in the road but missed, stubbing her toe on the hard ground. She cursed under her breath and walked the path to the front entrance, each step as downtrodden as she felt. There was no hope left in her, and she knew her only choice was to do what her grandmother had done and leave Vasterberg. By hook or by crook, she would find her own way in the world.

Her father was happy to see her, and Gwen accepted his long hug and tender kiss atop her head with humility. Much to her surprise, even her grandmother was welcoming.

"We've decided to allow you two more months to decide where you'll serve out your apprenticeship," Jacob announced after they'd finished the main course of their evening meal: roast beef and turnips.

"That won't be necessary, Father."

"Oh?" he responded.

Her grandmother set down the strawberry pie she was moving to the table to cut into serving-sized wedges and sat down in her chair.

"Yes. I'll never be the baker Gilly is. She should serve the apprenticeship with the Widow Crookstaff. She'll make a fine baker. That leaves the monastery."

"I see," said her father. His words held no enthusiasm, just resignation, but he smiled at her nevertheless.

Her grandmother, on the other hand, clapped her hands once, picked up the knife beside the pie tin, and plunged it into the center of the pie. "A wise decision, Gwendolin. You'll have a long and stable life as a monk. Which order will you serve?"

Her father looked down at his hands, which were clasped together and resting on the table. Gwen realized at that moment sending his daughter to a monastery hadn't been her father's first choice, but her grandmother's, and she was sad not to be surprised by the revelation. It also saddened her that her father didn't have more control over his household, particularly when it came to decisions concerning his own child. "I don't know. I thought I'd ask the schoolmistress for advice. She'll be in Vasterberg this week."

"Yes, yes. A wise decision, Gwendolin," her grandmother said, plopping a piece of the pie onto a plate and shoving it in front of Jacob. "She will know who you can speak with about the matter."

"If I might be excused, please. I'd like to clean my room before dark."

"But what about your pie? It's your favorite," said her father, his face wrinkled into an older version of itself.

"It smells wonderful, but I'm too full of roast to enjoy it. I'll have it tomorrow if nobody minds."

Her grandmother plopped two wedges out of the pie tin and onto plates, leaving the third one she'd cut in place. "Of course, child. It will be here in the morning and make a hearty breakfast."

"Thank you," Gwen said, rising from her chair and giving both her grandmother and father a kiss on their cheeks before heading for her room.

"It's good to have you home again," her father called out.

"It's good to be home," said Gwen. She felt a twinge of guilt for telling him a lie.

* * *

For the next three days, Gwen awoke early each morning and did chores before having breakfast. She even slopped the pigs twice, each time scolding them for charging at her but standing her ground even though she wanted to run away from their snuffling snouts and sharp, cloven feet. Once she'd completed all the chores she thought needed doing, for nobody had given her a list and she'd taken it upon herself to find tasks each day, she bathed and dressed for a trip into Vasterberg.

On the first visit to the village, Gwen found the schoolhouse empty. Using the underside of her apron to rub winter's grime off a window, she peered inside. Heavy cloth still covered the desks and chairs. Cobwebs stretched across corners where walls met ceiling and dangled from the unburned candles set into a wooden ring hanging in the center of the main room. Lessons would be delayed while the schoolmistress swept and dusted the room in which she taught lessons and tidied up the small room behind the main one. Like a cottage in miniature, the smaller space served as living quarters for the schoolmistress, who stayed from spring until winter's onset, when once again the lesson room's furniture would be covered and the building locked until after winter had thawed.

By the third day, when there still had been no sign of the schoolmistress's arrival, Gwen thought about which councilman would be amenable to unlocking the door so she could tidy up before Mistress Bourgogne arrived. She decided to approach the one who was an unmarried woodcutter. He supplied firewood for the schoolhouse and always seemed cheerful to chat with the schoolmistress while he unloaded his cart and carried the wood inside. Determined to do anything that would make the time before she could speak with the schoolmistress go more quickly, Gwen set off to fulfill her plan. She'd mastered the art of walking with her eyes cast downward while still being able to see far enough ahead of her to swerve around people before she encountered them, and so she easily slipped out of Vasterberg without speaking to a single person.

Before she reached the woodcutter's cabin at the edge of the forest, however, she caught sight of Gilly coming down the road toward Vasterberg . . . toward her! Thomlin walked beside her, and the two were talking and laughing. He was grinning like a fool and lugging a cloth-covered basket Gwen recognized as belonging to Mignon. Gwen wished he'd trip over his own feet, but more than that, she wanted to get away without suffering the humiliation of facing Gilly again, so Gwen dived into a hedgerow beside the road.

For what seemed like a lifetime in the bush, its prickly branches scratching her and snagging her cotton dress, Gwen waited for the pair to pass. As they approached, she heard Gilly's tinkling laughter and Thomlin's coarse croak.

"Are you going to talk with her about an apprenticeship?"

"Yes, I think I might. Mother says it would be a good way to improve my skills, and I trust her judgment."

"I think she's right. You truly are an amazing baker, Gillian Margaretta Bastwick."

Gilly giggled, and Gwen could imagine her friend blushing at the compliment. Thomlin had no right to use her mother's name, and it irked her that he did. Mignon had given her daughter her best friend's first name as a second name, and it was one that only those closest to her ever used. After her mother died, Gwen had found comfort in knowing her mother's name would live on in someone they both loved so much. Now the name that once soothed her pain had become a bitter reminder of a boy squirming his way into Gilly's life and displacing the closeness the two girls had built. He'd spoiled all the name signified for Gwen. She thought she truly hated Thomlin Frank.

The pair stopped right next to the hedgerow, and Gwen wanted to scream at them to just move along and leave her alone with her sadness, but she refrained and listened.

"Are you going to tell her?"

"The schoolmistress?" asked Gilly.

"No. Gwen. You said her grandmother and father wanted her to apprentice under the Widow Crookstaff."

Tears stung Gwen's eyes. How could Gilly have betrayed her and told *him, him of all people,* about the disagreement she'd had with her family? Gwen had half a mind to crawl out of the bush and slap Gillian Margaretta Bastwick right across her silly, blushing cheek.

"I don't think so. She'll find out soon enough. What is there to say, Thomlin?" Gilly's voice changed and became mocking, "Hello, Gwen. I'm going to take the apprenticeship you never wanted anyway. So for once in your life, don't be so selfish and compete with me for it. You'd make a poor baker anyway."

Gwen was stunned at the cruelty in Gilly's tone. It wasn't that she was wrong in what she said. Gwen *would* make an awful baker, and she had no interest in spending her life standing in front of a dough table or stoking a hot oven. But there was no need for Gilly to be so unkind about the truth.

As the pair continued on their way to Vasterberg, Gwen remained in the hedgerow. When they were well out of sight, she fought her way out of the angry branches, vowing to even the score with Gilly for her betrayal. Someday, somehow, she'd show her just how unkind someone could be.

* * *

Gwen's plan to clean up the schoolhouse before the traveling schoolmistress arrived went off without a hitch. She secured the key from the woodcutter with the promise of contacting him as soon as the schoolmistress made it to Vasterberg. In a mere two days' time, she transformed the grubby space into a fresh, inviting one. When the schoolmistress finally appeared in the doorway, her place of employ and her living space welcomed her, as did Gwen.

"Good afternoon, Mistress Bourgogne. We were beginning to worry that something had befallen you on the road."

The woman, who towered above Gwen and couldn't have been more her opposite in coloring and demeanor, looked around the learning room. Her olive skin and raven hair, pulled back severely into a tight bun on the back of her head, shimmered in the firelight. "Did you do this, Gwendolin?"

Gwen nodded. "Yes. I thought you might like to start lessons right away. The spring thaw was late this year."

"That was very thoughtful of you. Thank you."

Just then, a tall man wearing a black coat that reached all the way to his ankles entered behind Mistress Bourgogne. At his side hung a sheathed sword and dangling from each hand was a tapestry bag, which Gwen recognized as the ones holding books the schoolmistress brought with her each year.

33

"Look, darling. Gwendolin has readied the entire building for us."

Gwen realized she must have had her mouth hanging open because Mistress Bourgogne looked from the man to Gwen and her hand flew to her mouth. "Oh, dear. How rude of me. Gwendolin, meet Master Gabaldi, my husband. We were married at the new year. My name is Madame Gabaldi now. Darling, meet Gwendolin, one of my brightest pupils."

The man gave a polite nod to Gwen as he passed her then dropped the bags near the schoolmistress's large oak desk. Gwen gave him a smile when he looked her way, but there was something about his narrow eyes that made her uncomfortable, something as sharp-edged as his name.

"Will lessons begin tomorrow?" Gwen asked.

"I don't see why not," the new Madame Gabaldi answered.

"I'll see you tomorrow morning, then," said Gwen, who needed to get to the woodcutter and deliver the news about the schoolmistress before he found out for himself. He would be so very disappointed.

After dropping off the key to the councilman, who was, indeed, downhearted about the schoolmistress's marrying before he could court her, Gwen went home and after dinner slept fitfully. Images of the tall, dark Master Gabaldi and his slit eyes haunted her dreams. She awoke wondering what he was master of.

The answer came at the start of lessons the next day, when Madame Gabaldi introduced him to the class. "My husband will be working with those of you who choose to study weaponry."

When Gwen groaned, Master Gabaldi shot her a disapproving glare, and that was only the beginning of what turned out to be a long, painful day filled with reminders that she no longer had any reason to remain in Vasterberg.

As she'd dreaded, Gilly attended the lessons, and Thomlin stayed so close to his newfound love that Gwen wondered if Gilly could turn around without bumping against the boy. "Hmmph," she said aloud at the thought that bumping against Gilly was likely Thomlin's goal.

Her unsolicited noise earned another disapproving glance, this time from Madame Gabaldi, who was delivering a boring lecture on the responsibilities of citizenship in Greatland governance.

Gwen was further disappointed when Thomlin didn't move into the group of boys who got up from their desks and gathered around Master Gabaldi, who led them outside, which she assumed was for the purpose of wielding weapons. It didn't surprise her, though. Thomlin had never struck her as a particularly brave or agile boy. And besides, he would have had to let go of Gilly's apron strings, and Gwen could see that clearly was *not* going to happen. During their midday break, he'd stuck beside her like she was made of maple syrup and had even tossed the remainder of a hunk of bread to some pigeons so he could follow Gilly when she'd gone back inside the building well before Madame Gabaldi called the students inside to continue with their lessons.

Before dismissing the students, Madame Gabaldi asked Gwen to remain for a few minutes more. "I'd like to speak with you about your continuing studies."

"I want to join a monastery."

Madame Gabaldi had never been very good at hiding her feelings, and the look of surprise on her face told Gwen she'd still not mastered that skill. "Are you sure, Gwendolin? That is a lifelong commitment, and it isn't one to be taken lightly or for any reason other than devotion."

Gwen nodded. "I'm sure. I'm not sure, though, which monastery would be best or even how to go about joining."

The schoolmistress's expression of surprise flattened into concern. "Gwendolin, why? Why do you wish to join a monastery?"

"It's what my grandmother wants me to do, and I can think of no other study that would please her."

"I don't know what to say, dear." She reached out and placed a hand on Gwen's shoulder. "But I do know that you don't have to decide today." She offered a reassuring smile before turning and bending down to retrieve one of the tapestry bags from beside her. Lifting it onto the desk and opening it, she rummaged inside, pulling out book after book until she found the one she was looking for. "Ah yes, here it is!" She offered the hefty tome to Gwen. "It's a history of monastic orders in the Greatland and beyond. Mind you, it may be incomplete and contains some language you may not recognize, but you may find it helpful in making your decision. Some knowledge is better than none, no?"

Gwen took the book, which had a dark leather cover with the words *Piety and Ordination* tooled on its ribbed spine. It weighed more than it looked like it should, and Gwen had to hold it with both hands to keep from dropping it. "Thank you," she said, cradling it against her chest.

"Just one more question, and you may leave for the day. If your grandmother wanted you to join a monastery, where in the world did Gilly get the idea you might have wanted to study with Vasterberg's baker?"

Gwen gritted her teeth until she could answer without letting out the anger swelling inside her. Gilly had yet again betrayed her, this time not just to some moon-eyed boy but to someone she respected. She managed a nonchalant shrug. "Who knows? She's not been herself since she took up with Thomlin Frank. He's a bad influence, and I doubt her mother would approve of all the time they spend alone . . . in the woods."

"Oh," said Madame Gabaldi. "Oh dear. Perhaps someone should speak with Madame Bastwick about that."

Mustering an expression of sincere concern, Gwen replied, "Yes, perhaps someone should . . . for Gilly's own good."

A week passed before the fallout began.

Chapter 6

Some consequences do not manifest until those responsible are dead and gone.
--Von of the Elsics

* * *

Gilly leaned down until her face was so close, her breath warmed Gwen's flushed cheeks. "You're a miserable, jealous little witch who thinks she can do whatever she wants, no matter who gets hurt. What did he ever do to you?"

Gwen could feel the stares of the other girls who had encircled her and Gilly.

"Go on. Tell me." Gilly glared.

Though the top of her head reached only as high as Gilly's shoulders, Gwen stood as erect as she could and refused to answer.

"Miserable coward. What happened to you? You were my friend, and we delighted in each other's happiness. But now you've done your best to ruin any chance of me being happy. I hope that fortune-teller was wrong. All of the Greatland is lost if *you're* its only hope. There is no love in your heart, Gwendolin Ahlgren, and I pity you."

"Pity?" Gwen lashed out. "You're the one who deserves pity. You're so desperate for love that you'd take it from that lump of dough Thomlin."

A couple of the girls standing in the circle giggled.

"Plump Thomlin Frank. Remember the songs you sang about him? Remember how you said the sight of him made you want to never eat another piece of pie again in your whole life? What happened to *you*, Gilly?"

Gilly's face grew redder, and Gwen could hear teeth grinding. Gilly backed away and shook her head. "I grew up. You didn't."

"Ladies! Come inside. Your break is over," Madame Gabaldi called from the doorway.

"I'm warning you, Gwen. Leave him alone," Gilly said before she turned her back on Gwen and headed toward the schoolhouse, the circle of girls parting to let her through.

The other girls followed her, and Gwen was left standing alone. She was the last to reenter the building. The only desk left unoccupied was in the back of the room, and Gwen thanked her lucky stars she didn't have to walk past everyone and sit in the front of the class.

Master Gabaldi stood beside his wife next to the large oak desk. "There's been news from the south. Foreign ships have been scouting the coastline."

One of the boys raised a hand, and Master Gabaldi nodded at him.

"Aren't there a lot of Greatland ships that could chase them away?"

"Yes, of course."

"Then what does it matter to us?" the boy asked.

His gaunt face crumpled into a frown, and Master Gabaldi glowered at the boy. "It matters because the Greatland is surrounded by water. What's to prevent those ships from sailing around from the south to the Westland? And what would you do, boy? Defend your home and family?"

The boy stiffened. "Well, yeah. That's exactly what I'd do."

Master Gabaldi smirked and nodded. "With what? You're the son of a farmer. Are you going to use a hay fork against swords and bows?"

The room erupted with chuckles, and the schoolmistress's husband stretched out an arm. Pointing at another boy who had laughed, he asked, "And you? What strategy will you use to turn back a throng of foreign soldiers? Will you herd them into a barn like your father's cows?"

The second boy slunk down in his chair. As Master Gabaldi glowered at each of the other boys, they, in turn, also sank into their chairs. Gwen liked the schoolmistress's husband less and less with each glare.

"Lucky for you, I have some expertise and can take you to those who know how to train even the least warlike among you," he said as he looked directly at Thomlin Frank, "to defend your homeland, yourselves, and your loved ones."

Thomlin bolted out of his chair. "I'll go with you!"

"You'll have to untangle yourself from Gilly's apron strings first," Gwen said.

Disorder broke out. Raucous laughter erupted, and the students lobbed teasing insults at each other, but one voice rose above the rest, demanding to be heard. "Gwendolin Ahlgren!"

She'd thought it was Madame Gabaldi beginning a stern reprimand until she looked to her left and saw Gilly stomping toward her. Before Gwen could get out of the chair, her cheek felt the sting from Gilly's palm.

When neither girl would explain what had brought on the outburst and retribution, Madame Gabaldi had sent both Gwen and Gilly home with wax-sealed notes. "I'll see the two of you in a week. I trust you'll have resolved your differences by then."

Gwen walked straight to the butcher shop, all the while thinking there was absolutely no way she'd make up with Gilly Bastwick. At the shop, she found her father plucking a turkey while he sat on a low stool and hummed a merry melody.

"I'll be right with you."

He stopped humming when he looked over his shoulder and saw it was Gwen. His expression turned from pleasant, which it always was when a customer was in the shop, to surprise and just as rapidly to concern. "Are you ill?"

She shook her head and handed him the note.

His expressed concern at seeing her before the lessons should have ended for the day changed into a sour frown as he read the note, and a long sigh escaped his lips before he spoke. "What's happened between you and Gilly, Gwen?"

Gwen shrugged.

"It must be something. The two of you have been inseparable since you were wee tots. Go on, then. Tell me. I've never known Gilly Bastwick to raise a hand to any living thing." He looked back down at the turkey dangling from one of his hands and with the other continued to yank out the feathers, which fell to the floor in a pile that shifted with the air currents her father's meticulous movements stirred.

The answer burst out of her in an uncontrolled stream, along with tears of humiliation. "How can you say that, Father? She's vicious and cruel. She's taken up with plump Thomlin Frank and forgotten we were ever friends. She thinks she's going to marry him just because some stupid gypsy told her so. He paid that awful woman to tell Gilly it was her destiny. I'm sure of it! I hate him! I hate them both! They deserve each other!"

Jacob Ahlgren's fingers let go of the base of a feather he was about to pull out. He lowered the half-plucked bird onto the pile of feathers at his feet and spun around on his stool to face Gwen. "I remember your mother saying something like that when Gilly's father started courting Mignon. That was when your mother and I became friends, you know. It was when I fell in love with her, and it was the start of the life we'd share, the life that graced us with you, my dearest one."

Gwen sniffled and wiped her tears with the flowing sleeve of her dress before looking into her father's eyes. They bore a duality she'd seen on rare occasions, sadness and joy at the same time, the double-edged sword of memories of her mother. "But she pretends like I don't exist. And I heard them talking when they couldn't see me. She told Thomlin that I was selfish." Her passion deflated by the lingering thought of her mother, she all but whispered the most painful part of what had become of her friendship with Gilly. "She betrayed my trust. She told him something I didn't want anyone else to know."

Her father put his hands on his knees and leaned forward. "That you went to the carnival without permission and spoke with a fortune-teller?"

Gwen blushed and shook her head. "Something more personal than that, Father, and I don't want to talk about it."

"I see. Your mother said something like that too. But she and Mignon made up, and they were best friends until the day your mother-- What I'm saying is that true friends don't give up on their friendships, even when one of them has done something they shouldn't have. They work it out."

Gwen didn't know what to say. Part of her longed to be friends with Gilly again, and part of her couldn't find forgiveness for Gilly's betrayal.

Her father reached out and took her hand in his. "Have you considered that perhaps Gilly told Thomlin something private to earn *his* trust, and that maybe she was so caught up that she didn't stop to think about how you might feel about it? Look. It was a mistake. We all make mistakes. Sometimes we act selfishly, and that includes both you and Gillian." He kissed his daughter's hand and turned back around on his stool, resuming his work.

Gwen stood there next to him and thought about what he'd said. After a few minutes, she put her hand on his shoulder. "Maybe you're right. I feel awful we're not friends, and I don't really hate her or want anything but the best for her. If she'd just spend a little time with me and not every moment she has with *him*."

Her father chuckled. "So how about you take a delivery for me out to the Bastwick cottage and talk this out with Gilly?"

"I doubt she'll talk to me at all."

"Did Madame Gabaldi send a note home with Gilly too?"

"Yes."

Her father chuckled again. "I suspect Gilly will be a captive audience, then. Mignon will be beside herself about this."

When he'd finished plucking the turkey, he laid the limp carcass on his butcher block and washed his hands before retrieving a burlap sack from the cold storage room. Handing it to Gwen, he said, "Give this to Mignon and tell her I hope it is smoked to her liking. Say it just that way. We'll talk later about the rest of Madame Gabaldi's note."

"What else did she write?"

"Later, Gwen. For now, you go take care of what you need to. It'll put your heart at ease and Gilly's too, I suspect."

"Yes, Father."

Gwen's walk to the Bastwick cottage was filled with fearful thoughts of Gilly rebuking her or refusing outright to see her. Uncertain if she could handle such horrible outcomes to a sincere effort, she fretted with every step. By the time the cottage came into sight, Gwen had worked herself into certainty that nothing she could say or do would dissuade Gilly from severing their friendship forever, and she was relieved when her rap on the door was answered by Mignon.

"Hello, Madame Bastwick. My father asked me to deliver this to you." Gwen shoved the burlap bag toward Mignon, who took it. "He said to tell you he hopes it is smoked to your liking."

Mignon nodded and smiled. "Did he now? Gillian, come here, girl."

The command came without warning, and Gwen's eyes widened as her stomach knotted.

Gilly peered over her mother's shoulder but looked away when her eyes met Gwen's.

"Invite our guest in, dear. She's come from the butcher shop with smoked meat. The least we can do is offer her some tea."

"That's not necessary."

"Of course it is, Gwen. You've come all this way."

"Yes, ma'am, but--"

Her smile turned to a frown. "But nothing. Gilly, set the kettle to boil. And you get yourself in here and sit by the fire, Gwendolin Ahlgren."

When Mignon spoke in the tone of voice she'd used, the result was imposing words not to be ignored, and everyone who knew her was aware of that fact. Neither girl dared to protest the commands. Gilly took a seat near the hearth once she'd put the kettle on the iron hook over the blazing fire, and both girls sat in unyielding silence while Mignon tucked away the burlap bag in the cupboard and busied herself preparing herb bags for the tea.

Once the water began to boil, Mignon retrieved the kettle and poured its contents into three mugs, each with its own bag of herbs. "We'll let this steep and cool off a bit," she said nonchalantly.

Gwen silently bemoaned that water didn't cool as quickly as she wished it would. The moments already were ticking away interminably slowly.

"And while we wait," Mignon continued as she took the only remaining free chair by the fire, "the two of you will tell me what foolishness has erupted between you."

Gwen looked at Gilly, who was glaring back at her. "Madame Bastwick, I really should be going."

"You'll do no such thing."

"My father and grandmother will be worried if I'm not home before dark."

"You won't be going home tonight."

Gwen screwed up her face. "What do you mean?"

"Your father will tell your grandmother where you are."

"But how would he know that?"

Mignon chuckled. "Your father sent a message with you."

Gwen cocked her head. "The only message my father sent was that the meat was smoked to your liking."

"Exactly, and while that may not mean anything to you two," she said, giving each girl a haughty shake of her head, "it means a great deal to your father and me."

"I'm sorry, Madame Bastwick, but I don't understand."

"Neither do I, Mother," said Gilly.

"The tea should be cool enough to drink now." Mignon got up as if they'd not been in the middle of a discussion, leaving Gwen and Gilly sitting there in confusion. She came back to the fire with the mugs on a wooden tray, which she offered to each girl before taking the remaining cup for herself and sitting back down again.

"Mother, what's going on?"

Mignon raised the mug to her lips and took a sip, seemingly in no rush at all to respond to her daughter's question. "Perfect," she said. "Go on, girls, drink up. It's going to be a long night."

Gwen leaned forward and set the mug down on the low table around which the chairs were arranged. "I'm sorry, Madame Bastwick, I mean no disrespect, but I'm leaving right now," said Gwen with a twinge of guilt for having spoken so harshly to the woman who had never been anything but kind to her.

"You'll do no such thing, and if you'll quell your impatience for a few minutes longer, I'll tell you what's going on."

Gwen settled uneasily back in the chair.

"Drink your tea, child," Mignon scolded as she handed the mug back to Gwen, who took it in hand and downed a hearty swig. "And you," she said to Gilly, nodding at the mug in the girl's hand. Like Gwen, Gilly obeyed.

"Good. Now I'll tell you what's going on. Long ago, when Margaretta and I were about your age, we had something of a falling out. It was the first and only time we ever had harsh words between us. For weeks, we didn't speak to each other. We avoided being in the same place at the same time. Our other friends took sides too, and before long, what should have been a natural change in the way we expressed our friendship became a war between divided camps."

"What were you fighting about, Mother?"

"Your father."

"You both liked him?" asked Gwen.

Mignon laughed so unreservedly and for so long that Gwen and Gilly looked at each other and shrugged.

"Was that it, Mother?"

Mignon's laughter died down to a chuckle, and she took another sip of her tea before shaking her head. "Quite the opposite. Margaretta *despised* him."

Gwen's mouth fell open. "But Mother never intimated such a thing. I distinctly remember her telling me he was honorable and had a nose talented at sniffing out lies."

"That he did," said Mignon, who gazed wistfully at the fire. "She wasn't always that kind in her assessment of him, though. At first, she truly hated him, and I don't blame her for it."

"Mother. How can you say such a thing?"

Mignon looked down and swirled the mug so the tea sloshed in it before taking another sip and sighing. "It was our fault, your father's and mine, but mostly mine, to be fair. When we met, he exuded such charm, worked so hard to impress me. I couldn't resist him and wanted to be with him every moment, to wade in the river while he fished, to nibble apples under a tree while he braided hemp, to let him carry my herb basket when I made deliveries for my mentor. Before I knew what I was doing, he was the first thing I thought of in the morning, the only thing I thought of all day, and the last thing I thought of before I drifted off to sleep. I was smitten. With my head filled with your father's sweet words and gallant gestures, I didn't think of Margaretta or that my sudden obsession would leave her feeling abandoned and undesirable as my friend."

In the brief silence that followed, Gwen looked down and put her mug to her lips, tilting it so the hot liquid barely touched them. She stared into the mug as if it held something mesmerizing and shouted in her head that she wasn't going to cry. Her tightly closed eyelids squeezed out tears nonetheless upon hearing Mignon's gentle tone again.

"Those who are wise say children who do not learn from the mistakes of their parents are doomed to repeat them."

Gilly threw herself onto Gwen and sobbed, and Gwen sobbed along with her.

When the two girls finished apologizing and exchanging declarations of how much they'd missed each other, Mignon further explained that Jacob Ahlgren was responsible for quelling the quarrel between her and Margaretta. He had gone to Mignon's house and told her that his mentor, a portly butcher in Vasterberg, needed to speak to her about collecting some herbs she would recommend for smoking a ham. He'd gone to Margaretta with the same story. At the appointed time, which was at the shop's closing, both girls had arrived at the shop. Once inside, Jacob, who had already fallen hopelessly in love with Margaretta but hadn't yet declared as much to her, had set out a spread of dried meat, cheese, and hard bread. Then he'd roundly scolded them for their childish behavior and locked them in the butcher shop, telling them he'd let them out when they'd resolved their differences. As he closed the door, he'd nodded to the spread atop the butcher's chopping block and said, "I hope you find it smoked to your liking."

"So that's why he told me to say the words exactly that way," Gwen said.

"Yes." Mignon nodded and chuckled. "Your father was wise and crafty as a young man. He's no less wise and crafty now."

That evening, while the three of them ate and sat by the fire twisting twigs together to make a gathering basket, Gwen resolved to give her father an extra hug when she went home and not to doubt his wishes for her to have a happy life even if it wasn't the life she would have chosen for herself. Maybe there was something he saw in her becoming a monk that she hadn't yet seen, something truly fortuitous and joyful.

Chapter 7

Fairness is a construct of the weak.
--Argus Kind, usurper king

* * *

The two friends were practically inseparable in every moment of spare time they had for the next two weeks. Though she found it difficult at times, Gwen tried her best to tolerate Thomlin's indirect intrusions on what had once been her relished private time with Gilly, time the two could laugh and muse about their futures. Gilly's future seemed set. She had graduated from her lessons and begun her apprenticeship at the bakery, and with each passing day, she shared details with Gwen about the ways Thomlin was working his way deeper into her heart.

"Today he brought a whole peck of blueberries to the bakery. He said I could use them to make some tarts to sell and the only price I had to pay was to save the best tart for him. Wasn't that sweet? Mother and I could use the extra coins, you know. And can you believe the Widow Crookstaff said she only wanted one in ten of the sales?"

"That's wonderful, Gilly. I'm so glad your apprenticeship is working out this well. I knew you'd be happy there. You're a splendid baker, much better than I could ever hope to be." Gwen felt sincere about what she was saying, and she was slightly ashamed of sidestepping the question about Thomlin while also proud of not commenting on his motives. Putting her friendship above her own feelings was getting easier, but she still struggled with the resentment she felt toward the plump boy courting her friend.

"Thomlin's been coming by to visit most evenings."

"Oh? How does your mother feel about that?" She consciously stopped her jaw from tensing and ratcheting. Gilly would notice if she gritted her teeth.

"She's still miffed at the rumors about the two of us being alone in the woods, but she agreed to let him come with me to gather herbs on the Day of Rest."

Gwen's mouth dropped open. "She did?"

"Well," said Gilly, who bit her lip then blurted out in a breathless stream, "if someone else goes with us. But Mother doesn't have time, and Thomlin says Rolf agreed to go, but Mother says it has to be another girl. Would you come, Gwen? Please, please say yes. I know it's not easy to be around Thomlin, but please . . . for me?"

She thought about how handsome Rolf was. At least she'd have someone pleasant to look at while Gilly and Thomlin stared into each other's eyes like nobody else existed, but she wondered if she'd have to smack some of Rolf's arrogance off him. Of course, that would give her an outlet for the frustration she was sure to have just being around Thomlin Frank. Gwen nodded. "All right. If it's *that* important to you, I guess I can convince my father not to tell my grandmother I'm off in the woods with that arrogant son of a hunter, Rolf."

"I think your father likes him."

"Thomlin?"

Gilly laughed. "No. Rolf."

Gwen shrugged. "My father likes anyone who brings in meat at a reasonable price."

With a gathering basket in hand and a bag slung over her shoulder, Gwen met Gilly and the two boys at the Bastwick cottage at midday on the Day of Rest, just as she'd promised her friend she would do. No matter how the day turned out, she was intent on having something to keep her occupied, so she'd packed a sackcloth bag with a small spade and clipping scissors, the journal she kept for jotting down her observations about herbs and other plants, and the book Madame Gabaldi had given her. It had been easier to carry the weighty tome over her shoulder than to bundle it in her arms. Nonetheless, her shoulder had registered its weight with complaint by the time she reached the Bastwick cottage.

"Now aren't you all the picture of a fun day ahead," said Mignon as she handed Thomlin a picnic basket. "I've packed a few tidbits for an afternoon snack. Just some teacakes and honey."

"Oh, thank you, Madame Bastwick," said Thomlin, his plump cheeks growing rosy while his mouth grew into a wide smile. "I love your teacakes."

Gwen, who stood beside Gilly, rolled her eyes. Mignon smiled and turned her attention to Rolf. "You be sure to watch out for danger, boy."

"Yes'm. Always." He tucked a stray clump of hair behind his ear.

Mignon smiled again and shooed the quartet out the door, not nearly soon enough for Gwen, who wanted the day to be over sooner rather than later.

Once outside, Gwen put her arm in front of Rolf. "Let them go first."

Gilly grinned at hearing Gwen's words and grabbed Thomlin's hand. While the pair led the way, Gwen and Rolf lagged behind, and they soon arrived at the meadow on the edge of the woods, the very one where the four of them had run into each other the day Gilly and Gwen had been out gathering herbs.

"Over here," yelled Gilly, waving from under a tree with branches wide enough to stretch over a patch of low grass that thinned into a thicket on the woods side of the tree and disappeared into taller grass on the meadow side.

Gwen waved back.

"He's pretty taken by her," said Rolf, "and don't have much time for hunting anymore." He shrugged. "Guess a miller don't have much need for hunting, though."

She mulled over his words, the frankness of which had surprised her. "I suppose you're right. He needs a wife to help him at the mill, and it looks like that's just what he's up to hunting."

Rolf bellowed a laugh. "Good thing. He's got a lot better chance of catching a wife than bringing down a buck. That boy couldn't hit a barn if he was standing next to it."

Gwen laughed at the mental image Rolf had painted for her. "My father says you're a good hunter."

Rolf shrugged. "It's what my papa taught me. Gotta eat. Everybody's gotta eat."

"Speaking of eating, if we don't get over there, Thomlin will have finished off the teacakes."

The hunter's son laughed and nodded. "Yeah, he will." He took two rapid strides forward and then turned around to face Gwen as he continued to move backward. "Race you!"

"But you're bigger," she said, breaking into a full run that sent her long, raven hair streaming behind her as she passed him.

Cheating didn't matter. Rolf still got to the tree before Gwen did, and she arrived out of breath.

"And an equally good thing you're not gonna be a courier."

Gwen kicked some dirt toward Rolf, who jumped back. When he frowned, Gwen caught the twinkle in his eyes that gave away his expression as an obvious fake.

"Equally? What are you two talking about?" asked Thomlin, who sat at the base of the tree leaning back on it.

"I was just telling Gwen how you don't hunt."

Thomlin's cheeks turned rosy for the second time that day, and he looked down at his hands, which he was wringing. "Yeah. I'm not very good at that, am I?"

Gilly moved her hand to rest atop Thomlin's. "No matter. You're a good miller, and that's what counts."

"Really?" asked Thomlin.

"Really." Gilly smiled.

"I sure hope Master Gabaldi sees it that way."

"What do you mean," Gwen asked him.

"I got kind of carried away the day he asked us about training."

Gwen's dislike of the schoolmistress's husband roiled. "You mean when he goaded all the boys? That day?"

Gilly spoke up. "That's just what I said. It was unfair, and he shouldn't have to do it."

"Ummm. What are you three talking about?" Rolf asked, squatting down and clearing away some twigs before sitting on the hard ground.

"Master Gabaldi told us about some foreign ships and said we might need to defend our homes and . . ." He looked directly at Gilly. "Our loved ones." Looking over at Rolf again, he continued, "So he's training us to fight with weapons . . . real weapons."

"Like bows?"

"Not so much bows as swords. He says once we've learned how to not cut off our own legs, he'll take us to an expert for more training."

Rolf took a teacake and chomped down on it. "Interesting. So who's this expert?" he asked after chewing and swallowing.

Thomlin shrugged. "Some famous soldier he knows in Sutherhold."

"Sutherhold!" Gilly exclaimed. "You didn't say you were going to Sutherhold. When were you going to tell me?" She stood up and folded her arms in front of her.

"I've been trying to figure out how to get out of going. I really was going to tell you."

Gilly glared at Thomlin, and Gwen saw the boy's face pale. He opened his mouth to speak, but Rolf spoke up first.

"No need to get your knickers all twisted, Gilly. Sit down. We'll figure this out."

Gilly responded with an arched eyebrow and a hard stare directed at Rolf. "That's easy for you to say. You've never met Master Gabaldi."

"True," said Rolf. "So maybe I'll do that." He took another bite of the teacake then reached for the little jug of honey in the basket.

"Come on, Thomlin. I want to talk with you . . . in private," Gilly said, her arms still folded.

Gwen didn't think she'd ever seen Thomlin move so quickly. The boy all but jumped to his feet rather ungracefully and stumbled after Gilly, who walked past Rolf and Gwen without a word and tromped into the middle of the meadow before stopping to let Thomlin catch up with her.

"Whew. She's got a temper, that one," said Rolf.

Gwen laughed and rubbed her cheek. "Don't I know it. He's lucky she didn't lay into him."

Rolf nodded toward Gilly. She now had both hands on her hips and was clearly scolding Thomlin, who had tucked his chin onto his chest. "Looks like his luck's run out."

Seeing him at the mercy of an angry Gilly, Gwen felt sorry for the miller's son. "It's not his fault, really. Master Gabaldi is . . . intimidating."

"Yeah? How so?"

Gwen felt chills creep up her spine. "I don't know. He wears a sword."

"That don't make him scary, though. Lots of fellows carry swords."

"That's true, but he's different. It's his eyes. Something about them. I don't trust him."

"Guess I'll find out when I meet him, then."

"You're coming back to lessons?"

"I don't know. If the schoolmistress will let me train, maybe."

Gwen thought about the possibilities. "I'm sure Master Gabaldi will convince her to let you train with the others."

"We'll see," he said before popping the last of a honey-drenched teacake into his mouth and lying back. "You holler if you hear or see any trouble." He closed his eyes.

After taking the book out of her sack, Gwen settled herself on the ground and leaned back against the tree trunk. She flipped through the pages, looking for something that might interest her, but her thoughts flitted back to Thomlin and Gilly. She looked out to where they stood in calf-deep grass and early-season wildflowers, holding hands and just strolling along leisurely, clearly having made up. A twinge of jealousy stabbed at her. Rolf liked weapons and he would probably take advantage of the extra time Master Gabaldi spent training the boys who wanted to practice more after the other lessons had ended and his wife was preparing their evening meal. Having a good friend alongside him during those sessions might prompt Thomlin to stay too, rather than meeting Gilly at the bakery to walk her home. That would mean the two girls could spend more time together. Yes, she thought, Rolf's return to lessons might be a very good thing. But a twinge of guilt amended her thought. It couldn't hurt to have Rolf there to help Thomlin practice with a sword. The poor boy truly was clumsy, and even if she still wasn't sure she liked that he and Gilly were headed toward something more serious than friendship, she no longer wished him harm. Gilly deserved better than a miller husband who couldn't balance and carry a heavy grain sack if he had just one leg. Maybe Rolf could help him save his leg.

She sighed and went back to reading the book. There were so many descriptions of orders of monks and their philosophies that Gwen felt overwhelmed. How would she ever decide which was right for her?

Chapter 8
Favor the conscientious over the confident.
--Brother Ramirez, Cathuran monk

* * *

By midweek, Rolf had convinced Madame Gabaldi to allow him to train with her husband, but not without compromise. Her condition had been that Rolf would spend two hours practicing reading every night to make up for the years of lessons he'd missed and, at the end of each week, would leave training when the younger children ended their lessons and come inside to read for her while she cooked. It was a hard bargain, and Master Gabaldi, who at first had been critical of his wife's demand, stopped protesting when he saw how serious Rolf was about learning to use a sword as skillfully as he used a bow. The boy was the first to arrive in the morning and the last to leave just before dusk. Gwen's hunch had been right. Thomlin, always the follower and never the leader, fell into staying with Rolf to practice, and she and Gilly resumed their former dallying about town after the bakery closed for the day.

The new arrangement made Gwen happy, even if she did feel a little guilty because Gilly missed spending time with Thomlin and had expressed it on many an occasion. For her part, Gwen still hadn't decided on an order to join. Her grandmother was growing impatient with her indecision, and even her father had begun to press her more frequently about choosing her path. Spending time with Gilly helped relieve the stress of indecision.

One day Madame Gabaldi called her in early from their midday break and asked if she'd given the matter any more thought.

"All the time. There are just so many to choose from. Some of them are so severe and strict. Others seem too lax and unfocused, and I'm not sure they even exist anymore. And some just . . . well, they seem . . . I don't know . . . uninteresting."

"I'm sure it doesn't help that the book is so old. I was afraid this might happen, but a bit of fortune has come your way, almost as if the heavens have intervened on your behalf." She gave a bright smile.

"What fortune?"

"My husband and I attended a party last evening."

"Gilly mentioned that she and the Widow Crookstaff had been busy baking pies and tarts and all manner of delicacies."

"Indeed, it was a fine feast, and the young woman honored at the party, the one visiting Madame Grayston, has graciously agreed to take a message to a friend of mine in Sutherhold. You see, she's from Sutherhold, and she knows the temple where Jacques serves. I grew up with him. A sweet boy, always so scholarly. We've met on many occasions to discuss philosophy and history and to exchange books when I passed through Sutherhold. I've asked if he'll take you in for a while and help you learn about the many options you have. He's quite learned about the orders."

Gwen's heart thumped faster. "When will we know if he is willing to do it?"

"Soon. The girl left for Sutherhold this morning and promised she'd deliver the message as soon as she arrives home. Jacques won't delay." Madame Gabaldi smiled warmly and reached out, laying her hand atop Gwen's shoulder. "I'm sure he'll agree. He's devoted, and I can't imagine he won't be thrilled to help another along the path to devotion."

"Thank you. My father and grandmother will be so pleased."

That afternoon, Thomlin and Rolf were waiting when Gwen got out of lessons, and the three of them walked to the bakery, where they stood outside and waited for Gilly to finish her day's work.

"I'm probably going to Sutherhold," Gwen announced without warning.

"Why?" asked Rolf.

"To meet with a monk who will help me find a monastery I can enter."

Rolf blinked. "You're going to be a monk? I figured you for the next schoolmistress or hedge witch."

His assessment stung, a bitter reminder that she'd never be what she wanted to be. She shook her head. "No. A monk." An awkward silence filled the space around them.

Thomlin piped up. "We're going to Sutherhold too. Maybe we can go together."

Rolf answered the question Gwen had been about to ask. "To meet Master Gabaldi's soldier friend, remember?"

"I had forgotten about that. Do you know when?"

"Too soon." Thomlin's tone made it clear just how disheartened he was over the thought of going.

"Can you not just tell that bully you don't want to go?" Gwen's ire rose. She truly hated Master Gabaldi and the way he berated the boys who were becoming young men under his tutelage.

Thomlin shook his head. "He already spoke to my pa. He said I'd be back in time for harvest and that it was our civic duty to prepare to defend Vasterberg. What could Pa say?" His eyes widened. "Don't tell Gilly. Promise you won't, Gwen. Please promise."

Gwen shook her head. The miller's son was cut from the same cloth as his father. In their own ways, each was a victim of bullying. "When will you learn that it's better to tell her than for her to learn from someone else? What if one of the other boys says something? This village isn't big enough to spit in without someone seeing it and telling everyone."

Rolf snorted.

"I will. I will. I was going to tell her tonight when I walk her home."

"Well, you'd better, or she'll wail you if she hears it from one of those loud-mouthed braggarts who want to be heroes." Rolf punctuated his point with a nod across the road.

There, three of the other boys training with them stood outside the general store. Gwen watched and tried to listen but couldn't hear what they were telling two villagers. She surmised the conversation was about training because the boys drew their swords and clanged them together in slow motion, as if demonstrating some technique they'd learned. The men nodded, the boys resheathed their swords, and the group fell into conversation again.

Gwen looked back at Thomlin. "Tonight."

The reluctant trainee gave a wary glance at the group across the road then nodded.

A few minutes later, Gilly came out of the bakery, her curls bouncing and hands filled with muffins. "Madame wants you to have these. They're the extra ones we made for the party in case any burned." She beamed as she held out her hands and let each of her friends take one. "I made them. Apple and nuts and my special seasoning. Not a single one burned."

The muffins were, as Gwen expected, delightfully tasty and seemed to perk up Thomlin's mood by the time he and Gilly left for the Bastwick cottage and into what Gwen knew would be a difficult conversation for both of them. As she and Rolf watched them go hand in hand down the road as the couple she believed they'd become, Gwen gave a little sigh. "She's going to be so upset."

A pall of sadness blanketed every moment Gwen spent with her friends for the next two weeks. Gilly kept bursting into tears, and Thomlin had morphed into desperation, which made him even clumsier than normal. Even Rolf was affected. Quieter than usual, he seemed to Gwen like he was holding back a simmering resentment. One early afternoon, he confirmed her suspicions when Madame Gabaldi asked her to take a break from lessons and deliver a message to the seamstress. She stepped out of the building and heard Master Gabaldi's voice from inside the center of a circle of trainees. Gwen could barely make out his head above the crowd, but she could see the tip of his sword pointing outward.

"That isn't a bow, and you don't have the reach, boy."

"I don't need reach."

Gwen recognized the voice as Rolf's and rushed to the circle, pushing her way through the silent crowd.

"You think not?" The swordsman's tone was taunting.

Blood ran down from a cut on Rolf's forehead, and he shook his head to direct the stream away from his eye. "Yeah. That's what I think," he said and took a rapid jab at Master Gabaldi, sending the man scampering backward.

Gwen gasped, her hand flying to her mouth. She wanted to scream at them to stop, but she was afraid to distract Rolf, afraid her distraction might give Gabaldi an opportunity to strike.

The man growled. "Put it down and calm down. This will not end well, I promise you."

"You didn't have to do that. You're a bully."

Master Gabaldi laughed and took two steps forward, his sword tip meeting Rolf's. "Call me what you will. You'll thank me when you meet the enemy. Now put it down."

Rolf shook his head again.

"What's going on here?" Madame Gabaldi said from behind Gwen, who let out an audible sigh of relief. "And what's happened to you?" she continued as her lanky form broke through the circle of trainees, and she walked straight up to Rolf.

"Ask him." Rolf nodded to Gabaldi but didn't lower his sword. Gwen could tell from the stiff position he held that he wasn't going to yield.

"Well, that will be quite enough." She spun around to her husband. "Quite enough."

Master Gabaldi stiffened.

"These boys are entrusted to my safekeeping, and I say that lessons are over for the day. End this now, Husband." She stared directly into his eyes.

As he lowered his sword, Gwen caught a flash of seething in Master Gabaldi's returned stare.

"And someone call for a healer. Get Madame Bastwick. Come along, Rolf. We need to clean this wound and see how bad it is." She grasped Rolf by his upper arm.

Though he'd muscled substantially since Gwen had first seen him, Madame Gabaldi's frame was much larger than his, and her long fingers wrapped around his bicep with length to spare. He seemed to comprehend that she wasn't trying to hurt him and that pulling away from her wasn't going to give him any advantage if her husband chose to ignore his wife's command and attack. Rolf cut his stare away from Master Gabaldi. "Yes'm."

The schoolmistress led him into the back room of the building, and there she kept him until Mignon arrived with her healer's bag. Gwen ran the errand and stopped at the bakery to tell Gilly what had happened. By the time she got back with Gilly in tow, the other students had dispersed, and only Master Gabaldi remained. He sat next to the door on a stool while he fletched arrows.

"The healer's inside."

"Shame on you!" Gilly fussed, all of her anger at him taking her beloved Thomlin away clearly unable to be held inside any longer.

Gwen took hold of Gilly's hand. "Come on. Your mother may need help."

Gilly resisted but acquiesced and followed Gwen inside, where they found Mignon giving cleaning instructions to Rolf.

"And replace the poultice every day, do you hear me? Or you'll have an angry scar."

"Yes'm."

Gwen strained to get a look at Rolf when Mignon moved away from him and took her daughter's hand. "Come along, Gilly." She looked back at Rolf. "And you see that Gwendolin gets home safely too. Tell your father I'll be happy to fill him in on your care. If he has questions, he can stop by the cottage."

Finally, Mignon and Gilly moved out of the way. Rolf nodded and slipped a stray strand of hair behind his ear. On his forehead were two slashes that crossed each other, an X dead center, like a target.

"Before you go, Gwendolin," said Madame Gabaldi, "there's something I need to tell you."

Gwen's stomach knotted.

"I've received word from Brother Jacques. We'll be leaving for Sutherhold in three days, accompanied by my husband and the boys who will be attending further training."

Gwen shook her head. "When Father hears about what happened, he's not going to let me go on a trip with your husband at the helm."

"I know. That's why I'm going with you. I'll take you to Jacques myself and then return."

"But what about the lessons?"

"I spoke with Councilman and Madame Grayston at their party two weeks ago. Their daughter Esmerelda wants to pursue becoming a schoolmistress, so I'll let her take over while I'm gone. She'll do just fine with the young students, and the older ones are mostly in apprenticeships already anyway. Not to worry, Gwendolin. All will be well. I'm not going to let what happened today prevent you or any of the others from following your calling."

Calling? thought Gwen. That was laughable. Thomlin certainly didn't think of further training as pursuing his calling, and Gwen didn't consider being a monk a calling she longed for either, but it was the path she'd chosen to investigate, given her options. She'd even started to look forward to learning new things about the world, things she couldn't see and didn't understand, things alluded to in the book. "I'll tell my father."

"Good. And if he needs to speak with me, he knows where to find me."

Gwen led Rolf out the back door of the building, avoiding Master Gabaldi and a guaranteed confrontation. She could see anger simmering in the way Rolf set his jaw.

"What will you do now?" she asked him when they were well away from the danger of running into anyone from Vasterberg.

"Same as before, I guess. I'll go to Sutherhold."

"But how can you, Rolf? After what's happened? What will your father say?"

"Nothing."

"I can't believe he'll have nothing to say. His son is coming home with gashes put there at the hand of a man twice his size and three times as many years experienced."

"He won't say nothing, Gwen. Let it be."

Gwen stopped and held out an arm to halt Rolf. "What's wrong? There's something you're not saying. No father, not even one who doesn't come around other people, *especially* one who doesn't come around people, would say *nothing*."

Tears welled in Rolf's eyes. He looked away from Gwen and stared out across the rolling hills. "He can't say anything because he's dead. Ran into a waking bear a month ago and bled to death."

"Oh dear heavens! Why didn't you tell us?" She threw her arms around Rolf's midriff and squeezed him tightly, thoughts of how she'd felt when her mother had been killed by the wolf reminding her of just how much pain her friend must have been feeling now. It explained his anger, his quiet mood. It hadn't been because he was angry when Gabaldi had bullied the Franks into sending Thomlin for more training or even because Gabaldi had injured him. It had been because his father was gone. Gwen wanted to kick herself for not recognizing the symptoms of grief.

All she could do was hold his tense body and whisper, "I'm so sorry, Rolf."

Chapter 9

The trouble with purpose is knowing you might never achieve it.
--Mother Seema, Cathuran monk

* * *

That evening, Gwen's grandmother had been delighted to learn about the upcoming trip; her father, less so.

"I don't like what people are saying about Gabaldi," Jacob told his daughter as they sat near the hearth after dinner. "I've never known the hunter's son--"

"Rolf. His name is Rolf Rosenkranz, Father."

"I've never known *Rolf* to be less than coolheaded. Even the first time he brought me game. He was calm and a lot more grown up than the Frank boy who was with him."

"He was angry today, Father. I saw that myself."

"I heard that too, but what made him angry enough to challenge a master swordsman? The boy's smart as a raccoon."

"I don't know. By the time I got there, he was bleeding and angry. None of the other boys said a single word. And none of the villagers were there either, so they have no right to talk about this as if they were. But I do know something they don't. Like I told you, Rolf's father died a month ago. A whole month. And in all that time, he didn't tell anyone about it, not even his best friend. Since then, he's been quiet. You know the kind of quiet I'm talking about--the kind that's brewing a blow-up. It was like that. Maybe Rolf said or did something. Maybe it was an accident like Master Gabaldi told everyone it was. It doesn't matter because I won't be going to Sutherhold *alone* with Rolf Rosenkranz or Master Gabaldi. Madame Gabaldi is coming too."

Jacob Ahlgren all but snorted. "And what's *she* going to do if he attacks another one of you younguns? *Teach* him to death? Hit him upside his head with a *book?*" His smirk highlighted just how ridiculous he found the idea of Madame Gabaldi being able to protect anyone against a seasoned soldier.

Though tempted to laugh because what her father said *did* conjure humorous images, she recognized the critical need to keep the conversation serious if she was going to convince him to let her go to Sutherhold. She tilted her head the way she remembered her mother doing when she and her husband disagreed and he made light of something with sarcasm. Her father must have caught the similarity of expression because he blinked, and his smirk disappeared into solemnity.

"It won't just be Madame Gabaldi. The other boys will be there too. And even if they weren't, Madame Gabaldi would be just fine. You should have seen her today, Father. She stepped right between Rolf and her husband and gave that man a good tongue-lashing for letting Rolf get hurt. He hushed right up and put his sword away."

"Well, he's telling the villagers Rolf got frustrated and angry and tumbled into the sword, and that's what caused the accident."

Gwen bit her tongue and refrained from using her father's sarcasm to say, "Twice? In a perfect X? Some misstep, that." Instead, she asked in a calm, controlled tone, "And don't you think his explanation is the most logical? Father, training accidents happen."

Her grandmother had been silent after her initial reaction to the news about Gwen, but now she spoke up. "Jacob, you know it's true. Have you forgotten almost cutting off a thumb when you were an apprentice?"

Jacob shook his head. "I haven't forgotten, Mother."

"Gwendolin's not his apprentice, and if he's as vicious as you fear, then all the better she'll have someone like him to protect the wagons on the road, don't you think?"

"I suppose." Jacob stared into the fire.

Gwen's grandmother put her darning in her lap and reached over to Jacob, placing a hand on his arm. "I know it's hard, but it's time to let her go, Jacob. There's nothing for her here now anyway."

The truth of her grandmother's statement burned in Gwen's heart. If Vasterberg held nothing for Gwen, it had been her grandmother's doing. She'd cut off the option of an apprenticeship with Mignon and had forced Gwen to make a choice between the lesser of two evils. But now Gwen was committed to the choice she'd made, and the time had come to use one final tactic to win her father's approval for the trip. She felt guilty for the half-truth she was about to utter, but she was willing to carry the guilt. "I want to go, Father. I *have* to go. I'm *called* to go."

Her strategy tipped the balance, not quite as far as she'd have liked but far enough to elicit an agreement from her father to speak with Madame Gabaldi and give fair consideration to what the schoolmistress had to say. That night, Gwen crawled into bed hopeful, and by noon the next day, her father gave his reluctant permission. She was dismissed from lessons to start packing the one trunk she would be allowed to take with her.

They left the schoolmistress's private quarters, where they'd held their discussion out of range of the overly curious students Esmerelda Grayston was tutoring. Gwen walked with her father toward the butcher shop, passing the boys training outside with Master Gabaldi, who spoke to his charges in a calm, patient tone while he demonstrated a sword technique. She wanted to roll her eyes at him. He'd never treated the boys with kindness or understanding before the incident with Rolf, but then, nobody had called into question his suitability for educating Vasterberg's young men in the art of killing others. This was pure performance, and it made her dislike the schoolmistress's husband all the more.

"I didn't see the Rosenkranz boy," her father said when they'd put some distance between them and the training circle.

She lied. "I didn't notice. I'm sure he was there somewhere. Some of those boys are broad and tall enough to hide a pony behind them." The truth was Rolf's absence *had* been conspicuous. She'd noticed when she arrived at the schoolhouse and had watched for him. By the time lessons began and he still hadn't arrived, Gwen had begun to imagine the worst. She'd worried about him all morning. Now she was doubly concerned. Her father was under the impression Rolf would be traveling with the group, and he'd expressed relief in knowing someone he trusted with a bow would be near his daughter. Gwen wasn't convinced her friend would come back to training as long as Master Gabaldi was in charge, much less travel under Gabaldi's lead and command. She changed the subject. "Madame Gabaldi says we'll be leaving in a day and a half. I'd like to walk Gilly home tomorrow afternoon and say good-bye to her and her mother."

Jacob stopped at the door to the butcher shop. "Right, then. You go on home and spend the day with your grandmother. She'll miss you, you know."

She nodded though she doubted her father was right. As soon as she got out of the village and well beyond her father's sight from the shop window, she headed straight toward the spot where she and Gilly and Thomlin and Rolf had spent their first afternoon as friends together. Standing in the cool shade under the same spreading limbs of the elm tree they'd sat beneath, she called out Rolf's name repeatedly, hoping he would hear her if he was hunting in the woods. Each time, she listened for him to call back, but she heard nothing except the scurrying of woodland squirrels and the rustling of branches as birds took flight. Time was too short for her to trek into the woods to his cabin. If time and her skewed sense of direction didn't deter her, the thought of venturing into the woods alone stirred up memories of her mother's death and gave her goose bumps. While she continued calling Rolf's name from the moderate safety of the meadow and strained to listen for any sign of response, she picked some wildflowers haphazardly and looked warily over her shoulder at the edge of the woods with regularity. Though she delayed as long as she could, she finally conceded she had to leave if she was going to make it home early enough to avoid arousing her father's suspicions about Rolf, or more precisely, the apparently missing Rolf.

Gwen avoided her father and discussion of Rolf after dinner by excusing herself to begin packing her belongings. Deciding what to take proved easy enough. She had only one trunk. How much could possibly fit in it? She used the space as efficiently as she could and managed to get four cotton shifts, three nicer dresses, a pair of brown leather flats, a nightgown, and a shawl into the trunk before it became apparent that one of the fancy dresses was taking up too much space. She winnowed down her stash by one cotton shift and the space-hogging dress. In a small, wooden box, she placed her quill, ink crock, and plant snips. She put the box and her herb journal on top of the clothes, along with another small box containing her hair comb, a few pieces of ribbon, and a small square of rough cloth for washing. One box for her passion, the other for her pleasure. Although she had to shift the contents of the trunk several times and finally push down as hard as she could to make room for the book Madame Gabaldi had given her, Gwen closed the trunk before she heard her father's chair scrape the wooden planks near the hearth.

She blew out the lantern and hopped into her bed, her back to the door and her eyes shut. The thud of his boots grew louder, and when the hinges of the door to her room creaked, she could feel his gaze. After a few moments, the hinges creaked again, and the latch clicked. Gwen lay in bed awake for a good, long while, her gaze fixed on the growing moon, her mind filled with a mixture of anxious thoughts about what her life would be like, excitement about exploring the world outside of Vasterberg's confines, and sadness about leaving her father. She would miss his tender kisses atop her head and the smell of smoked meat in his hair.

By the time she awoke, dawn had come and passed into a bright midmorning, and the sounds of the Ahlgren homestead floated in through the open window. Nestling swallows cheeped for their second meals of the day from the rafters in the open barn, and the hogs she so despised grunted and squealed loudly as they vied for spots in cool mud hollows where they could settle down for their post feeding naps. Gwen found her grandmother chopping parsnips on the cutting table near the kitchen window, the old woman's eyes fixed on the maple tree near the fence that ran along the edge of the road to their cottage, her fingers pressing down on a parsnip and curled against the knife's edge as she lifted it up and down, slicing cleanly through the dense vegetable.

"Good morning, Grandmother." Gwen picked up a heated kettle hanging in the fire and filled her bathing bowl with steaming water.

"When the stew's in the pot, I'll go to the cellar and bring up some dried fruits. You'll be a week on the road to Sutherhold. Your pa's bringing home some dried meat too. You'll not be hungry getting there."

Gwen placed the kettle back in the fire and picked up the bowl. "Thank you, but please don't go to any trouble for me, Grandmother. I can go down to the cellar. You slopped the hogs for me."

"We've still got time to wash a few of your clothes if you don't take too long bathing." Her grandmother continued to chop and stare out the window.

"Everything I'm taking with me is clean but thank you. I'll wash the rest later and leave them out on the line. If you don't mind, would you remind Father to take them into town and give them to Esmerelda Grayston? She can see to it that any of the smaller children who need clothes get them."

"Fine. If that's what you want."

The awkwardness of the conversation urging her to walk as quickly as she could without sloshing the water out of the bowl, Gwen carried it into her room and shut the door. She bathed and towel-dried her hair before braiding it. Then she spied the treat she'd set aside for a day she wanted to remember always: her favorite dress, a blue one with a low neckline, off-the-shoulder sleeves, and a feature her Grandmother was known for perfecting--a delicate draping waist ruffle cascading with such gentleness as to look like no more than a shimmery shadow atop the blue fabric. But when the skirt moved, the ruffle shuddered, and its wearer looked ethereal. Gwen found it calming. Soon she would have to give up her worldly goods, and though she'd packed two of her best dresses to wear while in Sutherhold, she hadn't been able to bear the thought of a total stranger ending up with her favorite dress. She'd decided to leave it behind with her other clothing and let a needy student benefit from her loss. But for now, she thought as she slipped it over her head, she was going to enjoy every worldly pleasure she could, especially the finery that a girl from such modest family means rarely dreamed of, much less had.

Once she'd tucked a sprig of the wildflowers she'd harvested the afternoon before into the single braid hanging loosely at the nape of her neck, she folded the braid up and secured it with a wooden stick she wove in and out of the hair. Then she tidied up her bed and took the bowl of water out to the garden, where she tossed it into the nearest hollow in the pig pen. A plump hog, who clearly had no idea he would become next winter's ham, snuffled the mud with such content Gwen almost felt sorry for him.

Chapter 10

Different is scary until normal thinking repeatedly fails to solve the problem.
--Mignon Bastwick, hedge witch

* * *

Before leaving the cottage, Gwen gathered up a few things she wanted to give to Mignon and Gilly. She stuffed them in a plain sackcloth gathering bag with a reinforced leather strap long enough to sling across her body from shoulder to hip. A pile of cut parsnips sat on the cutting block unattended as she passed through the largest room of the cottage, and Gwen felt ashamed she was relieved not to run into her grandmother on the way out.

Her shame niggled at her all the way to Vasterberg, and it colored the short walk she usually enjoyed. The only birds she heard were crows, and their cackling clouded the fresh spring air with foreboding. Worry soon replaced her glumness, though, when she got to the schoolhouse. Master Gabaldi was talking to his group of trainees, who stood at attention, and a quick scan of the group confirmed Rolf wasn't among them.

The soldier dismissed the boys as Gwen approached, and she headed straight for Thomlin. "Where is he?"

"I don't know. He didn't show up yesterday or today."

"I looked for him at the meadow and called out for him yesterday, but he never answered."

Thomlin kicked at the dirt and looked down. "He's not coming back, Gwen."

When he looked up into Gwen's eyes, the degree of compassion she saw took her aback.

"I don't blame him for that, mind you," Thomlin said.

Gwen placed a hand on Thomlin's shoulder and squeezed. "Neither do I. He's probably better off anyway."

"Yeah. Probably." He hesitated. "I'll miss him."

The complexity of Thomlin's feelings made Gwen feel ashamed again, this time for thinking of him for so long as a simpleton motivated only by food and his affection for Gilly.

"So will I," she said. "I'm glad he's not going to have to deal with Master Gabaldi anymore, though."

"Yeah, that too." Thomlin nodded.

"Let's go find your sweet girl," Gwen said, trying to lighten both their spirits.

"I can smell her already," said Thomlin.

Gwen crinkled up her face.

"Not like that! When she bakes bread, the whole village smells like her. I've been smelling her all day. Do you know how hard it was to concentrate on Master Gabaldi's *important instructions?*" These last couple of words Thomlin said in mimicry of Gabaldi's sharp tone.

Gwen laughed, thankful she'd learned something good about Thomlin, though it made her sad to think of what he faced, what they both faced. At that second, she realized just how much like her Thomlin was. He, too, had no choice in molding his own future. Unlike her, he showed no resentment. Gwen wondered what it took to feel that way but doubted she'd ever figure it out.

Gilly's voice drowned out the tinkling bell as they opened the bakery door, along with Gwen's thoughts about Thomlin and destinies unchosen. "It's about time! I've been watching out the window for at least an hour."

"Pacing's more like it," said the Widow Crookstaff from behind Gilly. The wrinkled old woman stood behind a block of wood similar to her father's cutting block kneading a large mound of sticky dough with the strength of a much younger woman.

Gilly seemed to ignore the remark. "I'll see you tomorrow, Madame Crookstaff. Thank you for your generosity."

The baker's hands sank into the dough, and she looked up. "Safe travels to you both." She returned her gaze to the dough and resumed kneading. When the bell tinkled again, she said, "And we'll be seeing you in the shop again soon, young man."

"Yes, ma'am," said Thomlin. "You surely will. Nothing will keep me away from your late-summer cakes. I'll be back in time for those, don't you know?"

Though he grinned at Gilly, Gwen knew his expression masked doubt, fear, and sadness. Part of her clung to the notion that maybe, just maybe, some small part of his expression, just one tiny speck of it, held genuine hope for the future.

The trio's walk to the Bastwick cottage was solemn and intentionally slow. Gwen trailed behind the couple, slowing her pace periodically to stretch out the distance between her and them. When they stopped and turned to face each other, their hands laced together, Gwen wandered to the side of the road and stooped over, pretending to take an interest in something growing there. She chuckled quietly as she fingered the scraggly blades of scrub grass, which had choked out other plants growing there if ever there'd been any. The irony of it amused her. Every miller's bane to sort out of gathered grain, but at this moment, the scrub grass allowed the young man who would become a miller someday to speak words of devotion and adoration in private.

After a few minutes, Gilly called out, and Gwen stood up. Thomlin was walking toward her, and as the two met, he said, "Thank you and I'll see you tomorrow morning."

Gwen nodded and smiled and continued walking toward Gilly.

"I sent him home. Mother will surely want all your attention when we get to the cottage. I just want a few moments alone with you too."

Tears filled Gwen's eyes, and she wrapped her arms around Gilly, hugging her tightly. "Life won't be the same without you, Gillian Margaretta Bastwick."

Gilly, who had been hugging Gwen in return, pulled back and smiled. "Well, of course not, silly."

The two laughed and walked the rest of the way to the cottage hand in hand, as they'd done as children. Those days long past, their friendship had blossomed into something Gwen would cherish her entire life. Of that she had no doubt. As she entered the cottage, she clung to the one thin certainty she had amid thick confusion about what lay ahead for her.

Mignon met them just inside the doorway and threw her arms around Gwen. "You look more like your mother every time I see you." She released her and pecked Gilly on the cheek. "And so do you."

"She could do worse," said Gwen. "You're both so beautiful." Inside and out, she thought.

"Well, come in and shut that door. Bugs are coming to life again, and I don't want them infesting my herbs. I've got a few things for you. Go sit down."

The friends did as directed, and soon Mignon appeared out of the cramped work area to the side of the fireplace, mugs of tea in hand. The aroma calmed Gwen at first sniff. "Chamomile."

Mignon nodded and returned to the counter for her own mug and a small tow sack. Once she'd settled on a stool near the girls and placed the tow sack on her lap, she put her nose near the mug and inhaled slowly before taking a quick sip of her tea. She placed the mug on the floor and reached into the tow sack, which by now had filled Gwen with curiosity.

"I won't be needing this anymore, and I'd like you to have it. Even monks need to know about herbs and remedies. Maybe *especially* monks."

In her hands was the sum of Mignon's knowledge. Thrice the size of Gwen's plant journal, Mignon's bulged with uneven pages of sheepskin between two thin pieces of wood, all kept together with a long strand of leather looped through the sheepskin and the protective planks.

Gwen's mouth dropped open, and her heart raced. "I can't." The words stuck to her tongue and came out thick and muddy.

"Of course you can. You're the most talented herbalist I've ever known and will ever know, Gwendolin Ahlgren."

Her hand shook when she reached out to take the journal from Mignon. When she touched it, she heard the gypsy fortune-teller's voice, as low and foreboding and clear as it had been on the day she and Gilly visited her tent,

"Ohmahold."

Mignon's brow furrowed when Gwen looked up at her. "Whoever takes the apprenticeship will have to begin with her own notes. These are for you. I know you'll use them wisely and with an open heart." She let go of the journal and drew her hands into her lap and clasped them, as if she didn't know what to do with her hands now that she'd released the collection of notes she'd made over a lifetime.

Her words drowned out any thought of the gypsy's voice or what it meant that she'd heard it again. Tears streamed down Gwen's face. She loved Mignon and felt as safe and loved in her presence as she'd felt with her own mother.

"But what about you? Don't you want to keep them to look back on?"

Mignon laughed. "Do you think I need those scribblings now?"

Gwen shook her head and smiled, although she could see Mignon's hands still fidgeting in their forced clasp. "No. You don't."

"I've something else for you," Mignon said. Out of the tow sack, she pulled a dyed wool shawl that seemed to go on forever.

Gwen recognized it immediately. Mignon wore the long wool shawl wrapped around her neck, its ends hanging loosely down the front of her clothing to her knees. No matter the weather or season, she put it on when she left the cottage to tend to others, just in case she needed a blanket if she had to spend the night with a patient. Gwen thought it was a reasonable habit. Her departures, after all, were almost always in response to a messenger calling her to tend to some critically ill person, to someone like Rolf who'd been injured, or worse. Sometimes, the people of Vasterberg and its surrounding clusters of farms called on the hedge witch to do what they couldn't when someone had been mauled by a wild animal or lost part of a limb. At those times, the hedge witch would determine if healing--and more important, suffering through what it would take to heal--was possible. If so, she might take measures as drastic as amputating a rotting limb. If not, she would allow the patient the choice of dulling or ending suffering, and she used her herb lore to accomplish whichever the unfortunate patient chose. Gwen thought this was why the people of Vasterberg, people like her grandmother, looked down their noses at Mignon. A simple woman of humble means, she held the power of life and death in little pouches of herbs. The people of Vasterberg were in reluctant awe, fearing the very thing they needed from her.

Its softness surprised Gwen when she touched it, as she'd always assumed it heavier and more coarse. "Are you sure?" she asked, hoping Mignon was.

"Most definitely. It's more than a dependable shawl, though. It's my good luck charm, and I figure you could use a bit of that in your life right about now. It's time I make a new one anyway."

"Thank you." Gwen felt around the bottom of her shoulder bag until she found the presents she'd brought for these two people who'd meant so much in her life. First, she pulled out her gift for Mignon, a gathering basket. "Mother knew I had no interest in stitchery, so she bribed me into making a lining for a gathering basket. Of course, first she had to teach me to dye the thread for embroidery, and then she had to teach me to embroider. It took late autumn and all of winter to finish it, and I had thought it would take a day." Gwen looked down fondly at her handiwork, a piece of sackcloth, the edges and center of which had neatly stitched delicate flowers in shades of yellow, red, and green. "It's not perfect, but I know you can always use another basket."

"It's lovely," said Mignon, who swallowed hard enough Gwen saw it. "Thank you."

Mignon's sentimentality almost brought Gwen to tears again, but she pressed on, her excitement manifesting in a grin. She'd saved the best gift for last and looked forward to seeing Gilly's reaction to it. Reaching into the bag again, she pulled out a piece of sheer, white cloth with lace edging and handed it to Gilly. "It's Mother's wedding veil. I want you to wear it someday."

Gilly burst into tears. "It's the most beautiful thing I've ever seen."

"It is, indeed," said Mignon, who reached over to brush her fingertips across the fine cloth. "Your grandmother made this, and every girl in Vasterberg envied your mother for it."

"Now every girl in Vasterberg will envy Gilly," said Gwen, "as they should!"

Her friend fingered the delicate cloth and looked up at Gwen with wistful eyes. "Do you remember when we were little and your mother let us play with it if we promised to be careful?"

Gwen nodded. "I do remember and if memory serves me correctly, you were going to marry my father."

"He was the most dashing hero in my mind, a gentle knight."

The three of them laughed, and Gwen was grateful for the release of tension and overwhelming sadness she felt in saying good-bye. The ever-observant Mignon must have sensed how Gwen was feeling because she rose from her chair and scooped up the tepid tea mugs. "Gilly has a gift for you too."

"I'd almost forgotten!" Gilly said as she laid the veil gently into the darning basket next to her chair and followed her mother into the area where they prepared food and Mignon mixed her concoctions.

Gwen watched as the pair moved about the tiny space without bumping into one another or impeding each other's movements.

When they returned to the chairs surrounding the fireplace, both had something in hand for Gwen. Mignon held mugs of steaming fresh tea for them, this time steeped with peppermint, the aroma of which filled the entire cottage and made Gwen wonder just how strong the tea was. Gilly had a cloth bundle she held by its knotted ends. Thrusting it toward Gwen, she said, "Madame Crookstaff contributed the exotic beans. She says they're called cacao beans." She scrunched up her face. "If you don't roast them before you crush them, they're horribly bitter. But they add a delightful and energizing flavor to muffins. Oh, and there are hard bread buns too, enough to keep you full the whole way to Sutherhold and beyond."

Gwen took the bundle and put it into her shoulder bag, along with the other things Mignon had given her. "Thank you, Gilly. I'll think of you with every bite, and so will my stomach."

For the next few hours, the three of them sat in front of the low fire and reminisced about the girls' childhood, the mishaps and accidents, the silliness and laughter, the adventures they'd experienced together as the best of friends. When the sun had crested and started its decline, they cried their reluctant good-byes, and Gwen left the cottage for what she knew to be the last time.

Before she rounded the bend in the road that would inhibit view of the Bastwick home, she turned around and took in one last look at the modest abode--its thatched roof and hand-painted door and shutters, the pale smoke streaming from the chimney, vegetable and herb shoots just beginning to poke out of the soil in rickety wooden boxes lining the sunniest side of the house.

She closed her eyes and breathed in the smell of the nearby woods and the dusty road, and a vision filled the darkness. It was Thomlin on a horse, galloping past her to the door of the cottage then tumbling off the saddle. The door flew open, and Mignon and Gilly rushed out, helping him to his feet. As they entered the cabin, Thomlin dragging a leg behind and draping his arms over the shoulders of the women on either side of him, he breathlessly spoke as if answering a question Gwen hadn't heard, "They tried to take us. . . . The Zjhon, that's who! . . . I dunno. I think they got him. You should've seen what Gwen did." And the door closed behind the three of them as if by some unseen hand.

She opened her eyes, her heart racing and her breath held. The cottage was just as it had been. No horse. No Thomlin. Gwen let out a whoosh of breath and wondered what else Mignon had put into the tea.

Arriving home in time to wash and hang out the clothes as she'd told her grandmother she would do, Gwen went about the chore with an unusual appreciation and satisfaction in every movement. The task helped take her mind from the disturbing vision, which felt less and less real as time went on. When she finished draping the last of her dresses over the rope, she caught sight of the blossoming tree under which her mother's grave rested amid white crocuses; delicate violets; and the gangly, grasslike early spring wildflowers that were somehow just as beautiful as the other flowers. By summer, asters and violas and foxglove would surround the grave. Gwen had planted those herself after her mother's death because they were favorites of both of them. The tree's leaves would be waxy and lush green by then too, its flower petals long spent and rotting in the rich soil surrounding its roots.

Gwen thought about the garden and its perpetual change, and somehow that calmed her enough to approach the grave. She looked up at the tree and reached for one of its tender flowers. Once upon a time, her father had thought the tree frivolous, but her mother had planted it anyway, insisting its purpose was just as important as that of a fruit tree or wind barrier even if it didn't bear anything they could eat or use in their everyday tasks. It would remind them life ever renewed itself each spring.

She smiled at that thought, and as she ran her fingers gently over the surface of a velvety petal, she heard her mother's voice. "You will have everything you need, my dear, dear Gwendolin. I promise you."

Her hand shook and she was uncertain if she could withdraw her fingers from the flower. Muscles ached as the weight of her arm became unbearable, surprising her that her body would tire so soon. Ever so gently, she plucked the petal and lowered her hand, giving one last look at the large rock at the base of the tree, the one on which a mason friend of her father's had chiseled Margaretta's name.

Gwen's whisper echoed in her own ears and through the budding branches of what she vowed to think of evermore as Margaretta's Tree of Life, "Good-bye, Mother."

Chapter 11

Angry shouts often drown out reasoned argument.
--Barabas, druid

* * *

Gwen awoke light-headed and with prickling skin, a sense of foreboding looming. It took an unusually long time for her to feel fully awake, and she couldn't remember what she'd been dreaming when she'd first drifted out of sleep. But drifted she had and by slow, dull degrees, as if the distance between the world of dreams and the world of the living were a vast expanse of desert, barren of thought and physicality. Unpleasant memories dampened her mood but remained beyond her grasp.

Getting out of bed and dressing made her feel less detached from the living world, and by the time she left her room and joined her family for breakfast, she felt more like herself and less like a spirit trapped between dreams and consciousness. Her father and grandmother didn't say much during the meal, and Gwen followed suit, restricting her conversation to telling them about how much Mignon and Gilly liked their gifts, especially the veil.

"Your mother looked so beautiful in it," her father said, the smile of a happy memory stretching his lips before he bit off a hunk of bread and chewed silently.

Her grandmother chuckled. "My fingers bled when I made that. I was afraid I'd stained it, but I spit on it and got the blood out."

Gwen thought about what her grandmother said. She'd not considered how much work it took to stitch the veil, much less to tat all the lace. Though it had been her first attempt and sure to have taken longer than it would an experienced seamstress, Gwen had spent months dying thread and embroidering a small piece of sackcloth. She couldn't imagine how long her grandmother had taken to create such a beautiful piece of finery. "Gilly loves it. She always has. It's a dream come true for her to have it, and she'll look beautiful on her wedding day."

"Good. I hate to see it go to waste," her grandmother said.

The reality that she wouldn't be wearing it because she wouldn't ever marry struck Gwen in the gut, knotting her stomach with returning fears she had about living the life of a monk. *How lonely will I be?* she wondered.

Her father interrupted her morose musing by announcing it was time for him to load her trunk into the cart so they could leave for Vasterberg.

Gwen rose, and her grandmother took her plate. "You go on and get your things together, and don't forget the bag of food," she said as she rose and turned to carry the dirty plates into the kitchen. She nodded toward the butcher's block, atop which a small gunnysack sat, its midriff bulging and its open ends tied into a knot so the bag could be carried over a shoulder. "Your pa's put some meat in there too." She paused before turning her back and continuing with her task as if today were any other day. "Now don't you forget it, girl."

This was as close to saying good-bye as her grandmother was going to get, thought Gwen, and she could live with that. "Thank you. I won't forget it."

Thanks to the preparation she'd done the day before, gathering her belongings took no time at all. Gwen grabbed the bag with Gilly's breads and the one with meat and dried fruits and tossed Mignon's shawl around her neck, and she and her father left the cottage without fanfare in a matter of minutes. As the horse hitched to the cart turned onto the road, Gwen heard the hogs snorting and grunting. She wouldn't miss them at all.

During the trip to Vasterberg, she and her father chatted like they would on any other day, her father reminding her of all the things she needed to do to be safe.

"And don't go away from the caravan without somebody with you, not even to wee," he said.

Gwen wrinkled up her nose. "Eww. Do we have to talk about that?"

"Just be careful, Gwen. The world's not always as friendly a place as Vasterberg."

"I know, Father, and I promise I'll be cautious." She tried to shake off the mental image of someone standing nearby while she squatted behind a bush.

"I know you will," he said, but his tone said, "I'm afraid you won't."

"Really, Father. I promise." His worry palpable and making his forehead look like that of a wrinkled old man, Gwen wanted to comfort him, so she gave him an earnest look, repeating, "I promise."

"Right, then," he said. "Looks like they're getting the caravan all lined up."

Gwen looked around, her eyes filled with surprise. They'd arrived and she hadn't even noticed how far they'd come. She'd missed all the serene scenery she'd wanted to firmly plant in her memory. What lay before her instead was chaos. Master Gabaldi was parading on a horse in and out of a throng of trainees on horseback too. "Two of you get up front. No, not you, Frank. You're gonna drive the wagon."

"But, sir. What about my horse?"

"Tie him to the wagon, boy. Do as I say!" shouted Gabaldi.

His cheeks rosy with embarrassment, Thomlin scrambled down from his horse, the bundle secured to his waist belt bouncing wildly. He tied the reins to the rear of the wagon then climbed onto the driver's bench, where Madame Gabaldi sat with reins in her hand while some boys who would be traveling with them tossed trunks and sacks up to a couple of boys who stood in the bed of the wagon behind her. Gwen's father drew his cart alongside the schoolmistress.

"Good morning, Madame Gabaldi," he said.

She gave a warm smile. "Good morning, Master Ahlgren." She leaned forward so she could see past Gwen's father. "And good morning to you, Gwendolin. Are you excited?"

Gwen thought before answering. "A little nervous, but a little excited too." Looking past the teacher, she could see Thomlin and the pinched look of fear as he stared straight ahead.

The woman nodded as if she truly understood the mixed emotions Gwen felt. "You boys get her things," she called back to the two in the wagon's bed.

The lanky youths scampered down, crawling over what they'd already packed tightly enough that it wouldn't shift when the wagon started to move. They grabbed Gwen's trunk and hauled it to the wagon, but when one of the boys reached for the two bags she intended to carry--the one with Mignon's journal and Gilly's baked goods and the other with food from her father and grandmother, she stopped him by placing her hand on his, "Not those. I'll take those."

The two boys looked at each other, and one said, "You sure, Gwen? They're pretty heavy."

At that moment, Master Gabaldi rode up to them. "You boys leave her some room in the back of the wagon. That's where she'll be riding. And redistribute the weight. I don't want to break an axle because of an unbalanced load. It's too heavy on the port side." He pointed to a stack of crates.

"Yes, sir!" they shouted in unison before hopping into the wagon and quickly turning what had looked like a neatly arranged load into a jumble of trunks and sacks and crates.

While they lifted each piece of cargo to weigh and set down in piles before reorganizing the load, Gwen got down from her father's cart and hefted each of her two bags onto her shoulders. The boys were right. The bags were heavier than she'd remembered either being when she carried them out of the cottage. "Maybe you could put these next to where I'll be sitting," she called up to the two boys.

"Hand 'em here," said one, who took them and tossed them carelessly on top of one of the piles when Gwen offered them to him.

"I'll be right back," Madame Gabaldi said as she handed the reins to Thomlin and climbed down, disappearing into the schoolhouse.

"Git on up here," said one of the wagon loaders, "and let's be sure you're gonna fit and not fall out." He offered a hand to Gwen, who grasped it and was immediately lifted off her feet. It was as close to flying as she could imagine, and she squealed with delight just before landing on the wooden planks of the wagon bed.

"Sit over here," the boy said, patting a burlap bean sack that was stuffed behind the wagon seat at the front of the bed.

Gwen plopped down on it. She could barely see over the side rails of the wagon, but at least none of the stacked cargo was blocking her view or making her feel as if it would tumble down on her. The bean sack was hard and lumpy. Gwen knew it would be unforgiving of every bump and divot along the way. "This is fine," she said.

Her father had become engaged in a conversation with Master Gabaldi, and Gwen didn't think she could manage to stand hearing it, so she busied herself by standing up and retrieving the two bags she'd brought with her. Reaching inside, she took the bundle of breads out of one bag and stuffed it into the one with the food her family had given her but not before Thomlin caught the scent of Gilly's bread.

"She gave you bread too," he said, holding up a small bundle of his own that Gwen recognized as the same cloth Gilly had used to make her bundle. "She brought it over early this morning." He beamed.

"Yes. She's so thoughtful." Gwen resettled onto the lumpy sack and looked up at Thomlin, who was twisted on the bench so he could look at her while he spoke.

"I don't know what I'm gonna do without her around," he said quietly, as if ashamed.

"Well, maybe you could concentrate on driving that contraption," said a voice from behind Thomlin.

Gwen stood up, a broad grin on her face. In front of the wagon stood Rolf in a buckskin coat, his bow and a full quiver strapped to his back, his sheathed sword hanging from one side of a leather belt, his hunting knife hanging on the other side in its own leather sheath. In one hand, he held a small rabbit-skin bag.

"You made it!" squealed Thomlin, and though Gwen couldn't see his face, she could tell from Rolf's expression that his friend was grinning as widely as she was.

Rolf shrugged. "I got nothin' else to do, so why not?" He walked forward and tossed the bag up to Gwen, who noted how lightweight it was and wondered how anyone could subsist on so little. "Just some dried meat left over from winter. You keep that away from Thomlin. I don't trust him to be alone with it." He winked at Gwen, who laughed.

"Hey, if you give me some of it, I might give you one of Gilly's rolls. On second thought, never mind. I'll keep them all to myself," said Thomlin, who reached down and patted the bundle, which made both Gwen and Rolf laugh.

Madame Gabaldi made her way from the schoolhouse with a book in one arm and a well-worn pillow in the other. She handed her retrieved booty up to Thomlin and then hauled herself up. Taking both items from him, she tossed the pillow onto the bench. After sitting down on the pillow, she slid the book under the edge of it between her and Thomlin. Almost defensively in response to the looks she was getting from Gwen and Thomlin, she said, "In case the ride is boring."

Gwen regretted that she'd packed the book about religious orders in her trunk, but she cheered up when she remembered that Mignon's journal was in the nonfood sack. Panic struck her, and her gaze searched for her father when her thoughts about the journal were interrupted by Master Gabaldi shouting, "Get in line. It's time to go!"

Jacob Ahlgren got down from the cart and walked over to the wagon. Leaning over the side rail, he kissed the top of Gwen's head. "You take care now."

A lump formed in Gwen's throat and she nodded. "I love you, Father, and I will think of you every day."

Her father nodded and looked up at the sky. "It's gonna be a good day for traveling. Not a cloud in the sky."

She wanted to leap up and throw her arms around her father's neck, but she knew he was doing all he could to avoid breaking down and crying in front of others, so she tried her best to be unemotional. Her attempts failed miserably when he looked back at her. "Your mother would be so proud of you--*is* so proud of you." Gwen lost all control. She jumped up, dumping Rolf's sack onto a pile of other bags near her. She wrapped her arms around her father's neck, and he squeezed his arms around her waist. Gwen burned every second of that moment into her memory, the slightly smoky smell of her father's hair, the tautness of his arms around her. She wanted to remember what it felt like to feel so loved. At last, her father released her, and she did the same.

When Rolf started to climb into the back of the wagon, Master Gabaldi's voice rang out again. "No. I want you in the rear of this caravan. I need you to watch the road behind us."

The hubbub of villagers who had come to see off the young boys grew silent.

"I can watch from the back of the wagon."

"No. I want you *behind* the wagon."

Rolf's face screwed up in disgust. "What difference does it make if I'm *in* the wagon looking back?"

The crowd shuffled.

"He can ride my horse," Thomlin called out.

Master Gabaldi looked around at the villagers as if he were calibrating how far he could push Rolf without a rebellion. "Fine. Take the boy's horse, but you will ride behind the wagon."

Rolf shrugged. "Whatever."

Gwen let out a sigh of relief.

The hunter's son untied the reins of Thomlin's horse, mounted it, and guided it behind the wagon. Gwen knew he was being punished, and so did everyone else, she thought, based on some of the looks he was getting from the villagers. Gabaldi hadn't changed at all, and now he was putting Rolf in the worst spot to be in on the road with a caravan. The rear of the line would be the dustiest, dirtiest, and smelliest spot. Thanks to Thomlin's quick thinking and generosity, at least Rolf would be above ground level, where the dust and smell of horse manure wouldn't practically choke him every step of the way to Sutherhold.

Gabaldi galloped to the head of the line and shouted, "Forward!"

The wagon gave a little start as Thomlin clucked his tongue and shook the reins. The horses pulling the wagon took their first eager steps forward, jostling Gwen back into her spot atop the bean sack. From there, she watched the skyline of the village, knowing it wasn't the place but her childhood getting ever more distant and finally disappearing on the horizon as the wagon rolled away from Vasterberg.

Chapter 12

Make your opponent think you are weak; then use their confidence against them.
--Master Gabaldi, swordsman

* * *

The first day of their trip to Sutherhold explained why Gwen had awakened with a sense of foreboding. Master Gabaldi quickly proved he hadn't changed his attitude toward his trainees, particularly Rolf. No more than two hours into the journey, the soldier dropped back to the wagon and halted the caravan.

"I thought I told you to redistribute the weight on the port side, boy!" His sharp glare searched through the horses and their riders until it found one of the boys who had helped load the wagon.

"We did, sir!" the boy fired back. "Right there, sir," he said after he rode up to the wagon and pointed at a stack of crates and bags.

"You are an idiot. That's the starboard side. Port is the left side. Do it again!"

The boy's mouth hung agape. "Yes, sir." He slid off his horse, defeat in his limp movement, and climbed into the wagon. "I'm sorry but you'll have to get down while I do this."

Gwen nodded and moved to the back of the wagon to jump down. Rolf met her there and offered a hand. "C'mon up here with me for a while."

"You. Rosenkranz. Since you're so keen to help, you get up there and help this idiot straighten out the mess he made. Be quick about it."

Rolf's gaze stayed fixed on Gwen, who was looking at him and pleading silently for him not to put up a fight. "I'll hold your horse's reins while you do it," she said to him quietly.

Without a word, Rolf dismounted and helped Gwen onto stable ground before climbing up and assisting the boy in rearranging the cargo. His movements weren't gentle or slow, and Gwen could see him setting his jaw the whole time he was working.

"How's this?" he called out as he straightened his back and looked around at the stacks he and the other boy had made.

Gabaldi walked his horse around the wagon, each step almost a prance because the soldier would spur the horse then give enough quarter on the reins for only one step at a time before he yanked them up and halted the poor animal again. It was painful to watch, and Gwen was sure even more painful for the horse. If she'd needed another reason to hate Gabaldi, he'd just given it to her.

"Fine," he finally said and spurred the horse so hard that it reared up before galloping to the front of the caravan again. "Forward!" he yelled.

Thomlin hesitated shaking the reins just long enough for Rolf and the other boy to jump down before the wagon started moving again. Rolf climbed onto the saddle before leaning down and offering Gwen a hand. She put her foot into the stirrup that Rolf's boot had vacated, which gave her some leverage to help him pull her up, though he seemed to do so effortlessly. She concluded as she landed on the saddle blanket that the hunter's son was a lot stronger than his thin frame suggested.

Once they were again moving down the road, Gwen discovered the elevated height from being on horseback did little to dissuade the caravan's dust from choking them. That fact surprised her completely because she hadn't seen or heard Rolf cough at all. She decided he was being stoic to spite Gabaldi, and she also decided it was time to protect them both from the dust. She repositioned the shawl and loosely wrapped one end of it around her neck and mouth. "Here. Wear this. Don't you dare fuss either. You're not going to make it through this trip if you keep breathing in dirt. You'll get the consumption," she said as she wrapped the other end around Rolf's neck and mouth, tucking the fringed end of it into the wrap so it wouldn't fall down and letting the middle of the shawl droop down between them.

At first, she thought Rolf might protest but he didn't. Over the course of a few minutes, he slowly let the horse drop farther behind the wagon. When they were well out of hearing distance of the others, he spoke over his shoulder to her in a shawl-muffled voice, "So how come a soldier knows about which side of a ship is called the port side?"

"What do you mean?"

"That's why that boy James didn't know which side to rearrange. He didn't know what 'port' meant. He told me so when we were restacking the cargo."

Gwen thought about what Rolf said. "How do *you* know what it means?"

"My uncle was a sailor. He told me all about ships and sailing."

"Well, maybe Master Gabaldi had an uncle who was a sailor too."

"I don't think so."

"Rolf, you're looking for trouble where trouble need not necessarily exist."

"Is that what you think? Really, Gwen?"

She didn't know what to say to that. In a way, it was true though she could certainly understand why Rolf would dislike and distrust Gabaldi. She felt the same way about him. "No. Not really, but I don't think you can condemn him for knowing something about ships."

"It's not that he knows. It's that he used the word without even thinking about it, like somebody who uses it all the time."

"All right. What if he does have some knowledge of ships that's more extensive than we're aware of? What of it?"

"He told us he was a swordsman, not a sailor. It just makes me wonder what else he hasn't told us and why."

"I'm sure there are lots of things he hasn't told us. But what can we do about it? We're here and he's in charge, and that's not going to change."

"Yeah. Well, I'm just sayin' I don't trust him. Be watchful. Trust nobody."

"Not even Thomlin?" she said, hoping to inject some humor to lighten the mood. "I've heard he's a dangerous sort who can eat a bag of dried meat in one sitting."

"Yeah, especially Thomlin," said Rolf, who then let out a guffaw and spurred the horse to pick up the pace.

Gwen spent the first half day of the journey behind Rolf on Thomlin's horse. By the time the caravan halted at midday, a fine layer of dust covered the lightweight cotton shift she'd worn, her hair stank of dirt and sweat, and her eyes itched and burned. Rolf looked even worse, but she suspected his behind wasn't as tender as hers had become from sliding around on the saddle blanket. When she dismounted the horse, her legs wobbled and she felt unsteady. It took a few minutes to regain her balance, and during that time, she surveyed the trainees. Most of them looked ragged and worn out too. "However will we survive this journey?" she whispered under her breath.

They'd stopped near a slow-moving stream, and Gwen wasted no time in getting to it. Cupping her hands, she dipped them into the cool water and let it dribble between her fingers and back into the stream. After smelling her palms, she decided the water was fresh enough to drink. Again and again she pulled up as much as her hands would hold, gulping down what didn't seep through the miniscule spaces between her curled fingers.

"Slow down. You're gonna make yourself sick," said Thomlin, who crouched beside her and dipped his hands in the water too.

"It's horrible back there," she said quietly to him when she'd finished drinking her fill.

"I know. You should ride in the wagon facing backward. It won't be as bad that way."

Gwen cast a glance back toward Rolf, who was leading Thomlin's horse toward the stream. "I can't. I'd feel guilty. Rolf is going to be stuck back there the whole time. You know it's true. Gabaldi's going to make him suffer as much as he can."

"Yeah," said Thomlin. "Rolf's tough. He can take it. You can't, Gwen."

His words surprised her. "What do you mean?"

"I mean you're not cut out for this. Neither am I. Rolf. He's different," he said, his voice getting quieter and quieter as Rolf came closer.

"So what's all the whispering about?" the hunter's son asked as he stopped at the stream and let loose of the reins of Thomlin's horse. The parched animal immediately lowered his mouth to the edge of the stream and began to drink while Rolf stroked his neck.

Gwen didn't want to tell him what they'd been talking about, partly because she was a little miffed about Thomlin thinking her weak. She was relieved when he spoke up. "We were just talking about how long this trip is gonna be for those of us in the back of the caravan."

Rolf let out a roaring laugh. Gwen and Thomlin stared at each other in confusion, and Gwen wondered if Gabaldi had already managed to drive Rolf to insanity. "What's so funny," she asked him.

Rolf shook his head. "It doesn't matter where he puts us. He's going to make this trip as long and miserable as he can for me, for you, for all of us. That's how it's gonna be."

"But it's worse behind all the horses and the wagon," Gwen protested.

Rolf shrugged. "Better than being up front with Gabaldi. I told you. I don't trust him. Somethin's not right."

"I wish my pa had thought that," said Thomlin. "I'll take Buttercup and let him graze a while. You go ahead and get a drink and get cleaned up."

"Buttercup? You named your gelding Buttercup?" Rolf let out a giggle so contagious Gwen couldn't stop herself from giggling too.

Thomlin's cheeks flushed. "I was just a little kid. I didn't know he was a *he*."

At that, both Rolf and Gwen doubled over with laughter. Thomlin grabbed the reins and started toward a grassy spot nearby. "C'mon, Buttercup. Shame on them for makin' fun of you."

His one-sided conversation with the horse sent Gwen to the ground in fits of giggles and laughter, leaving her side aching and her dusty face tear streaked. After she regained her composure, she splashed the stream's refreshing water on her face and neck and nibbled on some dried plums, which she shared with Rolf and Thomlin when he returned. She offered it to him, and he took it with such false reluctance it made Gwen giggle to see him trying to pretend to still be put off by his friends' teasing. She could see why Gilly thought him so good natured.

Before long, the caravan resumed its trek along the road to Sutherhold with Gwen in the back of the wagon and Thomlin driving it. Rolf, wearing Mignon's stream-dampened shawl draped around his neck and mouth, followed behind on Buttercup, and Gwen watched him with guilt and thankfulness for a lumpy bean sack. She hadn't seen it when riding behind him, but his gaze darted constantly from side to side and up and down as he rode. Several times, he turned in his saddle, as if looking over his shoulder. He'd done the same thing when she'd sat behind him, but she'd assumed it was to hear her or so she could hear him above the rattle and clanks of the wagon and the clomping hooves. Now she knew differently. He was looking for something . . . or someone.

About an hour before the sun set, the caravan stopped to set up camp for the night. Madame Gabaldi directed some of the trainees to start a large campfire.

"Is there something I can do to help?" asked Gwen.

"Yes. Go to the stream and fill this with water," Madame Gabaldi said as she rummaged through a trunk near the back of the wagon and lifted out a thin pot. "Some of these boys don't have much food. We'll boil some of those dried beans you've been sitting on this afternoon."

Gwen took the pot. "Yes, ma'am." As she carried it toward the stream, all she could think of was how unappetizing it sounded to eat something her tired, sore rump had been sitting on. She would nibble some of the dried meat and fruit tonight, she thought as she knelt on a rock and dipped the pot into the water.

A twig snapped behind her, and her heart responded with a thud. "I know it's you, Rolf. You might as well give up. You're not going to--"

A rustle in the grass followed by the whir of an arrow, a shrieking growl, and a heavy thud on the ground brought Gwen to her feet. In the dim dusk light, she saw Rolf walking toward her, his bow in one hand. Thomlin was rushing past the hunter's son, his arms waving wildly, "Oh dear heavens! It almost got you!" He reached her out of breath and gasping for air.

Before he recovered, Rolf arrived. "Woodcat. He must've smelled the food and waited for one of the flock to wander off." He nodded to her left, where the body of a cat the size of a lamb lay with an arrow through its neck, blood coating its throat.

That was all it took for Gwen. Dizziness jolted her and her knees buckled.

She awoke to the smell of horse and burning wood and something wet Thomlin was dabbing on her forehead with a cloth. Madame Gabaldi's voice came from the right. "You're perfectly fine, Gwendolin. It was just a fright. It didn't harm you. And Thomlin caught you when you swooned. It was my fault for sending you to get water. It won't happen again, dear. I promise."

As the feeling of displacement started to fade, she could make out the schoolmistress sitting on the bean sack next to her. Under Gwen's neck was something soft, and when she moved her fingers up to it, she recognized the slickness. Buckskin. Rolf's coat.

"You didn't even hear him, did you?"

Gwen looked up at Thomlin, still disoriented. "I don't understand."

"He was fast, I tell ya."

"The woodcat?"

"No," said Thomlin, who resumed dabbing at Gwen's forehead.

He had spoken over his shoulder, which meant others were standing around her too. Most likely everyone, she thought, which multiplied how silly and embarrassed she already felt. She wondered if her cheeks flushed as crimson as Thomlin's.

"Well, yeah. It was fast, but Rolf was faster, I tell ya. I've never seen anything like that. I looked around and saw you. And then I saw the woodcat rare back to spring. Before I could yell, Rolf saw me lookin' at it, I guess, 'cause he turned around, drew his bow, and got off an arrow before that woodcat got all four paws off the ground."

Gwen braced herself with her hands and scooted up into a sitting position, her fingertips resting on what she now knew was emitting the scent of horse: several piled-up saddle blankets spread on a grassy spot near the campfire. One was lying atop her, and she folded it back.

"You should rest, dear. I'll have the boys make you a comfortable spot near me after we eat." Madame Gabaldi stood up.

From her ground-level view, Gwen thought she looked even more intimidating than the extremely tall woman normally looked. "I'm fine, ma'am. Just a little shaken. I'll have some food and stretch my muscles a bit so I don't get stiff. I really am fine."

"Very well. You do that, then, but stay with Thomlin and within the light of the campfire. My husband has stationed guards around the perimeter. We'll be safe near the fire. I'll still have a spot made for you to sleep next to me after everyone has eaten." She looked around at the boys, and from the way their chins met their chests or their gazes shot off into the distance, it was obvious the trainees got the message in her firm tone and in the look Gwen couldn't see but was sure the schoolmistress was giving them--the girl would be chaperoned at all times by Madame Gabaldi.

"Yes, ma'am," said Gwen.

Her agreement seemed to quell any concerns the schoolmistress might have had because she went about the business of finishing the meal she or someone she'd directed had already started over the campfire. The other boys dispersed in and claimed boulders for spots to lean on in the little clearing where they'd camped. The last few drifted off to sharpen swords and fletch arrows only after Thomlin promised to tell the story again at the campfire.

"Where is Rolf?"

He sighed. "Perimeter. He was the first to be chosen."

Chapter 13

Some things can only be known once the knowledge will do no good.
--Madame Verona, soothsayer

* * *

The morning light brought movement in the camp, and Gwen's first thought upon waking was Rolf. She got up from the sleeping mat Madame Gabaldi had ordered the boys to make for her and pulled on the buckskin coat Rolf had worn and which had served as a pillow after she fainted.

Water sizzled. "Take Thomlin with you." Madame Gabaldi's tone rippled through the smoke of the campfire she was dousing.

"Yes, ma'am," Gwen replied before spotting Thomlin and giving him a twitching nod in the direction of a spot at the edge of the encampment where she wanted to meet to ask about Rolf.

The two had barely reached the isolated tree when Gwen asked, "Did you see him yet? Did he come into camp?"

Thomlin's forehead was creased with worry. He shook his head. "Nothin'. I was the last to sleep, and he didn't come in before that. That's all I know. I've been askin' about him, but none of the others have seen him either."

Seething at Gabaldi's injustice toward Rolf, Gwen's tone turned as stern as that of the schoolmistress. "This is *not* acceptable. Nobody's seen him and nobody's looking for him. If it were anyone else . . ."

Announced by an accompanying rustle from behind a scraggly bush, Rolf's voice suggested an outcome different than Gwen knew she'd been worrying herself into believing. "It'd be the same."

"Oh, thank goodness," said Gwen in a long sigh.

Thomlin's reaction sounded less relieved. "What in a cow's udder happened to you?"

Rolf clearly found the expression distasteful because he crinkled his face as if he'd eaten something sour. It made his skin look even more drawn than it was and, combined with the dark circles around his eyes, gave him the appearance of a distressed raccoon. "Nothin'." He shrugged. "But I wouldn't bet somethin's not gonna happen to me--to us--all of us."

"What do you mean?" asked Gwen, on whom it suddenly dawned that her friend had been away from the warmth of the campfire for the whole night without his coat, the one she was wearing. She slipped her arms out of it and handed it to Rolf. "And thank you."

The hunter's son took the buckskin jacket and returned her dusty shawl to her but didn't acknowledge her thanks. When he spoke, Gwen understood why manners seemed unimportant at the moment.

"We're being followed. Ever since we got out of sight of Vasterberg."

"Who would follow us?" she asked.

"I dunno. I caught sight of just their scouts at first, but now they're getting bolder. This morning, I saw some uniforms."

"Uniforms? What do they look like?"

"Uniforms. Dark. Plain. Boots. All the same." He looked at Gwen as if she had asked the most stupid question he'd heard.

His dismissive expression and tone set her teeth to itching, and she placed a hand on one hip. "I know what a uniform is. I was asking if you could identify *whose* uniform it is."

"I've never seen a uniform except for the ones the mayor and Gabaldi wear. How would I know? I just know we're being followed by men mostly dressed alike who are great enough in number to afford sending out three scouts."

"How many days to Sutherhold?" asked Thomlin, his voice shaky.

"Six, maybe five if we travel as fast as we did yesterday."

"We should go back." Gwen's voice quivered just slightly too.

Rolf shook his head. "Bad move. Gabaldi's not going back, and that means we'd have to sneak off and do it alone. It'd be like a lamb leaving the flock. If that wolf Gabaldi didn't get us, those woodcats of soldiers would be waiting."

Gwen's cheeks flushed again at the thought of how foolish she'd been to wander off alone and at the fact she now was recommending doing it again. "You're right. So what do we do?"

"Wait. Watch. Keep moving with the caravan."

"And if they attack?" Thomlin asked.

"Get away. Let the others stand and fight if they want. They won't win, though, so why sacrifice ourselves for certain defeat?"

Something about the ease with which Rolf was willing to let the other trainees fight his battle and possibly die doing it didn't sit right with Gwen. "Maybe we should tell Madame Gabaldi."

Rolf's expression of doubt betrayed his thoughts before his words did. "I don't know we can trust her either."

"That's just not fair," said Gwen. "She's been nothing but kind and helpful to me, to everyone. She stepped into that crowd when he attacked you with his sword. She doesn't deserve this from you."

"All right," he said, holding up his hands in surrender. "Even if we *can* trust her, you know she'll confront her husband, and then *he'll* know *we* know about the soldiers following us. If he's in cahoots with 'em, we'd be as good as dead."

Gwen covered her mouth with her hand then rubbed her face with both hands, leaving her skin tingly, which only added to the overwhelming sense of being watched.

Thomlin's sudden commanding tone penetrated her thoughts and the fear creeping into her. "C'mon. Let's get back. I'll take Buttercup and ride behind the wagon. You drive, Gwen. And Rolf, you get some sleep."

Rolf practically staggered back to the wagon, which was ready to go by the time he and Gwen reached it. She had taken the seat next to Madame Gabaldi, and Rolf had barely clambered aboard and nestled in between three sacks when Gabaldi arrived as if on cue and glared at the wagon bed.

"Leave him be," Madame Gabaldi said to her husband before the man had a chance to speak.

The soldier rode off in a huff and signaled the caravan's front row of riders forward.

Stiff awkwardness filled the space between Madame Gabaldi and Gwen, who considered telling the woman about Rolf's discovery but decided against it. In fact, the tension was so thick she couldn't even bring herself to thank the schoolmistress for intervening on Rolf's behalf. Gwen wondered what she had done to put such distance between them.

From the time they started moving until they stopped at midday, Madame Gabaldi fixated on the book she'd brought out of the schoolhouse at the last minute. The horses seemed to know exactly where to go and at what speed to follow the horsed trainees, so Gwen found driving monotonous. At first, she found herself filling the time by looking around as she'd seen Rolf do, her gaze scanning ridges and breaks in the woods, but unlike him, she saw nothing. One would think the presence of nothing comforting, she thought at first, but later decided not seeing the followers brought no sense of security, only a persistent feeling of being unsettled. After a while, she felt such strain she thought she would crack and blurt out everything to Madame Gabaldi. Even as she considered doing so, she struggled to find the words.

As she thought about what to say and how to say it, the memory of her mother's voice filtered through as it had on the day before she left home: "You will have everything you need."

What do I need? Nothing came to mind as a direct response to the question, but her thoughts drifted to the vision she'd had of Thomlin passing her at a gallop as she left the Bastwick cottage. The image of him bouncing on the horse flashed in her mind, and then a nagging feeling crept up her spine. She turned around and looked at the miller's son following the wagon. There he sat astride his horse, which lumbered along under its rider's weight. And then it came to her. He wasn't on Buttercup in the vision! He was on a different horse. She stretched and strained to see the horses in front of her. None had the distinctive black and white speckled coat of the one he'd ridden in the vision. She found it hard to believe Thomlin could take a horse from an attacking soldier. So, if the horse carrying Thomlin wasn't the one he was on at present and wasn't another of the horses in the caravan, they might be safe for now.

Gwen turned around and gave a bright smile to Gilly's future husband, who cocked his head in such an exaggerated way it made his neck appear stuck to his shoulder. Gwen burst out in laughter, and Madame Gabaldi looked up from her book.

"I'm sorry. I didn't mean to disturb your reading. If I've done something to upset you, please tell me how to make amends," Gwen blurted out, the words coming of their own accord and proving her previous discomfort little more than a frivolous waste of time she could have spent thinking about something more positive and hopeful.

"You've not upset me. I do tend to immerse myself when I read. Was I being too somber? I'm sorry if you thought it was directed toward you."

"Oh, good. I thought maybe my carelessness yesterday had made you angry. I wasn't thinking, but I am now."

Madame Gabaldi smiled. "You always were a bit of a thinker. Have you given more thought to your choice of monasteries?"

Gwen confessed she hadn't had much time to think or read about her choices since she began preparations to leave Vasterberg.

"I'm sure Jacques will prove immensely helpful to you. He'll like you, and you will like him. I'm certain of it."

Meeting someone friendly and helpful, someone not treating them cruelly, someone not following them sounded perfect to Gwen. Right now, she'd settle for anyone not intending them harm, and if that was Brother Jacques, so be it. "I'm eager to meet him," she said with unreserved sincerity, for it was the absolute truth.

It came as no surprise to Gwen or Thomlin when Gabaldi sent Rolf out for the night's watch again and didn't arrange for anyone to relieve him halfway through the night as he did for the other trainees.

"I'm goin' out there. This just isn't right," Thomlin told Gwen privately after they'd eaten the bean and grain stew Madame Gabaldi had made for the travelers that evening. "He hasn't had a decent meal in two days at least."

"You know he's trying to find out who's following us and why," she replied in a whisper. "He's probably nowhere near the perimeter. How do you plan to find him?"

Thomlin shrugged. "I don't know. I just know it's not right to leave him out there all by himself the whole night."

Gwen put a hand on Thomlin's and tried her best to sound comforting. "I know you want to help him, but you said it yourself. You're not cut out for this. Let him do what he needs to do, and he can sleep in the wagon again tomorrow. I'll talk to Madame Gabaldi."

His expression turned from concern to hesitance, and he shook his head. "I don't know. What if Rolf's right and she knows more than we think or she says something to her husband?"

She squeezed his hand tightly. "I won't tell her what Rolf saw. I'll just ask if she can help Rolf in some way. Leave it to me, Thomlin."

The miller's son sighed. "I guess we have no other choice, do we?"

She shook her head. "If we stick together, we'll get through this. Just a few more days to Sutherhold. Just promise me one thing, Thomlin."

"What's that?"

"You ride on Buttercup the whole way. *All* the way to Sutherhold."

Thomlin shifted his gaze from side to side. "Um . . . why?"

"I can't explain it. Call it a feeling. Just stay on Buttercup when we're riding. For me. It would make me feel better. Please?"

He shrugged. "All right. I guess I can do that," he said as he stood up to go find a spot to sleep for the night. Madame Gabaldi had made it clear none of the trainees, including Thomlin, were to sleep near her and Gwen. "I don't see why it would make you feel better. What difference does it make if I ride Buttercup or drive the wagon? Are you sure you're all right?"

Gwen laughed. "Not really, but I'm not insane if that's what you mean."

"No, I didn't mean--"

Gwen's laughter cut off his backpedaling. "I just can't explain it right now. Maybe once we're in Sutherhold."

Thomlin nodded and walked away but kept sneaking periodic peeks over his shoulder at Gwen. She could hear him muttering unintelligibly to himself, and she was fairly certain she heard her name at least once. Although she understood why he'd be confused about her request, the thought of explaining to him or to Rolf that she'd been seeing visions and hearing voices made her uncomfortable. How could she explain what she didn't understand? Trying not to question her own sanity, she pushed the thoughts aside.

The next morning, Rolf didn't show up at the camp until the caravan was about to leave. Nobody had said a word about his not being there, not even Madame Gabaldi, which shocked Gwen and made her even more fearful that Rolf had been right about her. As the wagon's wheels creaked into turning, Rolf came running out of the woods and jumped into the back of the wagon. He held up a partially skinned rabbit by its ankles.

Out of breath, he explained. "This little guy was fast. I almost didn't hit him. I was right in the middle of skinning him when I heard the caravan leaving."

Although her father was a butcher and she accepted that animals were slaughtered for food, Gwen had never been able to stomach the sight of a skinned animal before it had been cut into indistinguishable pieces. Somehow, not recognizing the body parts made it easier for her to forget what she was eating. For that reason, she forewent eating poultry legs and wings and let her other family members eat them when they had the rare occasion to feast on a hen that had stopped laying eggs. "Eww."

Rolf laughed and positioned himself next to a railing, over which he finished the job of skinning the already gutted rabbit. He stuffed the skinned animal into a leather pouch and tucked it under one of the smaller bags. "I'd appreciate it if you'd cook this tonight, Gwen, assuming it doesn't spoil before then."

"Of course," she said, looking over her shoulder at him. When their gazes met, she knew he had news he couldn't share in the presence of others. She nodded toward Thomlin, who was opening the bag of baked goods Gilly had given him. He held the open bag to his nose and sniffed so hard Gwen and Rolf could see his nostrils wiggle, which sent the two of them into giggling fits. "Have some of the dried fruit and bread in my bag. That'll hold you over until later."

"Thanks," he replied before digging into her food stash and helping himself to some dried plums and a hard roll.

Gwen could tell he was chewing each bite for as long as he could, and she thought she heard his stomach growl more than once. Within an hour after eating, Rolf was sound asleep, and Gwen thought it a perfect time to broach the subject of his treatment with Madame Gabaldi. Nodding over her shoulder to the boy sleeping in the wagon, she said, "He needs to eat and get a good night's sleep, ma'am. Look at how gaunt he's getting already. He's our best archer. He needs to be strong. Is there something--"

In a clipped tone, the schoolmistress cut off her words. "What I can do is limited." Madame Gabaldi cast a glance back at Rolf then looked straight ahead. "You cook his rabbit, and I'll give you some food from the evening meal and a water pouch after everyone else has eaten. You *must* make certain *nobody* sees you giving it to him."

"Yes, ma'am," ended their conversation, and Gwen didn't press the schoolmistress again. She knew which "nobody" the woman meant.

Over the next four days, she and Madame Gabaldi spoke not a single word about Rolf or anything else. Madame Gabaldi read her book when the wagon lumbered along the road. Gwen held the reins and searched the distance for signs of the soldiers. They set aside food for Rolf every evening, and Thomlin stuffed it under his shirt, making a public scene of noting he needed to go into the bushes to relieve himself and smuggling the food and small leather canteens of water to his friend at the perimeter. Thomlin returned and told Gwen the news Rolf had shared. The soldiers were getting bolder each day, moving nearer and nearer to the road, slowly closing the gap between themselves and the caravan. Rolf showed up at the wagon every morning with empty canteens and a fresh kill, either a rabbit or a squirrel or a pheasant, but always an animal small enough to be cooked quickly.

Despite the threat of the soldiers, Gwen's sense of security remained mostly intact as long as Thomlin sat atop Buttercup. When the caravan stopped for midday and in the evenings, the sense of foreboding she'd felt on the morning of their departure loomed around her like dust from the caravan, seeping into her mood but also wearing her down physically, as if she were fighting with it and losing. The only bright spot in her days and nights became Thomlin. Thomlin atop his gelding. Thomlin sniffing Gilly's baked goods. Thomlin talking to Buttercup when he led him to a stream. Thomlin giving her a wink each night to let her know Rolf had received the food. She couldn't help but notice the irony in their situation. The boy who'd once upended her easy friendship with Gilly, the very boy who had become her torment, now gave her the only comfort and security she had in a world not of her choosing. And she loved him for it.

Chapter 14

Power is a lens that makes others appear insignificant.
--Mother Seema, Cathuran monk

* * *

The morning Sutherhold came into view over the rise of a hill already coming to life with late-spring grasses and grazing deer, Rolf had appeared with his daily kill and liveliness in his step. He met Gwen and Thomlin at the wagon.

"They're gone."

"The soldiers?" asked Thomlin.

"Yep. They hightailed it out of the woods last night and took to the road about a league ahead of us."

Thomlin frowned. "Do you think they're going to attack today?"

Rolf shook his head and grinned. "Nope. They're probably holed up in a brothel or a tavern by now. They rode into Sutherhold, and I suppose they were welcome because nobody put up a fuss about it."

Gwen's eyes widened. "They're in Sutherhold, where we're going?"

"Yep. Probably weren't even following us, just keeping an eye on what we were doing."

Although she thought she should feel relief, she didn't. "What if they're from Sutherhold?"

Rolf shrugged.

"Why would an army from Sutherhold hide in the woods and hills if they were returning home? Why did they leave the hold at all?" Her gaze demanded an answer.

"I don't know."

"Hey," Thomlin interrupted. "Some of the other fellows were talking about how Sutherhold has a lot of recruiters and more than one guild for soldiers. Maybe it was a training mission."

Rolf looked at Gwen. "Maybe. What's important is they're not attacking *us*."

Master Gabaldi's voice rang out, and the trainees scrambled to their horses. Rolf climbed onto the driver's bench of the wagon. "I'll take us into the city."

"But don't you need some sleep?" Gwen asked quietly as Madame Gabaldi walked toward the wagon.

"Nah. I got some sleep last night."

Gwen wondered why Rolf would sleep while on watch, but before she could ask, Madame Gabaldi reached the wagon and took her place on the bench next to him.

"Whatever you brought for tonight's meal may bring you coin in Sutherhold. My husband says we'll be arriving by midday."

Climbing into the back of the wagon and crawling up on the bean sack now a third of the size it had been when last she'd used it to cushion the rough ride, Gwen settled in for the last stretch of their journey.

"Is that a fact?" Rolf responded. "What will you be doing in Sutherhold while your husband's busy with us?"

Gwen caught a flash of anger in Madame Gabaldi's glance over at Rolf, who was watching the riders in front of the wagon. She presumed he felt the glare because he turned his head suddenly toward the schoolmistress and stuttered, "I m-m-mean while he and his contact are helping us train. No offense meant, ma'am."

Madame Gabaldi looked away from Rolf and pulled her book out from under the cushion she sat upon while responding in a tone without a hint of anger in it. "I've some friends in Sutherhold who have children they'd like me to tutor. I can do that and still have time to visit the guild libraries. I'll be busy too."

The schoolmistress was the second person who'd mentioned guilds that morning, and Gwen saw an opportunity to learn more of what she was about to encounter. "May I ask which guilds, ma'am?"

"I'd visit them all if I could, but I'm not sure anyone has enough time. It would take more than a lifetime to read all the scrolls and parchments collected in all the libraries of all the guilds in Sutherhold. I'll start with the libraries of the trade guilds. Some of these boys haven't decided which trade to follow when they return home. I'm sure the guild librarians will have books they can lend to help in the decision making."

Rolf snorted. Gwen thought of her own book and how useless it had been.

"Did I say something amusing?"

"What guild *wouldn't* want apprentices willing to serve without pay?" The hesitation in his speech gone, Rolf sounded more himself.

"None, of course. Were it not for the guilds, though, who would educate the populace and assure the trades continued to produce skilled labor? Who would build houses and carve furniture? Who would protect the citizens and enforce the laws?" She looked directly at Rolf. "Who would supply game?"

"Hunters have guilds?" Rolf asked.

"I do not know about that, but I do know of at least one guild for furriers and trappers. One would think hunters a natural fit among the membership. Why, in fact, one of my dear friends is a recruiter for such a guild, and I can ask him if you'd like. He has mentioned the guild's numbers have dwindled in the last few years, so it wouldn't surprise me if their requirements for membership have relaxed as well."

"Why fewer members?"

She shook her head. "Not as many new apprentices, I suppose. There has been an odd shortage of young men coming to the city and staying in the last few years as well."

"How come?"

"Nobody I spoke with last winter could say for certain. Young people aplenty come to Sutherhold, but few remain to complete an apprenticeship. Some, of course, try but fail to master the skills necessary."

Panic seized Gwen's gut. What if she failed as a monk? Failure hadn't crossed her mind until that moment. She forced out the words, "What happens if an apprentice fails?"

"They go home. They do what a skilled tradesman will not. They survive as best they can without the contracts a guild can offer." She twisted her body around and looked at Gwen. "There are no second chances. An apprenticeship is a privilege. That is why the decision to enter one is a serious affair, one that requires knowledge, knowledge such as that found in the libraries of the guilds themselves."

Questions raced through Gwen's mind. She couldn't go home, and she had no skills for surviving on her own. Where would she go? How would she live? That her livelihood and, indeed, her very life might depend on knowledge from a book as ineffectual as the one Madame Gabaldi had given her made her skin prickle with tension. If she failed, she had no alternative plan. She *couldn't* fail.

The schoolmistress returned to reading her book, and Gwen leaned back against the side railing of the wagon, lost in horrific images of starving and freezing to death in the alleyways of Sutherhold and only somewhat aware of how the sway of the wagon shook her more violently than it had on the movement-muffling, full bean sack. Nobody spoke until they heard scratchy, road-dry voices in a rolling echo from the front to the back of the caravan, "Sutherhold ahead!"

Struggling to get on her knees and look ahead in the space between Madame Gabaldi and Rolf, Gwen felt her dress catch under her knees and tear. She shifted her weight from knee to knee to free the cloth, teetering so far she almost tumbled over the wagon's side. The rip didn't appear to threaten any further unraveling. If she kept the shoulder bags in front of her, nobody would see it, she thought. She looked up to see the gate to the city right in front of the wagon. Gwen tilted her head back as they passed under it, spying the grating her father had told her was called a murder hole because it was the grate through which boiling oil could be poured down on invaders. The light of day shone through it, and Gwen wondered why no invaders had ever thought to shoot a fire arrow through it when the guards positioned the oil barrel for pouring. Bright light flashed and Gwen blinked, at first thinking she'd seen a vision of what she imagined would be the resulting explosion when the fire arrow struck the oil.

When she craned her neck over her shoulder and looked behind her, sunspots dancing before her squinted eyes, she realized the flash had been a sunbeam she'd passed through and looked into. The flash had been nothing more than an unexpected and unshielded glare of sunlight. She felt relief and she recognized as much. She wasn't certain if that relief came from arriving safely in Sutherhold or realizing there was a logical explanation for what struck her first as an unexplainable vision like those that had come before. The unknown made her uneasy and enhanced her feelings of being powerless. Madame Gabaldi was right. There was power in knowledge. That much she knew.

When she returned her attention to where they were going, she was awestruck. Buildings larger than any she'd seen stood crammed together in tight rows on either side of the cobblestone street. Two merchants to the right of the wagon pushed wobbly carts laden with turnips. Just beyond them, another merchant, this one standing under a tattered awning, yelled, "Copies of the Scripture! Know the path you must follow!"

Citizens of Sutherhold rushed about, their children in tow, and from her vantage point in the wagon, Gwen noted an astonishing rhythm to their movement. Those who walked or rode in the middle of the street seemed to sense the caravan's approach and adeptly moved to one side or another with prompting but also without inhibiting their own forward progress. With few exceptions, everyone seemed to be going somewhere. Before long, Gwen realized why.

Breaking out of its columnar formation, the caravan spread out into clusters as the first riders into the town square stopped, forcing those behind them to choose a flank or risk blocking the street. So many other streets poured into the square that Gwen couldn't have counted them if she'd tried. The whole city was a web, spidering out from this central point.

Master Gabaldi sat astride his horse facing the first riders in the caravan. Above the noise of the city, Gwen couldn't hear what he was telling them, but she saw him pointing toward one of the streets, after which the riders lined up their horses in columnar fashion once again and headed in the direction Gabaldi had pointed to on the far side of the square. Each cluster of the caravan followed suit, and soon the wagon was almost across the square in front of an imposing, pale limestone structure with statues lining its portico and arched entries taller than any building in Vasterberg.

"That is the cathedral," said Madame Gabaldi as the riders and wagon pivoted and filed past the magnificent building.

"Is that where I'll find Brother Jacques?" Gwen asked, already imagining how much more grandiose it must be on the inside.

Shaking her head, the schoolmistress replied over her shoulder, "No, dear. I'll take you to him once my husband and the trainees reach the guild.

Jacques resides not far from there."

As the caravan snaked its way out of the square, twisting and turning through street after street, Gwen took in every sight and sound and smell around her. She did her best to memorize landmarks so she could find her way back, for the desire to see inside the imposing cathedral tugged at her curiosity. Surely it held an impressive library any scholar would covet. The thought gave her pause about Brother Jacques, making her wonder why he would choose to live elsewhere.

The farther the caravan moved from the town center, the dingier and more cramped the city became. Like the streets, the houses were more narrow, though they still rose higher than any in Vasterberg. Ropes strung with drying clothes stretched across the road high above them, and there seemed to be even more people than in the larger, more open space of the main road. Most weren't rushing about like those on the road that led into town, though. Here, in this darker, more densely populated part of Sutherhold, people moved at a slower pace, many burdened with sacks on their backs or baskets balanced on their shoulders. The scent of bubbling stews, roasting meats, and sweet, braised fruits mingled with that of rancid chamber pots and rotting vegetables. Flies buzzed everywhere, it seemed, and Gwen swatted them away from her face as the wagon cut through floating swarms.

She drew in a deep breath of fresher air when the constricted street spilled out into another square, this one smaller and far less impressive than the one where the cathedral sat on its border like a guard watching the influx of visitors to its grand city. This one was more like an oversized courtyard. At its center sat a marketplace, out of which poured a cacophony of screeches, verbal assaults, and cackling. Gwen tried without success to tease out the specifics of what looked to be an argument between a cloth merchant and a woman whose hands were flailing wildly in the air as she yelled at the man holding up a bolt of sackcloth, shaking his head violently, and yelling back at the woman. When the two abruptly ended their disagreement with a handshake, she had to look twice to verify she wasn't imagining it.

The wagon followed the riders, circumventing the maze of stalls and tents, and its wheels ground to a halt in front of a stockade fence, its pickets topped off with sharp points. At first, it seemed like any other fence erected for privacy and security, but then Gwen noticed something off about it. Instead of its rails and posts on the inside, they faced outward. Whoever had built it had done so not to keep someone or something out but to keep someone or something in, and Gwen wondered who or what the sharp pickets kept inside.

The answer--shocking her into an open-mouthed, wide-eyed stare--came from the lips of Madame Gabaldi. "Ah, we have arrived. This is where we shall part company."

Rolf stared forward silently for a moment then spun around slowly and looked into Gwen's eyes.

While her gaze remained locked with Rolf's, Gwen was vaguely aware of Madame Gabaldi dropping the book into a bag and climbing down from the wagon. She didn't see where the woman went and didn't care. Rolf's resignation terrified her and broke her heart, but she couldn't look away.

Chapter 15

Courage is not the absence of fear but action in the face of fear.
--Arbuckle Kyte, Lord of Ravenhold

* * *

"You don't have to go," Gwen said in a low voice when Madame Gabaldi had gotten out of earshot.

Rolf broke their interlocked gazes and looked over Gwen's shoulder. "Yeah. I do. Who's gonna watch out for him?"

She didn't need to verify whom Rolf was referring to. She knew he was looking at Thomlin. "You can tell his father what you saw here. He doesn't have to go either."

"He will, though, because he can't go home to Gilly if he doesn't do this." Rolf finally shifted his gaze back to Gwen. "And you'll be here all alone." Worry made him look twenty seasons older.

Her stomach knotted painfully. "Not completely. Madame Gabaldi will be here and . . ." If she couldn't convince herself she wouldn't be alone, she certainly wasn't going to persuade Rolf not to worry, so she just stopped speaking and let the gravity of her situation, of all of their situations, fill the space between them.

"Where are you going to be?" he asked.

Her answer didn't diminish the concern on his face. "I don't know. Madame Gabaldi said it wasn't far from here."

"Give me a name," he said, his voice insistent as his darting gaze replicated the extreme wariness it had when he'd been watching for the soldiers that first day of their journey. "Who do I look for?"

"Brother Jacques. That's all I know about him."

He leaned in closer to her, and Gwen stretched up to get her ear as near to his face as she could manage. His voice just above a whisper, he said, "If I need to get him out of here, I'll find you. You just stay put for as long as you can."

Gabaldi's yells filtered back to the wagon, and several boys in front of them dismounted. The wagon's gate suddenly dropped open, and Gwen turned with a start to see two of the recruits climbing up. "No, that's mine. Please leave it," she said to one who reached for her trunk.

"Master Gabaldi says to empty it. Take it up with him," he replied as he grasped the trunk and shoved it to the edge of the wagon bed.

The schoolmistress's voice came from behind her. "Not to worry, dear. Brother Jacques will send someone for your belongings."

Rolf climbed down from the wagon and gave Gwen a knowing glance before walking toward Thomlin, who had dismounted and was stroking

Buttercup's cheek. Gwen assumed he'd fill in Thomlin on whatever scheme his brain was devising. For her part, Gwen couldn't think straight. So much was happening at once, and the din of the marketplace only amplified the sense of chaos swirling around and inside of her.

"Come along, Gwendolin," said Madame Gabaldi. "Brother Jacques has been on the watch for us. Let us not worry him unnecessarily."

Her breathing shallow and rapid, she croaked out, "Yes, ma'am." Gwen stood, her knees weak at first. She dropped the bunched-up skirt and reached for her shoulder sacks, which she held tightly against her until she made her way to the outstretched hand of one of the boys who'd been helping to unload the wagon. Still grasping the sacks with one hand, she balanced herself with a clasp of his hand then hopped down. The leather soles of her flats landed on cobblestones more uneven than they'd appeared from above, and the boy had to grab her by the waist to steady her landing.

She blushed when she followed his stare of disbelief at the fingers still gripping her midriff. "Thank you."

The boy let loose of her and stepped back. "Welcome." He fumbled over his own feet to get away from her and rushed around the wagon toward the other recruits, obviously shaken.

Madame Gabaldi called out from behind her. "Gwendolin. It's time to go."

"I just want to say good--" She looked behind the wagon, but neither Thomlin nor Rolf was in sight. Frantically she turned around and searched the crowd of recruits. No Buttercup. No hunter's son. No plump Thomlin Frank.

She gave a quiet squeak as Madame Gabaldi's hand touched her arm. "This way, dear."

Though she wanted to break away, to find her friends, to thank Thomlin for caring so much about Gilly, to leave the keep that now felt like it, too, had been built to hold in someone or something, Gwen did none of those things. With arms folded around her bags and in stunned silence, she walked alongside the schoolmistress and didn't turn around or look behind her. In truth, she didn't think she had the strength to do either.

When Madame Gabaldi veered off the street and into an alleyway, Gwen realized she'd not paid attention at all to the landmarks in this part of the keep. She might be able to find the Cathedral again if she could locate the guild where Thomlin and Rolf were training, but she didn't believe she could retrace her steps back to the stockade fence.

She let out a sigh of self-disgust for not being more alert, which was drowned out by a male voice chirping, "Praise be to the heavens. You've arrived safely!"

"Jacques!" Madame Gabaldi responded, her tone more cheerful than Gwen thought possible for the austere woman.

The hooded and gray-robed man stepped out of a gated entrance off the alleyway. The two embraced and kissed each other's cheeks. When the monk leaned back, Gwen got her first unobstructed view of him. Gaunt and dark with full lips and skin glimmering as if freshly washed, the monk had green eyes overflowing with kindness. The overwhelming sense she got when he reached out for her bag and touched her hand confirmed what she saw in his eyes.

"Let me carry those for you, Sister Gwendolin," he said.

His voice struck her as even more kind and gentle, but there also was strength underlying it. What came to mind as she tried to define his even, stable tone was an infusion of power. Peaceful, kind, and gentle, but powerful nonetheless, and Gwen found unusual comfort in it. It wasn't until after he'd relieved her of the bags and hung them over his shoulder that she remembered the rip in her dress and folded her hands over the torn spot, embarrassed.

Gwen felt certain Brother Jacques must have noticed because he looked away, craning his neck to look down the alleyway as if watching for someone as he spoke to them. "Come in and have some cool water and fruit. You must be hungry and parched from the ride on that dusty road."

"Indeed, we are. Thank you," said Madame Gabaldi.

Jacques dipped his head and folded his hands into a prayer gesture. "It is my blessing to provide sustenance and a soft place for you to rest, my friends."

His tone drew her in with its sincerity, and for the first time since entering Sutherhold, Gwen felt secure.

He led them through a narrow passageway and across a courtyard into a small building with a flat roof and a single doorway with open windows on either side. They stopped in the first room, the inner walls of which were lined with doors, each painted with symbols that varied in design and color. Between the doorways stood gray stone statues of people Gwen didn't recognize, but all of whom wore robes not unlike those of Brother Jacques. Modestly furnished with piled cushions surrounding a low table in the center of the room, the space smelled of lilac, the source of which she located and identified as a tightly wrapped bundle of dried branches with fully opened flower petals. She remembered Mignon calling such a bundle a smudge stick. The healer had used them to detoxify rooms in which the sick lay while she tended them, though she'd said coneflowers were the preferred plant for such cleansings. The smudge stick's stream of smoke drifted upward from a copper bowl on a small table next to the door and out the window. Gwen wondered why she hadn't noticed its smell as they approached.

No sooner had they paused in the room than another monk, this one wearing a tan robe, came out of the first doorway on the wall to their left.

"Brother Vaughn," he said, giving a friendly nod to the man. "This is my friend Madame Gabaldi and our new charge, Sister Gwendolin."

The monk folded his hands as Brother Jacques had and gave a warm smile and dip of his head to each of the two women. Something about the way the monk looked at her made Gwen feel as if he'd been there all along and had overheard their conversation in the courtyard. "I'll bring refreshments," he said before shuffling back the way he'd come.

"He is not accustomed to visitors, I'm afraid. We don't have many, and he's been here with us only a short time," Jacques said apologetically.

"No need for apologies, my dear friend. Tell me, Jacques. How are you these days?" said Madame Gabaldi.

Her tone bespoke what Gwen perceived as genuine fondness, and it made her all the more curious about how her teacher had come to know the monk.

"Come and rest." Jacques motioned toward the piles of white cushions as he set Gwen's sacks on the floor next to the nearest pile. When he folded his legs and lowered himself onto one of the piles, the fluffy pillows billowed around him. "I wish I could say that all is well in the monastery and . . . the keep." He accompanied his hesitation with a quick glance toward the door.

Madame Gabaldi plopped onto a pile and let out a sigh of delight. Gwen mimicked the monk's cross-legged lowering and positioned herself by degrees on a pillow, taking care to configure her dress so the rip didn't gape open. She was comforted when the cushions plumped themselves around her body, providing a cozy and safe-feeling haven for her weary body and her damaged dress.

"There's been trouble?" Madame Gabaldi asked.

Jacques shrugged. "Not directly, no. Mostly whispers. One cannot rely on them, of course, but there are many whispers, and that in itself is troubling."

"The border? The Zjhon?" she asked.

He nodded. "Among other stories, yes. There is much unrest among those in the orders as well. Concern swells about the zealousness of the Zjhon masters."

"They have always been zealots, no? Why would that be of concern now?"

The first door on the left opened, and Brother Vaughn entered with a cloth-lined tray holding a pitcher and three mugs, which he placed on the table.

"Please sit with us, Brother Vaughn. I believe you may have something to share with our guests."

Without speaking a word, the second monk did as the first had but descended so gracefully his robe seemed to pour over the seating like hot glaze. Gwen envied his grace even more when he reached out to the tray and poured them a drink. As it streamed into the clay mugs, even the water took on the smooth and delicate movement of the monk's fingers.

The first sip of the water flowed down her throat just as smoothly, Gwen thought, and she tipped the mug and drank until it was empty. She thought she caught a mild taste of lemon and honey. Immediately her scratchy throat felt rejuvenated, and she held up a hand in refusal when Brother Vaughn asked if she'd like more.

"Brother Vaughn is from the east. He has come for his last worldly rites before taking final vows. Tell them what happened to you at the cathedral, Brother." This last statement Jacques said while looking at the other monk.

His demeanor showing no emotion whatsoever, Vaughn began to speak. "I went to the cathedral a few days ago. Upon entering, I was ushered out of the vestibule in a most inhospitable manner."

Jacques interrupted in a whisper, "By Zjhon soldiers and rather roughly, I might add."

Madame Gabaldi gasped. "How dreadful. Soldiers in the cathedral?"

"I was taken to an antechamber and questioned at some length by one of the Zjhon masters."

"Tell them what he asked about," said Jacques.

Gwen was sure she caught a gleam of annoyance in Brother Vaughn's quick glance at the other monk.

"He wanted to know the names of other monks who do not worship the Zjhon gods."

"Why would he care what other orders do?" Madame Gabaldi asked. "Why is that his concern?"

"I do not know," Vaughn replied. "I told him I could not speak as to what others might or might not believe and that I was not yet a monk."

"And what happened then?"

"I was escorted out of the cathedral and informed it has been closed to those not of the Zjhon faith and would be henceforth entered only by those who follow the True Path of the Scripture."

Gwen remembered seeing the man in the streets yelling to passersby about a scripture.

Madame Gabaldi frowned. "I am sorry to hear that."

"So was I, Sister Gabaldi. The library in the cathedral holds some of the most rare manuscripts in existence. Or at least, that is what is rumored."

Brother Jacques broke the pensive silence that followed. "Of course, one cannot draw conclusions from such a singular incident or the exuberance with which it occurred. There are many orders of faith who do not interact with others. The Zjhon are not alone in such a stance."

The schoolmistress turned to Gwen and smiled. "Do you see? It is as I told you. He is the perfect mentor for you at this stage of your path to the monastic life. There is none more knowledgeable about orders of faith than my dear, old friend." She reached over and patted Jacques on the shoulder.

"You regard me too highly, Sister," he replied, his words delivered with honest humility.

"That's rubbish and you know it, Jacques." She laughed.

He shrugged and looked down.

"When we were in lessons together, Jacques was always the first to understand every subject. He could find the most obscure references. We all knew he'd become a scholar."

"You grew up together?"

Madame Gabaldi smiled. "Indeed, we did. Jacques was my first love." She giggled like a moonstruck young girl.

In his first ungraceful movement, Brother Vaughn reached for the pitcher of water and toppled it over, sending a wave of liquid splashing across the tabletop and onto Madame Gabaldi's lap. The monk rose to his feet and rushed around to the other side of the table, offering the schoolmistress the cloth from the tray. "I am so terribly clumsy, Sister. Forgive me." His face looked as if he were in pain from remorse.

Madame Gabaldi let out a loud laugh as she stood and dabbed at her drenched skirt. "Nonsense. It was an accident. There's nothing to forgive, Brother Vaughn."

"We can provide you with a robe, but I'm afraid that's all we have," he said to her.

"That won't be necessary," she replied. "It's just damp. It'll dry. I should be on my way now anyway."

"But you haven't eaten. Let us see to your sustenance, Sister." Jacques stood.

"Thank you, dear friend, but I should get back to the guild to gather my things. My friends will be awaiting my arrival, and I'm eager to assess their children's level of education. Sutherhold is a treasure for teaching the young. So many monuments. So much to see and do."

As Gwen also rose from her cushion, she watched Brother Vaughn, who folded his hands and stood silently next to Madame Gabaldi. He'd recovered the gracefulness in his demeanor, but Gwen noticed his expression had flattened. Gone was the anguish it had shown when he'd apologized. She wondered what had been so disturbing to him that he'd lost his poise momentarily and what had pained him so much. It was just a silly accident, after all, not some harm visited upon his guest. While she was thinking about him, Brother Vaughn looked directly at her with a disapproving glance before he gathered up the toppled pitcher and the mugs and placed them on the tray.

The look took her aback, and Gwen almost lost her footing amid the squishy pillows.

"Gwendolin has a trunk at the fighter's guild where my husband has taken his pupils."

"Say no more," interrupted Jacques. "Brother Vaughn, will you have two of the neophytes accompany Madame Gabaldi to retrieve Gwendolin's belongings, please?"

The monk gave an affirmative nod and left the room, carrying the tray. Two white-robed young men about Gwen's age appeared from the same doorway in what seemed like only an instant.

Madame Gabaldi approached Gwen. "I know you will find your destiny, Gwendolin Ahlgren. It is most assured by the guidance of Brother Jacques. He knows where I'll be residing until the boys are ready to return to Vasterberg. He'll send for me if you are in need." Assurance had underscored every word the schoolmistress had spoken, and Gwen appreciated it for what it was.

"Farewell, Madame Gabaldi. And thank you for all you've done to help me and . . . the others."

The woman nodded a silent acknowledgment and turned to Jacques. "Take care, my friend. I hope to see you again during my stay."

"As do I, Sister Gabaldi. As do I." He smiled at her and folded his hands in the now familiar prayer gesture before dipping his head, this time keeping it lowered until the schoolmistress and the neophytes had exited the building. Turning to Gwen, he said, "Let's get you a warm bath, a clean robe, some food, and a bit of rest. Follow me, Sister."

Jacques escorted her down a long hallway to a room filled with steam, which rushed out and blasted Gwen in the face when he opened the door. "That one," he said once inside, pointing to another door, "will take you to a passageway. The first door is where you'll stay while with us. The second leads to another hallway that'll bring you back to the reception room where we sat earlier. There is a robe for you." He pointed to a mound of folded cloth then left before she could thank him.

Gwen couldn't remember a bath feeling more soothing. She lay in the wooden tub, steam soaking her face and hair, until the water cooled and the steam disappeared. After dressing in the white wool robe, which was much softer than she'd expected, she combed her wet hair and went to the small chamber Jacques had told her about.

When her hair was almost dry, the neophytes arrived in her chamber with the trunk. They came and went without speaking a word, although both did smile at her before leaving.

The same two neophytes returned in a few minutes with a platter of fruit and more water, and once again, they came and went without speaking. As she nibbled on the fruit, she picked up a book lying on the bed. In the first few pages, she learned it was a book about the Varics, an order advocating knowledge and learning in all aspects of living but also free, open, and balanced public discussion of matters related to government and laws. The thought of such a mission made her head throb.

Gwen concluded the monastery must have been an outpost for the Varics, which seemed a good fit for a scholar such as Brother Jacques. Many of the ordination rituals she'd read about required neophytes to do the very opposite of what their orders practiced, so silence seemed a likely part of the neophyte phase of ordination in a faith such as that of the Varics, which encouraged free speech.

With a full belly and her muscles relaxed from the bath, Gwen's eyelids grew heavy. The bed looked as comfortable as the pile of cushions she'd sat on earlier, and she wanted to sink into it. First, she thought, she needed to find something to wear so she could return the robe to Brother Jacques after she'd napped. After all, she'd wear a robe for the rest of her life once she joined an order, she thought as she opened the trunk to take out one of the dresses she'd packed. Inside, she found the contents in disarray and not just from the wagon's tousling. The things she'd packed on top were scattered throughout the layers, and some of the clothing had been bunched up and stuffed into corners. Someone had searched her belongings!

Chapter 16
Baking is mundane only to those with full stomachs.
--Gilly Bastwick, baker

* * *

Who would do such a thing? she thought as she, too, rifled through the trunk, tossing items out into piles on the bed. Nothing came up missing, but she still found the invasion of her privacy alarming, and she couldn't comprehend what would prompt anyone to do such a thing. What could the person have thought to find in the trunk of a simple and poor girl from the Westland?

By the time she'd refolded her clothing and repacked the trunk, someone rapped on her door. "Sister Gwendolin?"

She recognized Brother Jacques's voice, and when she opened the door and saw him, she got the same feeling of security and power she'd sensed earlier.

"Have you rested?"

She shook her head. "I'm afraid not. I was distracted."

Brother Jacques peered into the room as if searching for what might have kept her from sleeping then looked at her questioningly.

"My trunk had been opened. Someone was looking for something, and I'd say they did it in a hurry." Or in a frenzy, she thought.

His expression became more somber. "I see. Was anything taken?"

She shook her head again.

"Well, that is something. Perhaps the trunk merely fell open while being moved?"

Gwen wondered if he was always so objective and looking for any and all possible answers before drawing a conclusion. "Perhaps," she replied, deciding not to make more of the matter.

"I should let you rest, then." He turned to leave.

"No, wait," she said, reaching out and touching his sleeve. A scene of a whip cutting across a bald man's clothed back flashed in her mind.

"Is something wrong?" he asked her.

"No, I . . . I don't think I could sleep just now."

"I understand, Sister Gwendolin. It is a new place, and it must seem very odd to you to be here."

"A bit, yes." She was relieved he'd not asked any more questions. Trying to regain her composure, she looked away and spotted the book on the bed. "I found a book about the Varics." She pointed. "Is that the order you serve?"

"Yes, it is. If you're certain you cannot sleep, then come with me, and we can talk about the Varic order if you'd like."

She welcomed further distraction from the vision and from the unsettling feeling she had about the trunk. "I would like that very much."

Brother Jacques smiled and continued out into the hallway. Gwen followed, glancing behind her at the trunk as she pulled the door closed.

For the rest of the afternoon, the monk spoke with her about the Varic philosophy and mission as the two of them walked the grounds behind the building she'd first thought was just a small one. From behind it, she saw multiple wings, and Brother Jacques told her each contained at least one corridor leading to rooms where the monks worked and lived. Gwen didn't fail to take note that as he educated her about the monastery, he also set limits on her involvement. The two rooms with the bath and bed, as well as the reception area, he'd told her, were the only ones she was allowed to enter.

"I'm afraid the others are reserved for the ordained and those farther along in their studies than you. If you have need of something that we have, I or one of the other monks will happily retrieve it for you. All we have is yours. Perhaps someday you will come back and visit so that I may show you the inner sanctuary. It is truly a place of peace and vast knowledge."

"You mentioned before the importance of knowledge to the Varics, and Brother Vaughn said the cathedral has a vast collection of manuscripts and scrolls. I am curious. Are the Zjhon not equally devoted to knowledge?"

"That is difficult to know for certain. They have the most extensive collection of written knowledge in all the Greatland, it is true. Some manuscripts and scriptures are said to be more than twenty centuries old." He hesitated and made the prayer gesture, bowing his head long enough to say, "May the gods forgive my envy of their holdings." Then he resumed walking with his arms crossed in front of his body, his hands slid into the opposite arms' cuffs, which left him looking like lumpy wool from head to toe. "Sadly I've come to suspect they harbor knowledge not for its preservation or to share with those who seek it but to keep it away from the populace they wish to convert."

"And you believe this because of what happened to Brother Vaughn?"

"Not wholly, no. What happened to Brother Vaughn is reprehensible, but my doubts about the Zjhon's conviction to education come from more than just one incident of an unknown monk seeking entry to study tomes about birds. I've overheard stories in the marketplace about the Zjhon masters turning away even their own youths seeking more arcane holdings in the cathedral's archives."

"But that isn't what they told Brother Vaughn, is it?"

He shook his head. "No, it is not. Why would any part of the archives be inaccessible to someone of the Zjhon faith if an order believes all knowledge leads to wisdom? Would not any shepherd delight in the wisdom of the flock? No, I fear the motivations for such restrictions are nefarious."

Gwen cocked her head. "Nefarious? How so?"

"Because there is no rational reason for such actions. Because I have witnessed a growing intensity in Zjhon conversion efforts. In every corner of the city, I hear the same subtle calls for reformation, 'Copies of the Scripture! Know the path you must follow!' *Must* follow."

"I heard a man in the streets calling out those exact words as our caravan passed." Gwen's spine tingled.

Brother Jacques nodded. "History has taught us intolerance gains power not just through repetition of words, but also through constraint and ignorance. I've witnessed a growing reluctance to question the Zjhon government in Sutherhold, even amid increasingly confining laws based on ancient myths and old wives' tales, the securing of territory, and the growth of the military. The people become ever more gullible and, I regret to say, more fearful of challenging authority. If we've learned one thing from the past, we know fear breeds complacency with aggressors when mindful inquiry, peaceful protest, and diplomacy would benefit all."

The monk stopped and sat on a stone bench overlooking a small herb garden. Gwen sat down beside him, crossed her arms, and slid her hands inside the cuffs of her own robe. At first, the position seemed awkward, and she didn't know where to place her hands. She fiddled with wrapping her fingers around her wrists then grasped the cloth in her fists. Finally she settled on placing her palms flat against her arms, after which she simply wanted to sit in silence and take in the heady scent of lavender, the sharp smell of rosemary, and a sweet scent she couldn't identify but would ask about later.

The herbs reminded her of Mignon, and homesickness plunged her into a contemplative mood. Gwen mulled over what Brother Jacques had just told her about history, and it rang true when she thought about how Master Gabaldi treated the trainees, particularly his intolerance of Rolf's questioning and the subsequent sword attack that had left the boy scarred. Her stomach knotted, and her throat constricted on the question she was afraid to ask. In a desperate attempt to not think about the danger her friends were in, she stared at the disorderly herb garden with its clumps of intertwining plants. One by one, she identified each stalk and leaf combination until she came upon one she didn't recognize. She stood and moved toward it then bent over and reached for its velvety leaves.

"No, don't touch that one. It's mother's root. Extremely toxic. It must be gathered only by gloved hands," she heard Brother Jacques say as his fingers grasped her wrist and stopped her forward motion.

Again, the shocking sight of a whip cutting into bloodied cloth on a man's back forced its way into her mind. This time the scene lasted long enough for Gwen to make out the fabric more clearly. Tightly woven gray wool. The robe of a Varic monk.

"You are as pale as winter frost. Did you touch it?" Jacques asked with a frightful tone that alarmed Gwen even more.

She shook her head, torn between telling him what she'd seen and not scaring him with what she thought couldn't possibly be anything more than sheer exhaustion playing tricks on her.

"What did you see?" Brother Vaughn asked from behind them.

Were it not for Jacques's steady hands and quick reaction, she might have toppled face first into the herb garden. The monk drew her away from the dangerous plant, one of her arms over his shoulder until she steadied herself. Then she burst into tears.

"Take your time, Sister," said Brother Jacques as he handed her a mug of cool water once the two monks had taken her back to the reception room.

Gwen saw him give a sharp glare to Brother Vaughn, who had opened his mouth to speak. The second monk closed his mouth and drew his body in, as if shrinking back into the robe and hood. While she drank, the two men sat patiently with arms folded and hands hidden inside their sleeves.

After she'd downed a full mug of the water, Brother Jacques spoke up. "Better?"

She nodded. "Yes, thank you."

"What did you see?" Brother Vaughn blurted out, and though she didn't witness it with her own eyes, Gwen felt the heat of the other monk's glare.

"I'm not sure, but I believe I saw a monk being whipped."

The answer didn't satisfy him. "It was more than that."

"Yes. It was a Varic monk."

"And you've had this vision more than once."

His frankness she understood. His accuracy confounded and frightened her. "How do you know that? And who are you? You aren't a Varic, and you say you aren't Zjhon."

"Brother Vaughn is a Cathuran monk, and he is our guest." Jacques said in a tone of agitation bordering on scolding. "As are you," he added as he shifted his gaze from Gwen to the other monk, who once again seemed to wither into his garment.

"I apologize. I didn't mean to be rude," said Gwen.

"What has upset you, Sister?" he asked. "If the gods have given you a message, then they also have brought you to us, perhaps so we might aid you in deciphering it. The gods rarely speak in ways we understand immediately. Tell us what has happened, and we will try as best we can to help you."

In every word he spoke, Gwen heard nothing but sincerity and an earnest desire to assist her. "Brother Vaughn is correct. I have had the vision twice, and . . . and . . . it was you, Brother Jacques, your back under the whip."

"And when did you have these visions, Sister?" Brother Vaughn asked.

"When he touched me. When Brother Jacques touched me."

"You're sure it was Brother Jacques in the vision? You saw his face?"

"Well, no. But--"

"Did you see any face at all?"

"No," she said with a sigh.

"And you have assumed it was Brother Jacques because you had the visions when he touched you?"

"Yes, I suppose I did." She felt ashamed and her cheeks flushed.

Brother Vaughn looked at the other monk. "Have you told her why I am here?"

The Varic monk's response was clipped with annoyance as he directed his answer to Gwen. "I'd hoped to give you a chance to recover from the journey here before we discussed that matter."

The sense of security she'd felt with Brother Jacques persisted despite knowing he'd not been fully forthcoming with her. "I understand," she said, her own words surprising her. "Why *are* you here?" she asked, turning her attention to the Cathuran.

"To accompany you on your trip to the monastery you will choose as your own order." His words couldn't have been more matter-of-fact. "When you are ready to go, of course."

"Who arranged this?" she asked.

"The leader of my order, Mother Seema."

Although she'd not found many specifics about the Cathuran, Gwen remembered Madame Gabaldi's book containing some information about them. They were relatively secretive and avoided the outside world. Their primary hold, Ohmahold, was almost as far from the Westland as a place could be and still be in the Greatland. "And what makes her believe I will choose to be Cathuran?"

"She didn't tell me what you would decide, only that I needed to accompany you to the monastery of your choice."

Gwen felt the fool again for assuming more than she should have. She'd made that mistake twice, and she intended to choose her words more wisely from now on. "Why? And why me? Who am I to warrant special attention? How did she even know about me or that I was coming to this place? I didn't know myself until a few days before we left." With each question, her spine tingled more intensely.

"You'll have to ask her, Sister Gwendolin. On the day I informed her of the destination I selected for my final communion with the mundane world, she told me only what I have told you and asked if I would help. If you do not wish my escort, then nobody will force it upon you, Sister."

"I don't know where I want to go," she admitted. "I just don't want anyone to get hurt." She glanced over at Brother Jacques and spoke words that came not from her thoughts but from her heart. "I fear for the Varic. I fear for my friends. And I don't think there's anything I can do to help anyone. I've no business becoming a monk."

Chapter 17

For the common person, there will always be hope. They are by their very nature common.

--Mother Seema, Cathuran monk

* * *

"You're here for a reason." Brother Jacques spoke reassuringly and reached for Gwen's arm but then pulled back his hand.

She stared at the sleeve his hand had almost touched. "I'm here because I had no choice." Painful memories of her grandmother's insistence and her father's complacency came into focus, and hopelessness pressed down on her. "And now I have no control over my mind either."

"There's a reason these visions have come to you, Sister Gwendolin. They are blessings from the gods even though we do not yet know what they may mean. Tell us what you know with certainty to be true. What has happened to you and these friends for whom you fear?" asked Brother Vaughn.

"It started with the gypsy fortune-teller," she said, and in a flood, she recounted for the two monks everything that had happened to her and her friends--the gypsy's prophecies, Master Gabaldi's cruelty, Rolf's father's death, the soldiers following the caravan, the vision of Thomlin, and the ones she'd had about the whipping.

Upon finishing, her body and mind ached, and Brother Jacques seemed to sense as much. "You've given us much to ponder, Sister. Perhaps you should rest now?"

"Rest? How can I rest? Rolf and Thomlin are in danger. I know they are. I *feel* it."

"This Master Gabaldi you spoke of is the husband of the woman who brought you here, is he not?" asked Brother Vaughn.

"Yes. I suspect Madame Gabaldi has seen him for what he is, but there's little she can do to stop him. She protected Rolf, but her protections will do him no good now."

The monk turned to Brother Jacques. "Do you know where this woman is?"

"Yes, yes, of course. She is staying with the Dempsy family here in Sutherhold. When she sent word of bringing Sister Gwendolin to us, she gave me the address where she'll be living while tutoring their children."

"And her husband? Where will he stay?"

Brother Jacques shrugged. "I assumed he would be staying there as well when he isn't training at the guild."

"I think I can find it again," Gwen said, "at least the way to the guild from the cathedral. I remember that part."

"So there we have it. You aren't as incapable of helping your friends as you thought. I can accompany you to the guild, and you can warn your friends." Brother Jacques smiled at her, and she realized for the first time that he must have been quite handsome in his youth. Despite the kindness in his gaze, his bright eyes also brimmed with curiosity and, if she hadn't thought it impossible for a mostly cloistered monk, a sense of adventure. She smiled back.

Vaughn spoke up. "It may be too dangerous for you to go, Brother. Until we can interpret Sister Gwendolin's visions, you and the other monks should remain out of sight." He paused then added, "For your own safety. As I remember, all guild apprentices attend scripture readings on the Day of Rest, do they not?"

"Yes, that is true," replied Brother Jacques. "A few come here sometimes."

"I know the way to the cathedral, and Sister Gwendolin knows the way to the guild from there. We'll find her friends--coming or going--and she can tell them of her concerns."

"Brilliant thinking, Brother Vaughn. You truly should consider becoming a Varic. It's not too late."

The Cathuran let out an unreserved and rolling laugh. "Mother Seema said you would try to steal me away from Ohmahold."

Brother Jacques shrugged and gave a good-natured smile. "An insightful woman, your Mother Seema."

"That she is," said Brother Vaughn. He looked at Gwen, and in his eyes, she saw a genuine admiration for the Cathuran leader. "*Truly* insightful."

The three sat in silence as the sun descended. When offered a meal, Gwen declined the food and excused herself for the evening. In the small, windowless room, which she knew the monks called a cell, she climbed into her bed and looked around. She thought the name befitting, for she felt trapped and isolated, a prisoner of Fate. To distract herself from further morbid thoughts, she read the Varic book by candlelight until she fell asleep. Dreams confirming her worst fears about Rolf and Thomlin disturbed her slumber, and she awoke feeling even more tired and defeated. After she'd bathed and dried her hair with a rough towel, she picked up a clean robe she'd found lying neatly folded near the wooden tub in the same place she'd found the first one. She wanted to wear her own clothing, but in deference to the monks' customs, she slipped the soft wool garment over her head and slid her arms into its loose sleeves. The robe tumbled to the floor around her, leaving her a formless lump practically indistinguishable from any of the other neophytes.

For the next two days, the monks talked with her and encouraged her to find work to busy her hands, and she felt grateful to them for doing so.

When she asked if she could gather some herbs and tidy up the garden, Brother Jacques clapped his hands in delight.

"I was hoping you'd ask," he admitted. "There are gloves in the potting shed. Be sure to wear them."

"I had almost forgotten about the plant you said was toxic. Does it blister skin?"

He shook his head. "No, but touching one's mouth after touching mother's root is enough to transfer the potentially toxic substance. It is highly potent. And unfortunately its sweetness is quite alluring. On occasion, we find a dead squirrel or field mouse whose hunger made the plant too tempting to resist. Poor creatures." He shook his head and looked down.

"Why do you grow it, then?"

"Given in a small dose, it has strong medicinal properties and is known to boost fertility in women. It can also slow a heart beating too rapidly, which also slows blood loss if a patient is bleeding heavily. Too much, though, will cramp the heart."

"Killing the patient?"

He nodded. "But there is an antidote, which should always be at hand when using mother's root. It takes time to steep thoroughly and has a lengthy list of ingredients and a complex blending method, but it can reverse the effects of an overdose if administered promptly. Even then, it's no guarantee." He shook his head and looked down again.

Gwen wanted to comfort him, but she feared physical contact would set off another vision, and she didn't think she could handle seeing him whipped again. "Well, then. I'll get busy," she said. "Perhaps this evening, you or one of the other monks could tell me how to prepare the medicine and the antidote. I'd very much like to add it to my plant journal."

"I'd be delighted," he said. He gave her a bow of his head and lifted his hands into the prayer gesture before leaving her alone in the garden.

She retrieved the tools, taking special care to bring along a thick piece of tanned leather to wrap around the mother's root once she'd gathered it, and set to work. As she turned over the black soil and pulled out tiny seedlings of weeds, she thought about how much Mignon would have enjoyed manicuring such a splendid garden. She wondered if the hedge witch had an entry for mother's root in her journal, and she made a mental note to look for one in Mignon's extensive collection. When she'd finished trimming and snipping the plants, she rinsed the tools in a bucket of water and took care to pour it then a fresh bucket of water along the outer wall of the monastery so nobody would pour it on the plants. She hoped she'd diluted it enough not to harm any animals. She had no idea just how toxic mother's root might be, and she had no desire to be responsible for someone's death. She washed her own hands thoroughly and retired to her cell, where she searched in vain for an entry in Mignon's journal. Not finding one had the double effect of exhilaration--excitement over learning about a plant Mignon hadn't yet discovered--and sadness because she couldn't share her find with the hedge witch who'd taught her everything she knew about plants.

During their evening meal of carrot soup and hard bread, Brother Jacques stood up and announced the order would remain cloistered for at least two weeks. He told the congregation of monks gathered around the table they would leave the compound only to administer to the sick and dying. In a perfectly level tone, he also said they should enter the outer sanctuary and courtyard only to receive a patient or to meet the messengers the families sent to summon the monks to a deathbed.

When he was finished, he sat down, and a murmur of quiet discussion began. The neophytes watched and listened while the ordained monks brought up related matters, such as their stores of rations and other necessary supplies. Quickly agreeing on their priorities, the senior monks then assigned tasks to the junior monks, who, in turn, assigned lesser tasks to the neophytes. Everyone remained calm; every plan made and word spoken carried an atmosphere of practical reason. To Gwendolin's surprise, nobody questioned Brother Jacques as to why he'd declared such a thing, and that was when it dawned on her the gentle man was the leader of the Varics, at least in the Sutherhold monastery--a leader who possessed the full trust of his order. And at that moment, she couldn't have felt more incapable or unworthy of becoming a monk Brother Jacques would respect.

After the meal ended, Brother Vaughn pulled her aside. "We'll leave for the cathedral early tomorrow morning. It would be best if you wore your normal attire and brought your shoulder bags with you. We can put them on the mule. It may be safest to travel if we appear like travelers."

"And what about you? What will you wear?"

"My robe. Monks often escort young ladies to their betrothed. People will think nothing of seeing us together."

Gwen agreed to meet the monk in the outer courtyard after breakfast, and Brother Vaughn left the reception room. Then she approached Brother Jacques, who sequestered her in a corner so they, too, could speak privately while the other monks rushed about to clear the table and return the room to its nonmeal state. "Thank you for helping my friends."

He looked down, the essence of humility in his expression. "I've been thinking about Madame Gabaldi."

"Yes?"

"I think she could be helpful too."

"How so?" Gwen asked.

"You said you believe she knows her husband's temperament."

"I'm sure she does."

"And you said she stopped him from further injuring your friend and made certain he had food during the journey."

"Yes, she did those things. I'm not sure she can help, though. She said she could do only so much."

"Yes, I remember you telling us that as well. Those limits may not apply now that she is in Sutherhold, however. If she knows something is wrong and those boys are in harm's way, she may be able to convince her husband to reassign them to aid her and the Dempsy family. She's a rather crafty woman, you know."

Gwen hadn't thought of Madame Gabaldi as clever in that way. Book smart? Yes. Somewhat clever in the face of injustice? Sometimes. But cunning? Then she thought about how the monks trusted Brother Jacques. "If you believe you can convince her to help Rolf and Thomlin, then I trust your judgment."

He smiled at her, and again she thought about how handsome he must have been in his youth. "Then it's settled. I will go to the Dempsy house after morning prayers and speak with her while you and Brother Vaughn go to the cathedral. I bid you good night, Sister Gwendolin."

"Just one more thing before you go, please?"

He cocked his head, and the warmth in his gaze let Gwen know he truly wanted to give her whatever she needed. "The mother's root. Will you have someone tell me how to prepare it and the antidote?"

His smile stretched into the same one he'd shown to Brother Vaughn when the monk had told him about Mother Seema's foreknowledge of his attempted recruitment. "Of course."

"Thank you, Brother Jacques. Truly."

The monk toddled off and spoke with one of the senior monks Gwen had seen puttering around in the garden. Soon the man approached her and rattled off the list of ingredients and the sequence of steps to make the mother's root concoction and its antidote. Twice he repeated warnings about the maximum dose and the symptoms of overdose. Details swirled in Gwen's head as he spoke, and when he'd finished, she repeated it all back to him. "Perfect," he said then walked away.

Gwen rushed to her cell and wrote down the details before she forgot them, taking care to double-check each number and word. When the ink dried, she closed the journal and packed it into her bag, along with the box containing her quill and ink. Before crawling into bed, she bathed and set out the dress she wanted to wear. As she smoothed out its wrinkles, she realized how much she anticipated wearing normal clothing again, feeling the silkiness of the fabric slide across her skin. However would she manage to wear a formless robe for the rest of her life? How miserable would she be?

Chapter 18
Strengthen the poor and they'll supplant you.
--Archmaster Dok, leader of the Zjhon church

* * *

While the monks ate breakfast in silence, Gwen nibbled on the hard bread smeared with a tangy jam and thought of Gilly, of how much lighter and more tasty her bread was than the crusty, dry rolls the monks baked. She ate halfheartedly, knowing she might never see her friend again. After the meal ended, Gwen retrieved her shoulder bags, put on Mignon's shawl, and met Brother Vaughn in the outer courtyard. He slung the bags over the saddle horn and offered to help Gwen onto the tan mule's back.

"Thank you, but I can do it," she said as she slipped her shoe into the stirrup and pulled herself up.

"From up there, you'll have a better view for finding your friends." He took the reins and led the mule out of the passageway and into the alley, stopping to close the iron gate leading into the courtyard.

As the pair exited into the street, the chant of morning prayers swelled behind them. Already the streets were filled with people dressed in their Rest Day finest. Families walked together, children laughing and mothers scolding them for straying too far or too near puddles. Before long, Gwen and Brother Vaughn arrived in the square and stopped in the looming shadow of the cathedral, the steps to which were lined with soldiers who stood watch while groups of the devout sputtered up the steps and into the cathedral.

"Which direction is the guild?" the monk asked.

Gwen looked around and gained her bearings. "That street," she said, pointing to the one she remembered.

"Good. Then we'll wait there and watch for your friends." He led the mule against the traffic pouring into the square and stopped in the first alleyway.

Her stomach tightened and Gwen mildly regretted eating breakfast, so she concentrated on searching for Rolf and Thomlin in the passing crowds. Her search ended when a column of soldiers approached and streamed past. She spotted Thomlin first. Dressed in a dark uniform with a stiff collar tight enough to choke him, Gilly's love marched with eyes forward. His eyes had lost their sparkle. Gwen scrambled off the mule. "That's him," she said to Brother Vaughn before rushing to catch up with Thomlin.

When she was next to him, she took up his pace. "What a fine day for a stroll," she said.

Thomlin looked straight ahead as if he hadn't heard her.

"Thomlin?"

The boy continued staring at the back of the head of the boy in front of him, but Gwen could see tears welling in his eyes.

"I have to talk with you," she said.

A voice nearby called out. "Hey, you! Leave the boy alone. He's got no coin to give you."

Gwen stopped walking, and the soldier who'd yelled at her gave her a gruff look as he stepped around her and continued to walk beside the column.

"Keep moving. No talking!" he yelled at the side of Thomlin's face.

As the column continued to file past a stunned Gwen, Rolf's voice croaked in a mock cough, "On the way back."

Thomlin's demeanor and his tears didn't allay her fears for her friends. If anything, seeing him made her more certain than ever he and Rolf were in danger. She returned to Brother Vaughn, who still stood in the alleyway with the mule, and she told him what had happened.

"They aren't wearing Zjhon uniforms," he said.

She hadn't noticed it, but now that the monk mentioned it, she remembered the uniforms of the soldiers on the steps at the cathedral and the ones Rolf and Thomlin wore. "You're right! Thank heavens. But if they're not Zjhon uniforms, then whose uniforms are they?"

"I don't know much about the guilds or soldiers. Armies are always political, and we Cathurans avoid politics, but I'd guess your friends' guild trains soldiers for hire."

Gwen's eyes widened in horror at the thought of Thomlin actually fighting with anyone, much less in an army. He'd be nothing more than fodder on the front line. "Master Gabaldi told Thomlin's father they would train so they could defend the Westland if need be, not become mercenaries."

"Some soldiers merely escort caravans and important travelers. Not all fight in wars."

She knew he'd meant to alleviate her fear, but Gwen thought Brother Vaughn naive for thinking Master Gabaldi had any intention other than recruiting the boys to fight other people's wars.

"At any rate," he continued, "we will wait for your friends to return."

Time ticked away sluggishly, but eventually Gwen spotted the column approaching from the opposite direction. One by one, the trainees passed by the alleyway, and with each passing uniform, she became more anxious. When the last one filed past, she turned to Brother Vaughn in sheer panic. "Where are they? They aren't with the others."

"Perhaps your friends are waiting at the cathedral?"

"I have to find them." She rushed into the street and stopped, staring at the back of the last uniform in the column.

"Psst. Over here," a voice called out.

From the other side of the street in another alleyway, Rolf motioned for Gwen to come to him.

When she reached him, she threw her arms around his waist and squeezed hard, closing her eyes. In a flash, she saw a young man tossing a giggling little girl into the air, and she heard Rolf's distinctive voice laugh as he said, "Bonita, my beauty." Then the image was gone.

"All right, all right," Rolf said. "You're gonna break something. Come on. Back here. Thomlin's with me. We can't stay long, though. We're already gonna get latrine duty for lagging behind the others."

The alleyway turned out to be a widening dead end, at the butt end of which rested a tall stack of crates. On an empty crate turned upside down in front of the pile sat Thomlin, who had unbuttoned the tight collar. He broke into a wide grin when he saw Gwen.

"It's good to see you, Gwen. I couldn't talk to you. I'm sorry. I just didn't want to get into any more trouble."

"I understand," she said. "I had to find you, though. I can't explain, so please don't ask me to, but you're in terrible danger. You need to go home . . . now."

"The only way we're going home is in a wooden box or on a litter," Rolf said. "At least not until they send us home . . . if they ever do."

Thomlin had dark lines under his eyes, as if he'd not slept in the few days since they'd arrived. Sighing at Rolf's words, he dropped his chin to his chest, making him look even more exhausted and depressed.

"You can't wait for them to send you home," she said, insistence and urgency in her tone.

"What do you propose we do, Gwen? Just walk out of here and all the way back to Vasterberg?"

"I don't know, but--" Her words were cut off by a sudden round of shouting and noise in the street.

Rolf ran to the edge of the alleyway and peeked around the corner. He ran back toward her and Thomlin. "It's a Zjhon officer. He's talking with Captain Browning."

Thomlin groaned. "Great. Now we won't just have latrine duty. We'll end up in prison for being deserters. Or they'll just hang us to scare the others. They might as well. I don't care anymore."

"Nobody's hanging anybody, least of all us. Come on! Think, man! There must be some way out of this mess." Rolf drew an arrow out of the quiver on his back.

"What do you think you're doing?" Gwen asked, alarmed by the ease with which her friend seemed willing to shoot the soldiers.

"Didn't you hear me? Pine box or litter. That's the only way we're gettin' out." He positioned the arrow for quick nocking.

She wrapped her fingers around the shaft of his arrow. "Wait. You said 'litter.' Does the guild send home those who are sick?"

Rolf shook his head. "Nope. Only the injured."

"That's it," she said, looking around. She spotted a long piece of wood, which she guessed might be a sliver off a rotted beam. She picked it up and came back to Thomlin. "Do you trust me?" she asked him.

Thomlin crinkled up his face. "Well, I suppose so."

"Good," she said. She stared at Thomlin's leg and then looked up at his questioning expression. What had seemed a way out of the mess they were in just a second before now felt wrong. How could she do this to him? And what if she missed or couldn't swing hard enough? His pain would be for naught. He'd been her good-luck charm and a good friend to Rolf during the journey. He was gentle and kind, and most important, he loved Gilly the way she deserved to be loved. Gilly would never forgive her. But if she didn't do it, Gilly would never see him alive again, and that was what mattered. Gwen steeled her nerves and took a deep breath. She wasn't hurting Thomlin. She was giving him and Gilly the future they deserved. Without giving him a warning, she drew her arms back and swung the beam at Thomlin's shin, letting every dram of hatred she felt for Gabaldi and the Zjhon and the injustice of their situation flow from her shoulders to her arms and into the force of her swing.

The crack of breaking bone echoed in the alleyway, and the boy folded over onto the ground with a scream. Gwen hurled the wood at the stack of crates. Several toppled over, barely missing her and Rolf, who stood with his mouth gaping.

"Litter it is," she said.

The noise from the street grew to a roar as someone shouted, "Hey, watch out! You're gonna trample somebody!"

Rolf grabbed Gwen's hand and dragged her to the stack of crates, shoving her behind the edge of the pile. "Stay put!"

"What the hell is going on here?" the deep voice of a male yelled from the entrance to the alleyway.

From behind the slats of wood, she could see the legs of a horse. Its rider wore black boots with a high shine on them. She didn't recognize the voice, and she was relieved it wasn't Master Gabaldi's baritone sternness. "What are you doing here? Shouldn't you be with your troop?"

"Yeah, but my friend tripped and broke his leg," said Rolf.

The boots thudded in the dirt. "You sure it's broken?"

"Yep. I heard it when he fell."

Thomlin writhed on the ground, trying to drag himself back up onto the crate.

"We need to get word to our commander," Rolf said.

"That won't be necessary, soldier."

"We're not soldiers. We just came here to train."

Gwen shuddered at the edge of irritation in Rolf's tone.

The man laughed, and Gwen heard the scuffle of boots and Thomlin crying out, "He's got a knife!" The scuffle died down into panting.

Her heart thumping against her breastbone, she stretched and strained as quietly as she could to get a glimpse of anything to clarify what had just happened.

"Well, you're gonna be a soldier now," the man said and laughed again.

Rolf spewed out an angry stream of grunts. "I told you already. He's got a broken leg. He can't fight!"

"I'm not interested in him."

"Our commander will be looking for us," said Thomlin.

The man laughed again, and this time he came into focus. No more than a step away from the crates, with his back to her, he had his arm around Rolf's neck. "You mean Gabaldi? *That* commander?"

"Yes," said Thomlin. "Master Gabaldi will look for us until he finds us."

The man replied, "We are in agreement, then. He will find *you*." He laughed and jerked his arm to move Rolf one step to the side. "When this one's settled, I'll come back for you, and I'll be sure your commander can identify the body. Not to worry."

"What's going on here?" Brother Vaughn's voice rang out from the opening to the alleyway.

It was the distraction she needed. Gwen squeezed out from behind the crates and removed the shawl. Holding it with one end in each hand, she took off in a full run and leaped onto a crate, propelling herself up and forward toward the man. At the arc of her leap, she raised the shawl up and swung it down in front of the man's face. And then she collided with his back, her face smashing into the hard bone on the back of his head. Gwen crumpled to the ground, and the man lurched forward, letting go of Rolf as he clawed at the shawl obstructing his vision.

Rolf spun around, his fist connecting with the shawl and the man's jaw beneath it. The soldier went down with a thud, sending a cloud of dirt into the area. The hunter's son wasted no time retrieving the rope looped over the horn of the man's saddle.

"Wait," said Brother Vaughn, who had now approached the three friends. "Get his uniform off first."

The monk's words took her by surprise, and for an instant, Gwen forgot about how badly her cheek and nose hurt.

"Good idea," said Rolf, who helped Brother Vaughn peel off the man's jacket, shirt, pants, belt, and boots. The belt that had held up his pants became a gag, and Rolf used the rope to tie the man's hands and feet together. When he was finished, the man lay curled up on his side like a sleeping baby. The two dragged him behind the edge of the crates.

Throughout the whole procedure, Gwen watched from the corner of her eye, too embarrassed by the soldier's nakedness to look directly at what Rolf and Brother Vaughn were doing.

"Now you switch clothes with me," said the monk.

"My clothes'll fall off you," replied Thomlin.

"It doesn't matter. We have to get you out of here," scolded Rolf.

"I don't think I can stand to take off my pants."

Gwen didn't see what happened because she turned away and faced the opening to the alleyway. Seeing a monk and plump Thomlin Frank naked was more than she could handle. Her face hurt, drops of blood from her busted lip soiled her dress, and one eye was swollen almost shut.

Restrained cries of pain slipped out of Thomlin, and Gwen imagined the other two men had reached the stage of pulling the pants off his broken leg. The rustle of cloth and thud of boots sounded from behind her, but Gwen kept her eyes forward.

When she heard Brother Vaughn say, "Good enough. Now strap this plank to his leg and help me get him onto the saddle," she turned around in time to see Thomlin placing a sandaled foot into the stirrup of the man's horse: a tall, black- and white-speckled gelding. From behind the crates came muffled yells.

The monk, who now wore the soldier's uniform, looked up at Thomlin, who grimaced. Gwen couldn't imagine how much pain he must have been in. "Say good-bye to your friends," said Brother Vaughn.

"Come with me," Thomlin said to Rolf, who had walked over to check on the prisoner.

"Naw. Nothin' for me there. You go take care of our girl."

"Gwen?" asked Thomlin, the word pitiful and filled with fear.

Her heart raced at the thought of going home, of feeling safe again, but she remembered the vision of Thomlin. He'd been alone when he galloped up to the Bastwick cottage. "You have to do this alone, but I *promise* you *are* going to make it home to Gilly. You have to believe that."

At the sound of his love's name, the fire in Thomlin's eyes reignited so visibly it inflamed Gwen's resolve. She wasn't giving up. She'd be damned if she would give up now.

"You truly must be going," said Brother Vaughn.

Gwen knew she could sway Thomlin to put his fear aside, and she gave him a confident smile. "I just want to know one thing," she said.

His attention fixed on her, she looked into his eyes and asked, "Did you pay the gypsy to tell Gilly you were going to marry her someday?"

Confusion washed over Thomlin's face, and an expression of concern for her quickly replaced it. "Huh?"

The man's muffled cries increased, and Rolf said, "Go now, Thomlin, before it's too late."

Gwen persisted. "The gypsy at the carnival in Vasterberg. Did you pay her to say that?"

Thomlin turned the horse around, and Brother Vaughn slapped its rump. As her friend passed her, he shook his head. "I didn't talk to any gypsy, but I'm darned sure gonna marry Gilly."

Gwen smiled. Brother Vaughn slapped the horse's rump harder, sending it and a robed, wincing Thomlin off into the street.

Gwen turned to Rolf. "We have to get you out of here too."

He held up a finger, picked up the man's boot, then stepped behind the crates. Gwen heard a thud before the soldier's muffled noises stopped. When Rolf reappeared, he tossed her shawl to her and shook his head as if answering some unasked question. "I didn't kill him."

"You have to go too. They'll be looking for you when they find him," said Brother Vaughn.

Rolf directed his response to Gwen, as if he knew she would be the one to protest his answer. "I'm stayin' here."

"Why?" she asked.

"I met this girl. She's . . . got the most beautiful eyes."

"Your life is in danger, and you're thinking about a girl?"

"She's special."

Gwen couldn't believe her ears. The practical, crafty son of the hunter had lost his mind. "Rolf, you have to go. They'll hang you for this. Think of Thomlin. If they catch you, they'll find out about Thomlin heading back to Vasterberg."

"You go on, Gwen. Get outta here. I'm staying for Zaffira. I'll figure out something. Just go!"

"But," she sputtered before Rolf cut off her protest.

"Just go! Get outta here."

Brother Vaughn tugged at her. "He's right, Sister Gwendolin. We must go now." He offered a hand to help her onto the mule again, and this time she accepted.

Wordless, she climbed up and settled onto the saddle. As the monk turned and led the mule toward the spot where the alleyway met the street, Gwen looked back at Rolf, who had nocked an arrow and was aiming behind the crates. She spun around, rearranging her shawl to hide the bloody spots on her dress, and she dabbed at her lip with her sleeve. With tear-filled eyes looking forward, she let the sounds of the busy street drown out what she knew would be the whiz of an arrow that wouldn't miss its mark.

As she and Brother Vaughn waited for a cart to pass so they could blend into the flow of townspeople in the middle of the street, Gwen heard a booming voice from the alleyway. "What's going on here? What's your name, soldier?"

She twisted around but couldn't see who had entered the dead end. It hadn't been a voice she recognized.

Rolf's voice responded, loud and confident. "Borga Jahn, sir. I caught this fella trying to desert. He was trading clothes with some pauper, who ran away when he saw me. I thought it best to stay here with him, sir."

"You finished him?"

"Yes, sir."

"Good job, son. No mercy for a traitor. I know a unit that could use someone just like you."

The voices faded as Brother Vaughn tugged on the mule's lead and it plodded down the street.

Chapter 19

A weapon forged in vengeance bites most deeply.
--Argus Kind, usurper king

* * *

Brother Vaughn led the mule back toward the monastery, and Gwen remained silent for the whole ride there, though she glanced around warily, stiffening every time she saw a man in uniform. But nobody stopped them, and there'd been no sign of Gabaldi or any of the boys she knew. No one seemed to be looking for a missing soldier or trainee.

When they arrived, the monk excused himself. "I must get into my robes and out of these clothes. I suppose I should burn them."

"Yes. If you'll wait to start a fire, I'll give you this dress too."

He nodded. "Very well. I'll meet you back here," he said, indicating the reception room.

Gwen went straight to the bathroom in her cell and peered at her face in the looking glass. She'd been right. One eye was swollen almost closed, and blood caked the split in her lower lip. After cleaning up, she put on another dress and bundled up the bloodied one. Then she headed for the reception room. She didn't make it all the way before meeting Brother Vaughn in the hallway.

His face wore worry. "The others tell me Brother Jacques has not returned."

"Maybe Madame Gabaldi has taken him to her husband to discuss Brother Jacques's concerns," she said, but saying that aloud didn't convince her it was true. It didn't convince the Cathuran either.

"I would not risk your life and mine on that probability," he said.

"What should we do?"

"Burn the clothes and prepare to leave. If Brother Jacques does not return by midday, we will take a less . . . well-traveled road out of the city. Be sure that anything you need is packed onto the mule."

"What about my clothes? The trunk is too large for the mule."

"Take what will fit in your bags and on your back, Sister Gwendolin. Now is not the time to fuss with unnecessary belongings."

Though it pained her to think of leaving behind her clothing, she saw the logic of a light load. Handing her bundled dress to him, she nodded and returned to her cell, where she rifled through the trunk until she found a simple cotton jumper and a heavier wool one. She folded and rolled them tightly. Using several of her hair ribbons tied together, she secured the roll. Fearful she might have ruined Mignon's shawl in the scuffle, she laid it out carefully on the bed and examined it. Happy she found no blood or rips in it, she wrapped the treasured shawl around her waist. Again, she didn't make it to the reception room before running into a breathless Brother Vaughn.

"We have to leave now. Come quickly and make no noise," he said.

Taking her by the elbow, he guided her toward the reception room. Gwen's stomach knotted and the moisture in her mouth dried up, making each swallow painful and dry. Rather than leading her into the courtyard once they'd exited the corridor, he turned sharply and veered toward a door on the back wall.

A loud clatter and yelling came from the courtyard. Madame Gabaldi's voice rang out, "You can stop all of it, Jacques. Just tell us where the boys have gone."

The voice stopped Gwen just as she and Brother Vaughn opened the door she'd been forbidden to enter. Looking over her shoulder and through the slats of the shuttered door, she saw Brother Jacques standing with his arms wrapped around the courtyard's single statue, his wrists tied together. Behind him, a short, dark Zjhon soldier held a whip poised to strike.

Brother Vaughn yanked her through the doorway.

"This is your last chance, Jacques. Tell Lieutenant Dempsy where they are."

A few seconds of silence passed, and then Gwen heard the crack of the whip and a painful cry.

"We have to stop her," she protested, jerking her elbow away from the monk's guiding hand.

His voice firm and unyielding, he whispered, "There's nothing we can do, Sister Gwendolin. We cannot defend this monastery. The Varics are already hiding. They will return when it is safe."

"But she's with the Zjhon. Don't you see? Rolf was right. She's been in on it from the start."

"We can do nothing to change this situation, child. We must leave Sutherhold without delay, or there will be no escaping the Zjhon." He closed the door, turned a key in its lock, and removed it, holding it out to her. "I can do nothing. The Cathuran do not intervene in politics. I was tasked with accompanying you to your chosen destination. And now you must choose your own way. If you wish to declare yourself Varic, then stay, and I will have fulfilled my promise to Mother Seema. There's no going back, Sister, only forward."

The Cathuran placed the key on the floor at Gwen's feet, turned, and walked down what Gwen realized was another of the long corridors without windows or doors. As she watched him take step after assured step, she weighed her options. The Varics were gone, and she didn't know where they were hiding. Eventually Madame Gabaldi would look for Gwen and do the same thing to her that she'd done to poor Brother Jacques, whose only sins had been kindness and generosity to the woman who'd once loved him. Even if Gwen had wanted to become Varic, that option no longer existed, at least not in Sutherhold. Gwen kicked the key as she took off in a run to catch up with Brother Vaughn.

The corridor twisted and turned, and Gwen felt as if she were being pulled downhill. When they reached the end of the narrow hall, Brother Vaughn stopped at another doorway. He pressed his ear against it, and Gwen waited, straining to listen for sounds other than the echo of her own thumping heartbeat.

"Stay behind the door and don't come out unless I tell you it's safe," the monk whispered before turning the key in the lock and opening the door, which creaked and groaned so loudly Gwen winced at the awful noise. He stepped out while Gwen waited behind the thick wooden door, her back pressed against cold stone and her breath held as she listened.

"Come quickly, Sister Gwendolin," the monk called out, his normal tone more reassuring than Gwen could have imagined.

She stepped from behind the door and peered out. The sweet scent of apples and pears and the heady smell of rotting fruit filled the air. Behind Brother Vaughn, who stood with the mule's lead in hand, sat perfectly aligned rows of flowering and fruit-bearing trees.

"Nobody is here. If we go quickly, we can reach the main road toward the north before dark. It will be safer once we are on the road." He took the bundle of clothing from her and held out a rolled-up robe. "You may be less recognizable if you wear this, Sister."

Gwen frowned and nodded. When the monk handed it to her, she slipped her arms into its voluminous sleeves and dipped her head into the opening at the robe's neck, letting the fabric fall down over her clothing. The result was a bulky, uncomfortable glob of fabric surrounding her body. Gwen knew her much-loved clothing bunched up under the robe would only make her miserable for the length of the journey, so she stepped inside the corridor and closed the door most of the way. In the dark, she removed the robe and her shift then put the robe back on with a sigh.

Brother Vaughn seemed to sense her sullen mood because he helped her atop the mule and silently led the way out of the orchard through dense undergrowth of ferns and pale-bladed grasses, stopping periodically to pick ripe pieces of low-hanging fruit, which he stuffed into a pouch hanging on the mule.

By late afternoon, they'd reached the main road and passed several clusters of people traveling by cart and horseback toward Sutherhold. Thankfully they'd not encountered any soldiers heading in either direction. At dusk, Brother Vaughn led the mule toward a stand of trees near the road. There, a small caravan was camped, and the monk approached them with a jolly, "Hey ho, travelers! Might you have room for two monks to sleep by your fire?"

Two old women and a short, pudgy man dressed in little more than rags sat around a campfire. The man called back, "That depends. Do you have food?"

"Not much, Brother, but we will gladly share what we have."

The man waved them forward. "Then come and rest by the fire. I'm Albert."

"Thank you for your kindness, Albert," said the monk. "I am Brother Vaughn, and this is Sister Gwendolin."

Shortly after they'd settled on the ground near the fire, what seemed to Gwen a horde of young children appeared from behind the trees. As raggedly dressed as Albert, they also wore the grime of the road. One little girl with tangled, dark hair knotted to clasp a ponytail approached Gwen and reached out to touch her hair. "So pretty. Like my mama's hair."

"You have lovely hair yourself," said Gwen. "And I have just the thing for it." She stood and took the little girl by the hand, leading her to the mule, which Brother Vaughn hadn't yet unpacked. Retrieving her rolled clothing, she carefully untied it and unknotted a strand of the ribbon. She dug around in one of her bags until she found a comb. Holding up both, she smiled at the little girl. "Your hair will look beautiful with a braided ribbon, don't you think?"

The child grinned, completely unselfconscious about a missing front tooth, the replacement for which had barely broken the surface of her gums.

Gwen led the little girl back to the campfire, where the child settled onto Gwen's lap and sat still and quiet while Gwen did her best to gently comb out the tangles in the girl's hair. Busying her hands and listening, she learned that Albert and the two old women were taking the children to an orphanage in the northwest.

"There are Cathuran outposts along the way," said Brother Vaughn. "Stop there and tell them that Mother Seema from Ohmahold would greatly appreciate it if you could rest there for a night. Most monks will happily take you in and feed you and give you a warm, dry place to sleep."

When she'd combed out the nest of tangles in the little girl's hair, she held out the ribbon in front of the child. The girl fingered the smooth ribbon and looked over her shoulder at Gwen, who said, "My mother gave this to me, but I think it will look better in your hair." The second toothless grin melted Gwen's heart, and she took extra care in threading the braid tightly so the ribbon wouldn't work its way out.

By the time she snuggled up with the little girl to sleep for the night, Gwen had given the older girls all of her clothing and had handed out all of the fresh fruit Brother Vaughn had picked in the orchard. After they parted company with the caravan the next morning, Gwen half-expected the monk to scold her for emptying their stores of all but the little dried fruit, nuts, and hard bread she had left in the bag her grandmother had packed for her trip to Sutherhold. To her surprise, the Cathuran said nothing about the matter, and the two traveled in silence for the entire day, which allowed Gwen's thoughts to roam. Although certain Thomlin would make it home safely, she still felt guilty about breaking his leg. She hoped he'd not suffer too much until Mignon could splint the leg properly, and she wondered what Mignon would think when she learned how the leg had gotten broken. Thinking about Rolf brought sadness and uncertainty about what would become of him. For his sake, she hoped the mysterious Zaffira would appreciate what he'd given up to be with her.

"How much farther is it to Ohmahold?" Gwen asked when they stopped and made camp for the night.

"The border of the Northern Wastes isn't far, and luckily it's not yet time for the snows to return. We should arrive in a week or so if the weather holds." There was a long pause in the conversation. Then Brother Vaughn added, "So you've decided on Ohmahold?"

The question surprised Gwen. "Yes, I suppose I have," she replied and at the same time felt keenly aware of a sense of curiosity. "How did Mother Seema know I would need a guide?"

Brother Vaughn smiled. "The same way you knew Thomlin would ride to Vasterberg on a speckled horse."

Gwen blinked. "How could you know that? How could she . . . ?"

"Mother Seema is blessed with insight. She can see and feel the energy of many things. Sometimes I know what someone is thinking, but I cannot claim to have tapped into such energies to the degree Mother Seema has. The range of my insights is severely restricted. Hers is not, but then, you should ask her about that yourself when you meet her. I am sure she has much to tell you, and you'd be wise to listen to her, Sister. Her wisdom is a treasure."

Gwen curled up and pulled one of the mule's blankets over her. She fell asleep pondering what it could possibly mean that this order of monks accepted without question her vision about Thomlin when even she could not understand what purpose such a thing could serve. Equally as odd to her was the way Brother Vaughn did not doubt his ability to hear the thoughts of others. But most of all, she mulled over and again why she had drawn any attention at all from such a powerful monk as Mother Seema.

When morning came, the monk repacked the mule's load and helped Gwen onto the blanket on its back. He once again took the lead and walked alongside the animal, the Cathuran's only words being, "We do not question the gifts we are given, Sister Gwendolin. As Mother Seema says, 'You will have everything you need.'"

Gwen and the monk exchanged glances, and she knew he knew what she'd thought when he'd repeated Mother Seema's words. Although she didn't know why, Gwen had no doubt Brother Vaughn was supposed to know she'd heard the words before in the voice of her dead mother, and somehow, that felt comforting.

Chapter 20

A perfect crust is useless if what's inside is unappealing.
--Gilly Bastwick, baker

* * *

From time to time during their journey to Ohmahold, Brother Vaughn shared stories about the Cathuran monks--their history, their beliefs, and some of their practices--although he stressed some specifics would not be revealed until Gwen took her final vows. The order closely guarded its most sacred rituals, and only those deemed ready to participate in them were privy to their details.

"Are you allowed to speak when you're in the monastery?" she asked to distract him from the arduous walk up a steep trail leading over the lowest ridge of a mountain, where the air had become thinner, and Gwen had wrapped Mignon's shawl around her to ward off the chillier air.

Brother Vaughn let out a snort. "Yes. Not during some of the rituals, though. Talking saps energy, and the rites often require more energy than you can yet imagine. Every pulse must be conserved."

"I'm not sure I understand what you mean when you say 'energy,'" she admitted.

"You'll learn." He offered no more information or explanation, and Gwen didn't push for more than he'd given.

Thereafter, she gave the bulk of her attention to their surroundings, ever seeking opportunities to pluck a tender shoot or collect wild berries for their meals. Remembering the warning Brother Jacques had given her in the courtyard when she'd almost touched the mother's root, she covered her hands and was careful not to touch anything bared-handed when collecting samples she didn't recognize. In the evenings, she added notes to her plant journal and pressed the samples between pages in the back so she could learn more about the unfamiliar plants after she gained access to the library at the monastery, which Brother Jacques had told her contained a substantial number of manuscripts and scrolls related to herb lore. She felt happy and excited at the prospect of being able to study plants, which she'd figured out was possible after the monk had explained specialization.

"An area of interest not directly related to spiritual practices, specialization is an allowance for continued study. Each Cathuran monk declares an area of specialization before taking final vows, and Mother Seema then sponsors one last trip to gather study materials outside Ohmahold. After that, any external documents or artifacts come only as a result of good fortune--either by a traveler bringing them to Ohmahold or by obtaining them while on a mission of a different kind, such as delivering supplies to another Cathuran outpost."

Herb lore would be her choice, as it always had been, Gwen had immediately decided.

As the mule and Brother Vaughn took step after labored step along a steep path, Gwen thought to ask him about what he'd chosen as his specialization.

"Creatures of flight."

"Birds?" she asked.

"Not exactly. Most are birds, yes. Others . . . I am not quite certain they would be called birds but most assuredly a distant relative of them."

"What flies but is not a bird?"

His eyes lit up with excitement. "Dragons."

Gwen almost giggled, but at the thought of it, she saw the monk's expression fall into embarrassment. His answer had sounded so sincere Gwen felt guilty for hurting his feelings. "Dragons aren't just stories to frighten children into not wandering away?" Her question rekindled the flame of inspiration in Brother Vaughn's eyes even though Gwen suspected he realized she was indulging him out of guilt rather than curiosity.

He shook his head. "I do not believe so. Only a few scrolls exist with any stories at all about them, but those that do tell of magnificent, terrifying creatures with skin like snakes and enormous, powerful wings. Some of the scrolls mention other scrolls with more information, but I have yet to find those. Perhaps someday . . . if ever I visit a library outside of Ohmahold again."

She didn't know how to respond to him. That a man who seemed so knowledgeable believed in dragons unnerved her and made her wonder just what kind of place this monastery might be if it harbored those who appeared common, if not slightly more intelligent than average, on the surface, but who unashamedly spoke such nonsense. "Doesn't the thought of being stuck within Ohmahold forever bother you?" Her stomach knotted at the idea of being forced to remain within the walls of a refuge for the touched.

He shook his head again. "No. I am ready to take my final vows. Wherever Mother Seema sees fit for me to be, there shall I serve at peace and with joy, whether in the confines of the monastery or somewhere else."

"Just *one* person decides what everyone else must do?" She wondered if life in the monastery would be any different from the life she'd left behind in Vasterberg. At home, she'd had no choice either.

He smiled. "Decides? No. She guides our paths."

"And if you disagree with her?"

"Mother Seema seeks counsel from all."

"But does she *listen* to it?"

Brother Vaughn stopped walking, looked forward and nodded toward something ahead of him. "You'll have to determine that for yourself."

Gwen looked forward too. They were at the edge of a bluff overlooking a valley surrounded on three sides by steeply rising mountains like the one they had just climbed. On its southern side, where the lowest ends of the eastern and western mountain ranges curved toward each other, a winding crevice between the mountains dead-ended at a wall.

"We are standing on the cliffs of Ohmahold, and just over there," he said, pointing down into the valley, "lies the city. Below us is a plateau of pastures where we keep goats and sheep. And there," he said, pointing toward the extreme other end of the valley, "lies the Inner Sanctuary of the Cathuran monastery. Home."

Between the city, which rested at the lowest spot in the valley, and the green area Brother Vaughn had identified as the Inner Sanctuary, which sat at a sharply higher elevation but still far below the three mountain ranges surrounding it, lay a walled-in massive stone building with a maze of narrow wings and a tower rising high enough to make the Inner Sanctuary accessible only by climbing the tower.

Gwen squinted at the vegetation covering the Inner Sanctuary. At first she thought it might be a forest canopy. On closer inspection, however, she realized there were no breaks between the clusters of leaves, which didn't seem possible, so she climbed down off the mule and walked to the edge of the cliff, where she scrambled down over boulders and ledges until she was as far as she could safely go. "It's one tree and it spreads over the whole valley," she whispered, awed by the sight of leaf-laden branches thicker than a cottage.

"Almost," said Brother Vaughn from behind her. Gwen could hear the reverence in his tone, and she felt the same way about the tree though she couldn't explain why.

"If you do not mind, Sister Gwendolin, I'd like to spend the rest of today and tonight here on the cliffs. It is my last unbound day, and I would like to end it with the memories I must set aside. Ohmahold will still be there on the morrow."

Gwen nodded. She could understand his desire to have one last night of freedom, even if he hadn't explained it just that way. She'd spotted some plants growing in between the rocky ledges on her way to the edge of the cliff, so she decided to spend the remaining daylight hours collecting them while Brother Vaughn made camp and did whatever it was he planned to do with his last hours of nondedication. She would give him the privacy he needed to be alone with his thoughts.

After retrieving her clipping shears, she traveled from crevice to crevice and snipped off stems and leaves and scraggly flowers, those open and those still in protective buds, just in case one form or another had special qualities. When dusk fell into evening, she watched as yellow specks of light flared and flickered on in the city below until it looked like a starry night twinkling below her. Sitting near a low fire Brother Vaughn had kindled for her before tromping off to a rocky ledge, where he sat with crossed legs and his back to her, Gwen felt surrounded by sky, and she couldn't remember having ever felt so tiny and insignificant.

Sometime well into the night, Gwen fell asleep and began to dream. Although she knew she was dreaming, her surroundings felt real. *On a rocky ledge of the cliff, a man in monk's clothing sat with legs folded in front of him and one hand resting on something Gwen couldn't quite make out. As she walked closer to the man, he stood and pulled back the hood of his robe. Slowly he began to turn around, but before he'd rotated enough for her to make out his face, her gaze fixed on the object in his hand--an arrow, on the shaft of which was crudely painted in blood red the words* Bonita's freedom. *She stopped abruptly. Unable to move, she watched the man complete his turn. By the time he'd finished, the robe had disappeared. Facing her in a Zjhon uniform was Rolf mouthing the words, "Forgive me."*

Gwen bolted upright, her forehead drenched in sweat, her hair plastered to her head and neck, her breath uneven and raspy.

Someone was calling her name in the distance, and she flinched when Brother Vaughn reached out to touch her arm. "Are you ill?"

"I don't know. I don't think so," she said as she struggled to widen the distance between dream and reality. Across the valley, dawn glowed beyond the eastern mountain range. "Can we leave now?" she asked, her voice shaky.

"Yes, of course. Let's get you to the monastery, where Sister Brunhilda can attend to you. You really do not look well, Sister."

The trip down the mountain was as precarious as the climb up had been, and their descent ended at the winding crevice. Gwen rode atop the mule in a half-sleepy stupor, the dream insistent on replaying in her head. Even more surreal was the ritual Brother Vaughn enacted once they were well into the narrow passageway in the crevice. He stopped to strike a metal sheet three times, its tones reverberating and echoing until they filled the narrow space around them. A guard appeared, and after the two spoke, Brother Vaughn led the mule forward.

By the time they reached a heavily guarded gate, Gwen teetered on the mule, distracted by the still-replaying dream and too upset to pay attention to anything around her, except to notice how foreboding the gate to Ohmahold looked as she passed through it--significantly more foreboding than the gate to Sutherhold and considerably more ancient. On the other side of the gate, the city was awakening slowly, and only a few people roamed, mostly young shepherds driving their flocks out to pasture. When they reached the entrance to the monastery, three monks came out to greet them.

"This is Sister Gwendolin. Sister Brunhilda will need to see her at once,"

Brother Vaughn said after each gave him a welcoming hug. One hurried back into the monastery, leaving behind a trail of dust. The others helped Gwen down from the mule and assisted her into the halls behind him. Inside, the flustered monk and a tiny, wrinkled old woman hurried toward them.

"Bring her to the first purification chamber and have my bag retrieved from my apartment. It's hanging on the wall beside the door," the old woman said, "and tell Mother Seema she has arrived."

That was all Gwen remembered about reaching the monastery when she awoke in a basin filled with pebbles.

Chapter 21

When the fields are sown and the animals fed, a farmer eats with an unburdened soul.

--Jacob Ahlgren, farmer and butcher

* * *

For what she estimated to be the next several weeks, Gwen remained naked while she underwent purification after purification--the shaving of her body except for the hair on her head, which she was told would be shaved when she undertook her final vows. The attending monks, two young women not much older than she, placed steaming rocks on her skin and washed her body with hot cloths; they massaged her skin with oils and melted candle wax in her ears; they lathered her in mud and peeled it off when it was dry and cracked. Upon each purification ritual's completion, she slept, sometimes in a basin filled with stones that caved around her body as it sank into them, sometimes on a pallet on the stone floor. Upon waking, she drank small amounts of water from a glass placed on a stone table while she slept, and although she ate very little of the small bits of bread left for her intermittently, she didn't feel hungry. The visions didn't cease, though, and they often interrupted Gwen's sleep, leaving her tired and frustrated and worried when she awoke. But each day, those feelings were erased by whatever purification the monks delivered.

Finally the day came when the rituals ended. After a final shave, bath, and massage, the two attending monks dabbed at Gwen's skin with a warm towel and helped her put on a blue robe. She thought it prettier and thinner than the coarse, tan one Brother Vaughn wore and the darker tan ones the other monks wore. The two monks who had attended her left the room, and an old woman dressed in a white robe entered, gently closing the door behind herself.

"I am Mother Seema. I've waited long for you, Sister Gwendolin."

Gwen sized up the woman, who was about the same height. Her gaunt face made her appear frail, and though wrinkles framed her eyes, they didn't lend any harshness to her countenance. In fact, her face bore serenity, and her gray eyes exuded kindness and wisdom. Gwen could understand why Brother Vaughn felt the way he did about the leader of the order. She looked easy to love. "How did you know I would come here?"

Mother Seema smiled. "I dreamed you would. From the time I came to Ohmahold, I knew you would follow."

"I don't understand."

The woman smiled softly again, the empathy on her face making Gwen long to embrace her. "I know you don't, but you will. I promise. You've a long day ahead of you. First you will break your fast with us. You must be famished."

Gwen's tummy rumbled at the thought of a meal.

Mother Seema chuckled sweetly and grasped Gwen's hand so tenderly it almost made the girl cry. "Come with me, dear sister. First we eat, and then we'll talk more."

She led Gwen out of the room and down one shadowy corridor after another, all of which seemed identical. Finally they entered a large room lit by only candlelight in iron sconces along the walls. In the center of the room sat the longest table Gwen had ever seen. Simple wooden chairs lined all sides of it. In the chairs, the robed monks of Ohmahold sat in silence with perfect posture and hands resting folded in their laps.

Releasing Gwen's hand, Mother Seema placed an arm around her shoulder. "Sisters. Brothers. I am so very happy to introduce you to Sister Gwendolin. I know you will assist her in any way you can. Let us celebrate her arrival."

The group broke into wide smiles and pleasant nods, with some calling out "Welcome" or "Well met, Sister Gwendolin."

Gwen shifted and grasped the ends of her sleeves in tight fists as if holding on to the courage she needed to take in the sea of faces, shaved heads, and robes awash in shades of tan and brown.

Mother Seema motioned to a chair to the immediate right of the empty one at the head of the table, and Gwen wasted no time in getting to it. The old woman had no more than barely sat on her own chair before a stream of blue-robed monks poured out of a door at the back of the room. Like a line of azure ants, they encircled the table, trays and tureens in hand.

Brother Vaughn, who was sitting across from Gwen, stood up and looked first at Mother Seema then down the table at the other monks.

Gwen took note that his robe was the same darker tan as that of the other monks. He'd taken his final vows, and from the serenity he, too, exuded, Gwen could see he seemed at peace with his decision. She saw no sign of the delusional excitement he'd shown when he spoke about dragons, and she wondered if perhaps he'd just been teasing her and had put on a show of false dejection when she'd blurted out her question about their being real. His new sense of calm and stability reassured her that she wasn't in a place full of the touched.

"Let us take a moment to be thankful and to reflect on how we might best serve those in need this day." He bowed his head and closed his eyes, as did the others, and Gwen followed his example.

Time ticked slowly for Gwen, and the scent of food tugged at her hunger. Her eye twitched. Her nose itched, which only made her aware of it and the aromas it had caught. She tried to push the thought of eating out of her mind and concentrate on Brother Vaughn's instruction, but the smell of parsnips and rosemary teased her. She squeezed her eyes shut even more tightly to stop their twitching.

Just when she was sure she couldn't keep her eyes closed a second longer, Brother Vaughn sang out a long baritone note, which began as a quiet tone then rose in volume to clear, steady pitch before diminishing to nothing. When the note ended, he spoke again. "Let us now celebrate the safe delivery of our beloved sister."

Gwen opened her eyes, a little surprised by how bright the candlelight now seemed. Brother Vaughn sat smiling across from her. A blue-robed monk placed a platter of fresh berries between her and a young female monk to her right, who turned in her seat to face Gwen. "Welcome to Ohmahold. I'm Sister Lucinda."

Gwen recognized something familiar about the woman's face: a scar in the spot where an eyebrow would have been had it not been shaved off. "I have a vague memory of you. You came to my chamber during the purifications."

Sister Lucinda nodded. "Yes. I did. I must say you tolerated it well."

"Thank you for your kindness. You must tell me what's in the oil you used on my skin. I thought I caught the scent of honeysuckle?"

Mother Seema laughed. "Very good, Sister Gwendolin. You've a well-trained nose." She leaned toward Gwen and spoke quietly, "It's my favorite segment of the purification rituals too."

Gwen hadn't thought of it that way, but once Mother Seema had said it, she knew it to be true. The honeysuckle had been both invigorating and relaxing, and it had been her favorite part.

She enjoyed each bite of the fruit and cheese, every drop of weak vegetable stew she ladled out of the closest tureen, and every luscious nibble of dense ginger cake topped with a dollop of fresh goat cream.

The monks chatted among themselves and let her eat without asking questions. When their feast had ended, Mother Seema took Gwen by the hand once again and led her through the winding corridors to a chamber with a bed and a chair next to a bare window low enough to see out of when sitting. The view included a young fruit tree with small dots of green hanging from its branches.

Mother Seema stood beside Gwen. "We call it the Tree of Plenty. Brother Bastian grafted it himself. It bears apples and pears, each with a distinct flavor. I hear he's growing some saplings for another of his experiments--this time, one that will bear a large variety of pitted fruits. I can't begin to understand how the process works, but then botany was never my specialization or interest, to be honest."

"It's amazing," Gwen said in a stuporous gaze at the tree. "I'd never have imagined such a thing possible. I wonder if the same could be done with plants." Her mind had already begun to work through the steps of such a process, and it had already halted and backtracked when reaching a dead end.

"Perhaps. You should speak with him when you return."

Gwen blinked away her thoughts and stared at Mother Seema. "When I return? Where am I going?"

"South. To the harsh, dry lands of the south."

She'd worried she would fail at being a monk, and now her fear seemed confirmed. "Why? What have I done to be sent away?"

Mother Seema took Gwen's hands gently into her own. "My dear sister. You are not being sent away. I am dispatching you with Brother Vaughn into the Southland. It will be your final journey before taking vows."

"Vows? So soon? But I know practically nothing about being a Cathuran monk."

"I know. I am rushing you. It isn't fair and I apologize for that." She frowned. "I told you I had foreseen your coming. What I did not tell you was the role you will play here, and I still cannot tell you everything about it. I can say only this: the survival of many in the Greatland will depend on your understanding of what it means to love, to truly love with heart and soul. I know it makes no sense to you yet, but it will. I promise you it will . . . someday. We have only a few years to prepare you for a task more burdensome and more joyous than words can describe, a destiny awe inspiring in its simplicity and exquisite in its complexity. Will you trust me, Sister Gwendolin? Will you do this thing because I ask it of you, because it will turn the tide for the survival of so many, including your Cathuran Brethren and Sisters? Will you travel to the Southland to meet your destiny?"

Gwen strained to speak, and her voice came out the same way she felt inside: in incomplete, jagged shards. "I . . . I . . . If . . ." She was suddenly aware of moisture on her forehead and palms; she could hear her voice saying, "Yes," but no air had passed between her lips. Light-headed, her nod made her dizzy.

"It is your choice, Sister Gwendolin. Yours only."

"Yes," Gwen said. "I choose 'yes.'"

Chapter 22

Though art can bring joy, it is often born of pain.
--Gemino, sorcerer and artist

* * *

For the next week, Gwen spent daylight working alongside the monks and evenings in solitary repose in the little apartment where she gazed out of the window at the Tree of Plenty while mulling over her dreams and Mother Seema's words. In truth, she found the routine peaceful even though she uncovered no meaningful answers as to what the dreams signified. She threw herself into learning all she could about the plants in Ohmahold from the two monks who specialized in them, splitting her working hours between assisting Sister Brunhilda in the potting shed during morning hours and helping Brother Bastian in his greenhouse in the afternoon.

Sister Brunhilda, aware of Gwen's impending journey to the Southland, gave her a list of rare plants to locate, which reduced Gwen's anxiety about setting off to meet her destiny, as Mother Seema had so onerously defined the purpose of the trip.

"This is a crude drawing of Terhilian skullcap," Brunhilda said, handing Gwen a piece of parchment.

Gwen studied the image. To her, it looked just like the image in her own plant journal--mintlike leaves with hooded flowers and distinctive seed pods. "Terhilian? What makes it different from common skullcap?"

The old monk smirked. "Common skullcap can be helpful for settling nervous conditions, itching, irritations of the skin."

"Yes, that is what I was taught," said Gwen.

"Terhilian skullcap aids in vision quests."

Gwen cocked her head. "Aids? Do you mean it induces hallucinations?"

Brunhilda shrugged. "Who can say? But it is extremely powerful as a relaxant, and some who struggle with clarity in visions claim Terhilian skullcap has helped them slip into the dream state more easily."

"I see. I'll make a note of that." Gwen handed the parchment back to the monk. "Does it grow in the same places as common skullcap?"

"No, and that is why we must not miss this chance to get some while you are in the Southland. I've heard it prefers areas where the land is alternately marshy and wooded but with no more than half a day's sunlight, not full sun."

"I know nothing about the Southland and its landscapes or climate."

"But Brother Vaughn is quite knowledgeable about such things. I have heard he will be traveling with you on his way to Drascha Stone to deliver a message and pick up some artifacts. That means you will pass through remote areas of the Southland, and as luck would have it, those areas are ideal for the herbs, seeds, roots, and cuttings I'd like you to gather." She handed Gwen another parchment, this one containing a long list of plant names, some with specific instructions for the stage of growth they should be at before collecting them.

Gwen reviewed the list quickly. "I'm not sure what some of these are," she said.

Sister Brunhilda reached into a drawer below the potting table and pulled out a stack of drawings, which she held out to Gwen. "Sort through these and copy any you need for your own journal. In fact, you can put the pages in alphabetical order while you're at it. My eyes are not what they used to be. And be careful," she added as she set the pile into Gwen's hands, her own reluctantly drawing back. "These are the only copies I have."

Gwen's eyes widened at what she suspected were hundreds of individual sheets. "Of course, Sister. Thank you for lending them to me. I'll have them back to you by morning if that suits you." She had no idea how she'd get the task done but knew Brunhilda would be uncomfortable with her keeping them for more than a day.

"That will be fine. Now off with you," the old monk said. "Brother Bastian will be waiting."

"Yes, Sister." Gwen turned and walked toward the greenhouse.

Before she shut the door behind her, she heard Sister Brunhilda call out, "And drop those in your apartment before you go to his grimy greenhouse."

Gwen sensed some jealousy about Brother Bastian's more spacious workspace. She nodded from the doorway. "I will." As she closed the door, the thin glass insets that allowed extra light to flow in through the potting shed's door rattled. She made a mental note to ask which of the monks specialized in carpentry and could reseal the edges of the panes so none fell out if a brisk wind caught the door and slammed it shut. Maybe sprucing up the shed would make Sister Brunhilda feel more appreciated.

As promised, she set the stack of parchments on her bed before walking the distance to Brother Bastian's greenhouse, taking care to follow the directions she'd been shown. She'd quickly learned most of the corridors inside the monastery looked alike, and she'd been warned not to wander because some of them contained death traps. Only some of the sisters seemed to understand the designs marking which halls were safe and which weren't, which restricted the movements of everyone else, and so Gwen, not being among those who understood what the designs portended would lay beyond, had stuck to the routes she knew would take her only where she needed to go to safely eat, meditate, sleep, and work. In the back of her mind, she wondered if something should be done to prevent monks from accidentally taking a wrong turn and ending up maimed or dead, but she kept her thoughts to herself.

The second she opened the door to the greenhouse, the scent of pears filled the moist air. It reminded her it was past midday already and she hadn't eaten since early morning.

"Hello, Sister Gwendolin. Please shut the door before the bees escape."

Gwen hurried in and closed the door behind herself, noticing the panes in the door panel didn't rattle when the door clicked shut.

"Brother Vaughn tells me you will depart for your journey tomorrow."

Her stomach knotted. It explained why Sister Brunhilda had given her the list. But why hadn't Brother Vaughn or Mother Seema told her?

"The Southland has an abundance of fruit trees and shrubs, and though I'd very much like specimens of all of them, I'm afraid you won't have the means to carry them safely back. There's simply no need to overburden the mule and uproot samples if they won't weather the trip. I'm eager to experiment with some of the more exotic seeded fruit trees. I suppose I'll have to settle for a fig and a pomegranate this time, as I suspect dear Sister Brunhilda has requested a hoard of herbs."

A smile sneaked onto Gwen's lips, but she said nothing.

Like his apparent rival had done, he handed her a single parchment, his not a list, however, and much more elaborate than any of Brunhilda's drawings. His bore images of two trees and their fruits, but his sketch also included carefully labeled, colorful cross-sections showing the layers of skin, flesh, and seeds of the fruits, as well as the pattern of the root system. "I'd like young saplings, as they'll stand a better chance of surviving, but be sure to gather some near-ripe fruit from larger trees too. Not completely ripe or they'll rot before you get back. I'll study the seeds and preserve what I can. Experiments do fail and extra seeds may be needed. Wrap the base of the trunk and all of the roots in this," he said, handing her a roll of rough burlap tied neatly with twine. "And be sure to wet it first. Keep it moist or the roots will go into shock. Oh, and leave a small amount of soil on the roots. They will need the nutrients."

Gwen nodded. "I understand."

Brother Bastian put a hand on her shoulder. "Am I asking too much of you, Sister Gwendolin?"

Flustered, she sputtered out, "N-no. I just hadn't expected to leave so soon."

His face glowed with a warm, comforting smile. "I understand. Perhaps you should go back to your cell early today. I'm sure you have packing to do."

Gwen smiled back. She liked Brother Bastian, and she appreciated his kindness. "Thank you. I can stay if you need me, though."

He shook his head. "Nothing is urgent today. In fact, I'd like to watch the bees for a while and see which flowers they prefer. When Sister Ellena relocated them here, she said they might be a bit confused at first and that I should be certain they have enough of whatever they like until the colony has settled in." He turned his head and squinted. "There goes one now." As he crept away from her, peering into the rows of potted trees and shrubs in search of the bee, he spoke more loudly, "Travel safely, Sister Gwendolin. And thank you. You'll do a fine job bringing back the trees, I'm sure."

"Good-bye, Brother Bastian," Gwen called out as he disappeared behind a row of thick, flowering bushes. She let herself out of the greenhouse, taking special care not to open the door until she was certain no bees were nearby.

Her apartment, which had seemed cozy and comforting, felt cramped as she sat on the tile floor in the small amount of open space between the bed and chair. She spread out Sister Brunhilda's parchments in a circle around her and began sorting them alphabetically, a task that proved exceedingly more difficult because the monk's penmanship reflected a shaky hand and uneven pressure. Smudges distorted some of the letters, and Gwen had to use the images as aids for identification. Some plants she recognized on sight; others eluded recognition. She gnawed on her lip as she studied the parchments and flinched when she accidentally bit down too hard and drew blood.

As she licked the tender spot and tasted the saltiness, at first strong then dissipating, the vision of Rolf holding the arrow and silently begging forgiveness flashed in her mind. She stiffened when she heard her name spoken by a woman.

"Forgive me for interrupting, Sister Gwendolin."

She blinked away the vision and looked toward the sound.

Mother Seema stood in the open doorway. "We missed you at our evening meal." The monk motioned, and one of the blue-robed neophytes entered with a tray, atop which sat a pitcher, a mug, and a plate covered with a tea towel. "I thought you might be hungry."

The silent, young monk placed the tray on Gwen's bed and left the room, gently closing the door behind herself.

"I see Sister Brunhilda's keeping you busy," said Mother Seema, a grin twisting her lips.

"I don't mind. I'm thankful for the distraction."

"Are you nervous about the journey, Sister Gwendolin?"

"A little, I guess." She looked down at the disorderly pile of parchments and avoided eye contact.

"I'd be a lot more than a little nervous, especially if I were having visions I didn't understand."

Gwen made eye contact. "How do you know that?"

Mother Seema smiled. "Some of your more perceptive friends here are worried about you because you aren't discussing your troubles with anyone. I count myself among those friends, Sister. I can't know what your visions portend, if anything, but I do have an empathetic ear and do care to lessen your worries if I can."

"I keep seeing an image of a boy I knew. A hunter. But he's in a Zjhon uniform, and he's holding a bloody arrow." An immediate sense of relief washed over her.

Mother Seema sat on the bed, steadying the tray to keep the pitcher from toppling. "A hunter with a bloody arrow. While the vision isn't a pleasant one, I'm not sure why you would find it disturbing." She lifted the edge of the tea towel and peeked at the food on the plate before covering it up again.

"In the vision, I can't hear him speak, but his lips move. He is saying, 'Forgive me.'"

"Hmm. And has your friend done something warranting forgiveness? Something you might know about?"

Gwen shook her head. "No." She remembered the Zjhon soldier behind the crates in the alleyway. "Well, maybe. I didn't see him do it, but I think he might have killed a Zjhon soldier when Brother Vaughn and I were in Sutherhold."

"Brother Vaughn has told me about the soldier," Mother Seema replied, her voice calm and nonjudgmental. "He said the man was tied up, though, not killed. And didn't your friend put on his uniform?"

"That was the other friend. And . . . well, I'm not sure my friend Rolf didn't kill him after Brother Vaughn and I left the alleyway. Rolf stayed behind."

"I see. But you're also not certain he did the soldier any harm."

"There's more. Before all of that happened, I had a vision of Rolf holding up a little girl. A little girl named Bonita. He was older and I think the child was his."

Mother Seema's expression was the picture of serenity as she listened. "Go on."

"The shaft of the arrow in the other vision had words written on it-- *Bonita's freedom.*"

The expression of serenity faded, and Mother Seema said, "I do not see a connection between the two visions and what happened in Sutherhold. You said your friend was older. Perhaps you merely saw a glimpse of one possible future, one in which he might do something warranting forgiveness? The line of time is not unbending, Sister Gwendolin. Unrelated memories and assumptions often cloud the meaning of a vision. I am sure you'll decipher what you need to help your friend, most likely when you least expect."

Though she found no comfort in the lack of resolution about the visions, Gwen did feel better for having revealed the details to Mother Seema. "You're right, of course. Maybe I'm just a bit more anxious about this trip than I thought."

"I don't profess to infinite knowledge or even a shred of wisdom on most days, but I do know you have undergone a great deal of turmoil-- leaving your home and family, discovering your teacher was not what she claimed to be. No wonder you have disturbing visions." She stood and reached out to Gwen.

Gwen got up and clasped Mother Seema's hands. "Thank you for listening."

The monk smiled warmly and squeezed Gwen's fingers tightly. "Know this, Sister Gwendolin: This journey will change forever the course of your life, just as a similar journey turned the tide of mine. You will know joy and love. Above all, love." She let go of Gwen's hands and nodded to the piles of parchment on the floor. "I should let you return to your work. Sister Brunhilda will not be denied." She winked then exited the room, turning to say, "May your travels be safe and bountiful," before closing the door and leaving Gwen in a room filled with the warmth of her kindness.

Chapter 23

To crush the creative spirit is to rob the world of beauty.
--Madame Gabaldi, teacher

* * *

A few hours before dawn, Gwen finished copying the notes she needed from Sister Brunhilda's parchments. She also put the pages in order and bundled them neatly with one of her long, green hair ribbons, which she thought not much of a sacrifice since she'd have no need for a ribbon until her hair grew out again. Under pressure to get the work done before morning, she resisted taking time to read and learn about plants she'd not previously encountered, but she made a list so she would remember which parchments to study and copy upon her return. She surveyed her handiwork and considered sleeping. Knowing she couldn't still her worries enough to rest, she packed one bag with her plant journal and writing implements, an extra robe, and her plant snips. Then she slipped out of her apartment and took the bundle to Sister Brunhilda's potting shed, where she laid it on the potting table, along with a note thanking the monk and promising to return with all of the requested samples.

At daybreak, she met the other monks for a light breakfast and said her good-byes, but not before asking Sister Lucinda to make certain the door panes in Sister Brunhilda's potting shed were resealed.

Brother Vaughn led her to the stable where two pack mules awaited them. "They'll take us to the ship."

"Ship?"

"Oh, yes. Summer wanes and we haven't enough time to travel by mule all the way to the Southland and back before the winter snows. We'll be sailing to Mundleboro then traveling east by mule to an outpost in the Southland."

Without fanfare, they departed the monastery, making their way through the city and out through the crevice before turning eastward and heading to a small port on the coastline. There, Brother Vaughn negotiated their fares, and not more than two days after leaving the safety of Ohmahold, Gwen found herself on the deck of a cargo ship looking out over the vast sea, feeling no sense of security whatsoever and missing home.

"If we met the rising sun, we'd land in the Godfist," the monk told her, which didn't make her feel any less homesick. "But we're heading south and sailing around the tip of the Greatland. We'll make landfall on the southern tip of Mundleboro in two or three days."

The trip turned out to be four days, and miserable ones at that. A light storm rocked the ship side to side and shoved it over crests of crashing waves. Gwen, who had never even stepped foot on a boat, much less a ship, spent much of her time heaving up what little tepid broth she could get down. She had never appreciated solid ground so much as she did on the day the clouds broke up, the fog thinned out, and the Mundleboro coastline came into view.

After the ship dropped anchor, a handful of sailors rowed Gwen and Brother Vaughn to shore in a small boat they'd lowered over the side of the ship. Two more boats brought the mules, neither of which seemed to appreciate being hobbled, placed in slings, and lowered into the boats. Both brayed incessantly, and by the time they reached shore, the sailors hurried to secure ramps and release the complaining beasts. Gwen pitied the sailors almost as much as the mules. Once freed from the hobbles and their reins handed over to Brother Vaughn, who whispered in their ears, they settled down and let the monk repack and affix their loads with the assortment of mostly empty bags and baskets brought to carry the bounty Gwen would harvest for Brother Bastian, Sister Brunhilda, and, of course, herself.

The pair trekked through southern Mundleboro without event in a little more than two days. By noon of the third day after making landfall, the relentless sun had begun to tire Gwen, and she'd resorted to covering her head with the hood of her robe despite the discomfort of the excess heat it caused. She was thankful when they reached an isolated cabin on the remote western side of the Southland. As they approached it, two monks in dark brown robes and straw hats looked up from their work of weeding a vegetable garden.

"Is this Drascha Stone," Gwen asked her companion.

"Oh, no. Drascha Stone is in the far south. This is just an outpost through which the established monasteries relay messages and Cathurans stop when seeking shelter temporarily while traveling," he replied before waving at the monks. "Greetings, Brothers!" he called out then dismounted the mule.

The pair dropped their tools and met the travelers with warm smiles. "You're just in time for the noontide meal, Brother Vaughn, Sister Gwendolin. Come inside. We've been expecting you and were beginning to fear the weather had caused you harm. Storms have been blowing eastward for the last week."

"Yes," said Brother Vaughn as he handed the reins of his mule to a third monk who had joined them, "we encountered them at sea."

Gwen dismounted and handed over her reins, as well, choosing not to think about or comment on the stormy weather, which had caused her to be so very ill on the ship.

Once inside, they sat at a table and were served bread and cheese, followed by a mixture of fresh tomatoes and onions in a tart vinegar. Gwen found it refreshing. She listened as the monks exchanged news, none of which surprised her.

"The Zjhon have increased their presence throughout the Greatland. Even the minor cities report frequent patrols passing through. Sylva, Lankland, Astor, and even the Westland."

Gwen's stomach knotted. "Have you any news of Vasterberg?"

The monk at the head of the table, a middle-aged man named Frederic, who sported an orange-red beard, clapped his hands together. "Vasterberg! Oh my!" He stood and retrieved a folded parchment from a desk in the corner of the room. "Please forgive me, Sister Gwendolin. A week ago, a monk who passed through Vasterberg brought this message for you, and I'm afraid my sun-addled brain almost forgot about it. I would have sent it on to Ohmahold, but we knew you were coming and thought it would get into your hands sooner if we held onto it." He handed the parchment to her.

Gwen saw her full name on the outside of the parchment. At once, she recognized the handwriting as her father's. She took a deep breath and unfolded the parchment.

My dear, dear Gwendolin,

It is with a heavy heart I write to you, and I shall not delay in informing you of the sad news of your grandmother's passing. A month after you departed, she left this world peacefully during her sleep. We buried her frail body under the tree next to your mother. I am certain they are happy in being together again, and I am at peace knowing that is true.

Thomlin Frank has told the whole village about the horrors in Sutherhold, and we fear for the sons and brothers who still have not returned. I regret not recognizing for what it was the deceit Master Gabaldi perpetrated. I can only pray you and Rolf are safe.

The Zjhon have passed through Vasterberg twice since you departed, and each time, they have questioned the villagers and taken at least one young boy. Conscription, they call it. More like kidnapping, I say! Oh, but had I listened to your protests. Forgive me, dear daughter, for my lack of foresight.

For more than a fortnight since you departed, I have pondered the wisdom of my decision to force you to marry or to join the monastery. After seeing the joy Gilly and Thomlin expressed at their wedding just two weeks ago, I regret even more my decision, not because your grandmother and I wanted security for you and thought the monastery a safe haven, but because I did not give you time to explore other options. The limits of my imagination became your limits by force, and I regret that.

I miss you. I miss your laughter and your antics. I miss you dodging the pigs when you slop them. I miss kissing the top of your head before you sleep. I even miss your horrible cooking.

I do not know if you have taken your vows yet, but if you haven't, I want you to know you can come home, and I will welcome you with open arms.

With all my love and prayers for your safety and happiness, I am always your loving father.

"Excuse me," said Gwendolin, folding up the parchment and rising from her chair. Her voice cracked more than she'd meant to allow. "I'd like to be alone for a bit."

None of the monks said anything, and Gwen wondered if Brother Frederic or the others had read the letter. If they had, they showed no sign of it. No sympathy or condolences on the loss of her grandmother. No discussion of the news about the Zjhon in Vasterberg.

Gwen walked out into the midday heat and looked west. Home. She could go home. Her grandmother's voice teased at the corner of her memory but eluded her. Inexplicable sadness seared her, like visible heat waves floating across flat land in the distance.

"Sister Gwendolin?" Brother Vaughn's voice interrupted her thoughts.

She handed him the parchment, which he unfolded and read while she continued to watch the heat waves.

"I'm terribly sorry for your loss. Shall I make plans to guide you to Vasterberg?"

Gwen's heart thumped, and she turned and looked at him, surprised by his question but even more surprised by her own doubt. "You have business in Drascha Stone, don't you?"

"Yes, but I can send one of the other monks if you'd like me to take you home."

"I promised I would gather some things for Sister Brunhilda and Brother Bastian. There's no rush to get back to Vasterberg. I can do nothing for my grandmother now. You go ahead and take care of your business, and then we'll figure out what to do after that."

He placed a hand tenderly on her shoulder. "Are you sure, Sister?"

She nodded and lied. "I'm sure. Thank you for asking."

Brother Vaughn squeezed her shoulder and then returned to the cabin, leaving her alone with thoughts of home.

That night, she slept in a bed roll under the stars. As she had when she'd inhabited the little cottage with her grandmother and father, she watched the moon rise and crest before she drifted off to sleep.

She awoke to the ruckus of arguing.

"I tell you she should not be alone here. She's not even one of us," said a male voice she recognized as one of the Cathuran monks, but she wasn't sure which.

Brother Vaughn's voice then belted back, "Mother Seema has so ordered, and you'll follow her directions, as will I and every monk who serves the Cathuran order. I'll hear no more of your poisonous words. You should be ashamed to have spoken them! The girl has lost a loved one. Have you no compassion?"

Gwen got out of the bed roll and walked to the cabin, where she found Brother Vaughn standing with a stiff posture facing the eldest of the monks at the outpost. Neither saw her enter, and they both jerked their heads in her direction when she calmly said, "It's true I am not yet officially Cathuran, Brother . . . I'm sorry. I don't even know your name."

"Brother Mason," he replied, gruffness drawing his eyebrows close together.

"Your words are true, and I will say only that I trust Mother Seema's judgment in all matters. She sent me here for a reason, Brother Mason, and I do not yet know what that reason may be. Whether you leave me here alone or otherwise, I will remain until I know, even if it means I must sleep on the dirt and scrounge for food and water. What you do is of no concern to me."

The monk looked at Brother Vaughn, flustered and red faced. "See how she speaks to me? She is yet petulant and lacking humility."

Brother Vaughn's posture relaxed, and his voice lowered to his normal, calm tone. "You doubt the wisdom of our Mother. What does that make you, Brother Mason? I am one of mind with Sister Gwendolin. I have faith she can care for the outpost for the short time we'll be gone. I depart for Drascha Stone tomorrow morning . . . with or without you and the others."

One by one, the other monks approached her throughout the day and showed her around the little outpost, pointing out the few chores she'd need to do in their absence--water and weed the vegetable garden, pick any ripe vegetables and store them in the cold cellar, scatter feed for the chickens, and milk the cow before feeding her and making sure her water trough remained full. Everything else, they told her, could wait for their return. She said a silent prayer of thanks when she discovered they had no pigs to slop. With only a few chores to do each morning, she'd have ample time to accomplish the tasks she'd promised to do for the Ohmahold monks.

As he'd said he would, Brother Vaughn left for Drascha Stone the next morning just after sunrise. All of the other monks, including Brother Mason, went with him.

Once they were out of sight, Gwen acknowledged an odd sense of comfort knowing she'd be alone for a couple of weeks. She set to her morning tasks without delay and actually enjoyed talking to the cow while milking her. She named the gentle creature Tinkles because nobody had told her the cow's name and because the bell around her neck, unlike those of field cows, was so tiny its ring was barely audible. Gwen laughed with delight when the cow mooed in response to the name. Once she'd finished the rest of the chores, she retrieved her plant journal and gathering tools and walked in the direction of a grassy knoll dotted with bushes and wildflowers.

It didn't take long before she found a wild blueberry bush, from which she picked enough berries for a pie and a couple of light meals. Nearby she spotted a thick cluster of broadleaf plantains where the soil had become compact from poor drainage. She snipped the youngest leaves and plucked the seeded stalks from every plant in the patch, and she sat cross-legged on a clump of short grass and opened her journal in her lap. The growth pattern of the plantains had struck her as unusual because the plants had been more tightly compressed than she'd seen in the Westland, probably, she noted, because the soil in the Southland was more dense and less fertile. She speculated the leaves and possibly even the tender seed stalks would taste more bitter, as well. She held up a stalk with one hand and started drawing it in her journal.

"Broadleaf plantain if I'm not mistaken," a baritone voice said.

Gwen let out a squeak and threw up her hands so violently the stalk and her quill went flying into the air. The quill came back down, nib first, splotching her sleeve with ink. As she tried to stand, her feet got caught in the robe, and she ended up on all fours, trapped in her own clothing, and looking up in alarm at the most handsome man she could have imagined. If he were going to murder her, at least she'd die looking at something pleasant.

Chapter 24

To achieve a peaceful life, one must be at peace with themselves.
--Mother Seema, Cathuran monk

* * *

Leaning forward, the young man offered Gwen his hand. "I'm sorry. I didn't mean to frighten you. Let me help you up, Sister."

Gwen fought with the robe to untangle herself while she sized him up. Though he had a sword, he'd secured it in its scabbard. He hadn't given her any looks that made her uncomfortable, and he hadn't acted rudely or in a threatening manner. Still, she thought exercising caution the wiser course. "I can get up by myself, thank you, and I don't need any company. So you can just be on your way."

"Please," he said, offering his hand again and topping his offer with an irresistible smile upstaging a cut and bruise under his left eye. He didn't wait for an answer. Stepping closer, he reached down, hooked his arms under Gwen's armpits, and lifted her onto her feet without effort.

Her robe fell into place, and there she stood not a long step from him, face-to-face, close enough to smell the musky scent of a traveler's sweat. Gwen reached for her hair and blushed when she realized it was barely more than dark stubble.

"Thank you," she said.

He stepped back, looked around on the ground near them, then bent over and picked up the quill. Examining it, he said, "Looks like it didn't survive, Sister. I can make you a new one."

"That won't be necessary."

"Sure it is. It's my fault it got broken. It's the least I can do after giving you a fright like that."

The thought of having nothing to write with annoyed her, and she frowned.

"Was I right?"

"Right about what?"

He nodded toward the gathering basket. "Broadleaf plantain. That's what you were drawing, right?"

"Oh. Yes." She tried to gather her thoughts, but his voice, which carried an unusual accent, clouded them. "It's broadleaf plantain."

"Good for the gut if I remember correctly?"

"Among other uses, yes."

His dark eyes lit up with interest. "Other uses? Such as?"

"It depends on the part of the plant you're using, of course, but leaf extracts stop bleeding and encourage healing without scars."

He scratched his chin. "Hmm. And other uses?"

"In the Westland, wet leaf compresses have been used with some success to draw out snake venom . . . the degree of success dependent on the species of snake, of course. I'm not sure what purposes Sister Brunhilda has in mind for it, though. Now that I think of it, I'm not sure the Northern Wastes have any snakes. It's probably too cold for them."

He broke into a grin and shoved his hand toward her. "Benjin Hawk."

"Gwendolin Ahlgren. Gwen," she said, placing her hand in his. When he shook her hand instead of kissing it, she drew her hand back and looked at it, embarrassment warming her cheeks.

"I thought monks gave up their surnames."

"I'm not a monk. Well, not yet." He lifted an eyebrow, and Gwen felt compelled to explain. "I haven't taken any vows. In fact, I just learned that I might be going home and not becoming a monk at all." She wanted to bite her tongue. Why was she telling this stranger something so personal?

Thunder rolled in the distance.

"Just my luck," Benjin said. "I was hoping to get to shelter. The past week's been one storm after another, I swear."

She knew it broke every rule of safety to invite strangers into one's home, every rule of propriety to be alone with a man she didn't know, and every rule of hospitality to bring a stranger to a home that didn't belong to her, even if it was one of the homes of her order. She broke the rules anyway because it also seemed inhumane to leave a stranger out in a storm when she could offer shelter. "We've a barn. It's not very large, an enclosed pen, really. And you'll have to share it with Tinkles and the chickens, but you're welcome to stay there until the rain has passed."

"Tinkles?" he asked.

"The cow."

"Your cow's named Tinkles?"

"Well, she isn't my cow, but that's what I call her."

"Tinkles?"

What started as a giggle turned into full-blown laughter, and Gwen's heart swelled. "What's wrong with Tinkles? She likes it!"

Her protest made Benjin laugh harder, and Gwen soon found herself laughing with him.

"We'd best get you back, Sister . . . Gwen. Weather happens fast here. I've never seen it blow in so fast as it does in the Southland."

Benjin helped Gwen gather her belongings, and she pointed in the direction of the cabin. As they walked, she asked, "Where is your home, Benjin Hawk?"

"To the east."

His accent didn't sound like any she'd heard from Endland, nor from Astor, the only lands east of the outpost, except for the eastern reaches of the Southland, and Benjin's comment about the weather had made it clear the Southland wasn't his home.

"Where in the east?"

"Across the sea," he said. He stopped walking and reached out to touch her arm. "Please don't tell anyone. I'm just tryin' to get home."

Home, she thought. Home. Before the Zjhon. Before . . . She shut off the memories. "What brought you to the Southland?"

The light-hearted expression she'd seen earlier disappeared, replaced by a troubled frown. "A fella back home. Damned fool. I should've stayed put and let him come alone."

He resumed walking. Gwen caught avoidance in his downcast eyes and anger or something like it in his plodding steps. "What is your trade, Benjin Hawk?"

"A little of this. A little of that. I never studied anything for long. I can farm and hunt and track and fish, and I suppose I can defend myself if I have to. I'm a pretty decent herbalist, but my knowledge is limited. I'd like to learn more."

"Would you?" she asked. "Truly?"

"Oh, yes, miss. What you said earlier about the plantains made me want to take down some notes. My memory's awful and I wouldn't want to get a concoction wrong. I've seen what can happen."

He gave a shudder, but his darker emotions--the avoidance and anger she'd seen--had disappeared, displaced by liveliness and genuine interest despite the dark subject of overdosing. Gwen found herself longing to nourish the positive feelings he now expressed so freely. "Well, then. Perhaps while you're waiting out the storm, we can talk about some of the plants from your homeland and mine."

"I'd like that," he said and gave her another of his devastating smiles. "If our chat won't keep Tinkles awake, that is." He winked at her, and Gwen laughed.

By the time they reached the cabin, the clouds had gathered, darkened, and let loose a fury of lightning, thunder, and rain. They were still laughing as they entered the modest log cabin.

Benjin looked around. "You're alone."

Gwen walked to the fireplace and picked up the poker, stabbing at the logs the monks kept at a slow burn. "The others will return."

"They left you alone here? Don't they know the Zjhon have patrols combing the countryside for unprotected spots just like this one? They take what they want."

"This is a Cathuran outpost. They wouldn't dare--"

He interrupted her. "If you believe that, miss, you're making a grave mistake. The Zjhon respect no property, persons, or gods but their own."

She didn't want to admit he was right, but Gwen knew he spoke truth.

She'd seen the forceful way they preached their religion in Sutherhold and the way they'd recruited young men for their army. "I'll be just fine," she said, reassuring herself if not him. "Would you like some tea?"

"Tea." He said the word with the fondness one has for something long unexperienced but once loved.

Gwen smiled and leaned the poker against the stone face of the fireplace. "I know just the thing." She'd spotted some chamomile leaves in the cupboard, and so she crushed them and steeped them in the hot water the monks had left in a kettle hanging over the fire that morning. After straining them, she poured the liquid into clay mugs and set one down for Benjin.

He closed his eyes and leaned forward over the mug, letting the steam rise into his nostrils. "Chamomile. Calming, soothing."

"That's right. You've a good nose, Benjin."

"It's one of my favorites. I'd forgotten how much so."

"Would you like some honey in it?"

He shook his head and took a slow, long sip of the tea. "Perfect just the way it is."

Gwen grinned.

"You've a knack for working with plants. I've tasted chamomile tea so bitter it made me spit it out, but this is perfect. Utterly perfect. Thank you, Sister."

"Just Gwen."

"Thank you, just Gwen."

They laughed, and while they drank, they shared some of their favorite recipes for combination teas. The storm raged through their teatime conversation and through a light evening meal of bread, broth, and fruit, which Gwen prepared and shared with Benjin.

"How did you injure your eye?" she asked him.

"I fought someone's fist with my face."

"After dinner, you should let me take a look at it. Comfrey root will help it heal more quickly. The cut looks like it's on the verge of infection."

Benjin rubbed the spot. "I'll give it a good wash. It'll be fine."

"Now you're the one being silly," she said.

He shook his head. "Do all women do that?"

"Do what?"

"Remember every word a fella says and use those words against him?"

Gwen chuckled but didn't answer. She couldn't speak for other women. For her, though, Benjin's every word landed in her memory as naturally as the raindrops falling on the rooftop. And in her thoughts, she already played them over and over again.

When dinner was over, Benjin volunteered to wash the dishes, and Gwen retrieved the comfrey root she'd found in the cupboard. Standing beside him, she worked in a clean spot on the counter next to the washbasin, and all the while he watched her work. She chopped the raw root with a cleaver and used a wooden mallet to mash it into coarse mush, which she mixed with a small amount of honey in a crude stone bowl she found in the cupboard as well. She made a mental note to have a proper mortar and pestle sent to the monks in gratitude for their hospitality. By the time she finished the preparation, Benjin had dried and put away the dishes.

"Sit down and pull up a chair in front of you so I can see what I'm doing." She set the mixture on the table, retrieved a clean cloth from the cupboard and dampened it with water from the kettle, turned up the fire in the oil lamp sitting on the table, and took the chair he'd positioned in front of his own. Knee to knee, they faced each other as Gwen brought the wet cloth up to Benjin's face and dabbed at the cut.

He squinted but didn't flinch.

"It's painful, isn't it?"

"A little," he said, averting his gaze.

"Because it's getting infected, and it doesn't hurt a little. It hurts a lot. There's pus around the cut."

She pressed the cloth against the wound. "Hold this for a moment. I'll have to lance it to drain the infection."

"Uh. You sure that's necessary? It's just a little cut."

She got up and returned with the sharpest knife she could find in the cupboard. While she thought the knife would suffice, she wished she had one of her father's knives, all of which he kept sharpened to a fine edge, which would make the lancing quicker and less painful. Nothing hurt worse than a dull knife, and the last thing she wanted was to hurt Benjin. Placing the tip of the knife in the flame of the oil lamp, she heated it until it glowed red then sat down facing Benjin once more. "Move the cloth," she said calmly.

Benjin's eyes looked wild, like those of a spooked horse.

"I'll be quick about it. My father is a butcher. I can handle a knife. I promise."

As he was letting out a sigh betraying his nervousness, she reached up and slashed the cut with the tip of the knife. Blood and pus spilled out of it, and he pulled back. She tossed the knife on the table and grabbed the cloth out of his hand, placing it beneath the cut to catch the ooze dripping from the wound. Then she pressed all around the incision and bruise, making sure all of the infection came out of the cut.

"Ouch," he said, wincing and trying to get away from the pressure she applied. "I thought you said it wouldn't hurt."

"That's not what I said. I said I'd be quick about it." She pulled the cloth away and inspected the wound. "It looks better already."

"It stings."

"The poultice will fix that," she said, putting the cloth aside and dipping her fingers into the sticky preparation of comfrey and honey. She smeared it on the bruise and the cut and added another layer of the mixture on top of the first before Benjin said anything.

"You're right. It does feel better. Less pressure around my eye."

"Yes. I'm afraid if left unchecked the infection would have blinded you, if not worse."

Benjin's eyes grew wide. "Really?"

She nodded. "Infection can spread quickly, particularly near the eyes." She leaned back and looked at her handiwork. "I made only a small cut, and the comfrey root will heal it without a scar." That thought pleased her, as she hated to think she'd be responsible for scarring such a handsome face.

Benjin took her hands in his. "Thank you, Gwen."

That was when the vision took over. She saw the blow landing above his cheekbone and the brawl that had ensued, along with flashes of a beautiful young woman standing off to the side yelling at Benjin and the man hitting him to stop. Then Benjin was on the ground alone, the woman comforting the other man and yelling at Benjin. "What's wrong with you? Why can't you just be happy for us?"

"Gwen? Gwen? What's wrong?" Benjin's voice grew louder as the vision faded.

She blinked and looked down at the hands holding hers.

"You're shaking," Benjin said.

Her eyes filled with tears as she understood what had caused the fight. The woman Benjin loved didn't love him back.

"I'm fine," she said, rising and gathering the supplies she'd used. Standing in front of the washbasin, she looked out the window and listened. "The storm has stopped. You can take my bedroll to the barn." She pointed to the roll she'd left beside the door.

"Are you sure you're all right?" he asked.

She nodded but couldn't bring herself to look directly at him. She needed to think. "Good night, Benjin."

"Good night, Gwen," he said, rising from the table and repositioning the chairs before he picked up the bedroll and left the cabin.

Once he'd shut the door, Gwen grabbed the edge of the counter and braced herself. For the next hour, tears streamed down her face and she sobbed quietly, as much for herself as for the pain Benjin carried. Sleepless, she tossed and turned on one of the mats the monks usually slept on, but by morning, she had resolved to make Benjin forget about the woman who'd rejected him. She knew now why Gilly and Thomlin had acted the way they did. Love didn't let lovers choose. It chose for them. And on its own terms. For Gwendolin, that realization had come too late. She'd already fallen in love with Benjin Hawk.

Chapter 25

Dragons and magic are much alike. If they do exist, the powerful will take them and use them against the weak.

--Argus Kind, usurper king

* * *

"Good morning," Gwen said as Benjin approached her in the vegetable garden.

"Feeling better?" he asked.

"Yes. I'm sorry about last night. It was just . . . the sight of blood reminded me of something unpleasant." She looked up at the sky as she stood with a basket full of ripe beans. "It's a beautiful day. I thought we might do some gathering. I've a number of herbs to collect for Sister Brunhilda."

"Sure," he replied.

"I left your breakfast on the table."

"You're too kind, Gwen. Let me do some of the chores for you, and then I'll come in and eat. I feel like such a freeloader."

"All right, then. I've already milked Tinkles. If you could feed the chickens, that would be helpful."

"Sure enough, miss."

When he'd finished, he came inside, where Gwen had already begun shelling beans.

He sat down and devoured the bread and cheese she'd left for him. Touching the spot where the comfrey and honey paste had dried and crumbled away from his skin, he said, "It feels better today."

Gwen smiled broadly. "Good. You'll need both eyes to help me spot some of these plants." She took Sister Brunhilda's and Brother Bastian's lists out of her pocket and handed them to him. "Are you familiar with any of them?"

Benjin's gaze traveled down the list and he nodded. "Mm-hmm. And I know where to find some of them; I saw some on my way here. We'll have to walk pretty far, though."

"As long as we're back by nightfall."

"Plenty of time, then," he said.

After he'd eaten, they set off toward a nearby valley, where Benjin said he'd found a small patch of woods and marshland. While walking at a steady pace meant to make ground, they talked leisurely, and Gwen learned Benjin had left his home to go on an adventure with a friend named Wendel. Now he regretted the decision. It had brought him nothing but pain and suffering, he admitted, but he didn't divulge the specifics of how and why. Gwen didn't press him for more information. She already knew what he'd say even though he hadn't mentioned the fight with Wendel or the girl in the vision.

Benjin's ability to remember the landscape around him, down to the tiniest details of the plants and amounts of water and sun available for them impressed her. She steered the conversation away from anything to do with the girl or Wendel and focused instead on leveraging Benjin's knowledge to find the items on her lists.

"I think the most difficult to find will be the trees."

"Aren't there any fig trees in Ohmahold?" he asked.

"If there are, they must not be the kind Brother Bastian needs. He's growing the most unusual trees, ones that bear more than one kind of fruit."

"I didn't know that was possible," he said, shaking his head as if sloughing off disbelief.

"Oh, yes. I've seen it myself. He's managed to grow a tree with both apples and pears on it."

"Is the fruit sweet?"

"The apples taste like apples, and the pears taste like pears. It's really quite amazing."

"Truly," he said.

"Perhaps you'd like to come and see for yourself?"

Benjin laughed. "Nah. I'm headed for the Godfist. It's time for me to go home. I'm tired of traveling and ready to settle down."

"Have you considered staying in the Greatland?"

Benjin stopped walking and surveyed the landscape around him, as if gaining his bearings. "Yeah. I considered it. That didn't work out." He pointed west. "This way," he said and fell silent.

Gwen wanted to kick herself for reminding him of the girl again, but part of her also wanted to leap for joy. He had at least considered the possibility of staying. Maybe she could make him want to remain . . . with her.

The day's trek netted about half of the plants, roots, and seeds Sister Brunhilda had requested. It also netted more ease in their conversations, as Gwen avoided pushing Benjin about his past and his future.

The next day went much the same, as did the day after that and the one after that. Days turned into a week, and Gwen became accustomed to spending her waking hours with Benjin doing the thing she loved most. While he helped her locate and collect specimens, she helped him by writing down information about the plants foreign to him, including preparation methods and antidote instructions. They discussed the medicinal and cooking uses for common plants. Although Gwen felt she knew more about plants than did Benjin, she still learned things she hadn't known. When she told him she appreciated his sharing his knowledge so freely, he accepted her thanks with grace, and she could tell it gave him confidence, which filled Gwen's heart with a joy she'd not known before meeting him. For the first time in her life, Gwen knew the true meaning of fulfillment.

Then one morning while they ate breakfast and planned their day's trek, the Zjhon arrived.

Benjin had been the first to hear horses' hooves approaching, and when he peered out of the window, he announced, "If they take me, I'm dead."

"Then they aren't taking you. Quick," she said, retrieving her extra robe. "Put this on and cover your head."

Gwen grabbed a kitchen knife and slid it inside of her sleeve. While Benjin put on the robe, she met the Zjhon before they reached the vegetable garden.

"Greetings," she said to them with a nod, her arms crossed and hands hidden inside each sleeve in the monkish pose she'd seen so often.

"Sister," the man responded gruffly as he looked at the property around him, clearly appraising it.

"You're welcome to water your horses," she said.

"Thanks." He motioned to the others in the patrol, who dismounted and walked their horses over to Tinkles's trough.

"What brings you to our humble outpost?" she asked.

"We're looking for someone."

"Anyone in particular?"

"A fella with a funny accent."

Gwen chuckled but her stomach knotted painfully, and she doubted she could pull off hiding her fear for long. She responded loudly enough that Benjin would hear if he were listening, which she was certain he was doing from inside the cabin. "I'm afraid you've come to the wrong place, then. I'm not a fella, and Brother Bastian is mute. The others are in Drascha Stone, but I can't say any of them have accents much different from my own."

"Where's this brother of yours?" He dismounted and motioned to a younger soldier standing nearby, who was waiting his horse's turn at the trough. The young man walked over and took the reins of the horse.

"Inside."

The man took a step in the direction of the cabin.

Gwen stepped in front of him and frowned. "Meditating. You do realize this is a monastic outpost, don't you? Sacred ground."

The man snorted. "Uh. Yeah. Whatever you say, heathen." He pushed past her, and she followed him into the cabin.

On a straw mat, Benjin knelt with his palms and forehead pressed to the wooden slats of the floor.

"You. Get up," the man yelled, shoving him with the heel of his boot.

Gwen held her breath.

Slowly Benjin rose and stood in front of the man, head down and arms folded in front of him.

"What's your name?"

Benjin looked up at Gwen and brought his hands up in front of him and began twisting and turning his fingers in awkward motions.

"I told you. His name is Brother Bastian," Gwen said.

Once again, Benjin moved his fingers.

The soldier frowned at Gwen. "What's he saying?"

Gwen wanted so very much to say, "That you're an idiot." She refrained. "He said you look parched and asked if you would like a cup of tea."

Benjin's eyes widened then went back to normal when the man looked from Gwen to him.

"Sure," the man said. "Why not?"

The soldier sat in a chair from which he could keep an eye on Benjin.

Gwen watched as he took down a crock from the cupboard and plucked off leaves from the plant inside it, dropping them onto a square of cheesecloth, which he tied in a knot and placed in the mug.

"So . . . any fellas you don't know pass through here?" the man asked.

Benjin put the crock back into the cupboard and poured hot water from the kettle into the soldier's mug.

"You're the first person we've seen in weeks," she answered.

When Benjin set the mug in front of the soldier, Gwen caught a whiff of its contents. Panic set in. What was he thinking? When the senna took effect, the soldier would surely know the tea had made him ill. She turned her head so only Benjin could see her eyes, and she gave him a brief glare. He didn't react, but she could see the mischief in his eyes. He resumed his meditation pose on the mat.

"You don't look well, sir. Are you overheated?" she asked the soldier.

The man picked up the mug and took a sip of the tea. "Naw. Ain't nothin' wrong with me."

She'd planted the seed of doubt. Maybe he wouldn't make a connection between the symptoms and the tea. At least, she hoped he wouldn't.

A voice called out from outdoors. "Sergeant Blackwood. Horses watered and ready to ride, sir."

The soldier downed the remainder of the tea and set the mug on the table, its weight thudding on the worn wood.

"If that fella shows up, you be sure to hold him 'til we get back this way. Two, maybe three weeks at most."

"Does he have a name?" asked Gwen.

"We don't know his name, just that he speaks with a funny accent. He's not from the Greatland."

Gwen nodded. The soldier tipped his hat then walked over to Benjin and kicked him in the side, toppling him. Benjin doubled over and rocked but didn't make any sounds.

"Why did you do that?" she yelled at the man.

"Just makin' sure, Sister." He smirked and exited the cabin. Gwen slammed the door behind him and tossed the knife she'd hidden in her sleeve onto the table.

She heard the chickens squawking and the sound of hooves beating on the hardened dirt.

Benjin motioned for her to look out the door, and only after she'd gone outside and come back in did he speak. "Sorry son of a . . ." He held his side as he stood slowly by degrees with her help. Through gritted teeth, he spoke. "Have you got some cloth to wrap me in? I think he broke a rib."

As gently as she could, she helped him take off his robe and shirt. As she wound the ripped strips of bedsheet tautly around his chest, Gwen struggled not to stare at Benjin's muscled torso, back, and arms. "I didn't stop to count, but I think they took at least two hens. He'll regret eating once the senna sets in and he can't control his bowels."

"Zjhon scum. He deserves it," he grumbled.

"Why are they looking for you?"

"Wendel and Elsa. They insisted on taking something from the cathedral in Adderhold. I told them not to, that it was too risky, but they wouldn't listen. The way Wendel and I talk . . . no way to hide that. I knew the Zjhon would put it together eventually. I don't even know if those two made it any farther. Maybe the Zjhon snagged them after we split up. It'd serve them right."

The last sentence sounded unconvincing to Gwen. "Wendel is your friend from the Godfist?"

Benjin shrugged. "I wouldn't call him a friend. But yeah. He's the reason I came here in the first place."

"And Elsa? Who's she?"

Benjin's body stiffened.

"Is she the girl you and Wendel fought over?"

His eyes widened. "How do you know about that?"

It was too late to take back the words. "Why else would you and your friend have fought? Isn't it always over a girl?"

"She's not just a girl," he said, defensiveness making his voice as stiff as his posture.

"I'm sorry. I didn't mean to pry." She knelt in front of Benjin and held both ends of the strip of cloth. "Take a deep breath. This is going to hurt."

From the wincing he did when he drew in air slowly, Gwen knew it hurt more than he was letting on. "Deeper."

Benjin groaned but expanded his chest with more air, and Gwen pulled the ends as hard as she could and then tied them in a knot. She wasn't wholly sorry it hurt him. "There. That should hold the rib in place. No more lifting or bending over for a while. It could just be a deep bruise; I didn't hear a crack when he kicked you. But you shouldn't take any chances. Give it time to heal."

"How long?"

"At least a week."

For the next two days, Benjin grumbled and groaned and brooded. Gwen did her best to make the straw bed in the barn more comfortable for him, but he came inside the cabin every morning looking like he hadn't slept at all.

On the third day after his injury, Benjin ripped off the bandage. Gwen scolded him for it, but after conceding she couldn't change his mind, she made a compress to soothe the bruises darkening his entire side. It stank like carrion, and she took some delight in seeing him periodically gag when a gush of wind would blow the stench up his nose.

On the fourth day, she returned to gathering Sister Brunhilda's specimens. Benjin fashioned a walking stick out of a dead tree limb and insisted on accompanying her. He walked well with the stick balancing him, and Gwen surmised his injury had not been a broken rib. Still, his rib cage remained tender and his movements slow. At noon, they stopped near the edge of a stand of trees and nibbled on blueberries, bread, and cheese.

Benjin stared into the distance, and when Gwen couldn't take his moody silence any longer, she blurted out her thoughts.

"Do you believe in destiny?"

He shrugged. "I don't know. Why do you ask?"

"Mother Seema, the leader of the Cathuran order, told me I would meet my destiny in the Southland."

"And have you?"

"I think so," she replied. Stopping to reconsider her words, she wanted to be more honest. "No. I'm sure I have."

"I thought I knew what my destiny was when I met Elsa Mangst, but that didn't turn out to be the case, now did it? How can you or anyone else, for that matter, know for sure?"

Gwen set her jaw at the mention of the girl's name. "Elsa wasn't your destiny, Benjin. She was Wendel's destiny."

"How do you know that beyond all doubt? How can we ever know our futures, if there is such a thing?" His voice carried agitation.

"I feel it in my heart and in my spirit." She stopped short of telling him she'd fallen in love with him and wanted to spend her days making him happy and chasing after a brood of little Benjins.

He shrugged. "I don't know. I love Elsa. I will always love Elsa. Does that make her my destiny? Maybe in some twisted way, I suppose."

Gwen's heart ached to hear him say he loved someone else: her. "You're a fool, Benjin Hawk." She stood, annoyed with him. "And maybe you're looking in the wrong place for your destiny."

Before she took a step, she saw it not more than a foot from where they'd been sitting--mother's root, a plant so rare she hadn't seen any since Brother Jacques showed it to her in the garden of the Varic monastery. She reached into the basket to retrieve her gloves and caught movement out of the corner of her eye as Benjin stretched out his hand toward the plant.

"No!" she yelled, slapping his hand away. "It's dangerous. Even the slightest contact can kill."

"Surely not. I can smell how sweet it is from here," he said, rubbing the back of his swatted hand.

"Yes, well, that's the danger of mother's root. Its sweetness, both in scent and taste, masks any hint of its lethal nature when too much is taken." Gwen put on the gloves and opened a pouch in readiness for the plant. "It must be isolated. The essence is easily transferred." After digging up the plant, which she intended to cultivate and was certain would impress Sister Brunhilda, she placed it in the pouch and put that pouch inside another one before she removed the gloves, remembering to turn them inside out so any traces of the plant's oils remaining on them wouldn't come into accidental contact with anything else.

"Tell me about it. You called it mother's root. What an odd name for something that could be lethal."

"Maybe later," she snapped at him. I need to collect the last of the herbs for Sister Brunhilda." Her annoyance with him unhidden, Benjin gave her wide berth for the remainder of the gathering excursion, which suited her just fine.

By the time they returned to the cabin, Gwen had worked herself into a frenzy of thoughts. How could he not see that she was his destiny, a woman who would love him, care for him, share everything with him? Why would he love so foolishly a woman who loved another?

Inside, they discovered Brother Vaughn, Brother Mason, and the other monks.

"Sister Gwendolin!" Brother Vaughn said. "I was concerned you'd run afoul of the Zjhon. We saw them on the road a few days ago and managed to hide in a culvert until they'd passed. Brother Mason thought he recognized the two dead chickens hanging from one of the soldier's saddle horns. I feared the worst when we arrived and discovered some of the chickens missing but had a measure of hope when I saw fresh water in the cow's trough and a cooking fire still burning. Thank the heavens you weren't harmed."

"Benjin didn't fare quite as well." She turned and motioned to her companion, who held the walking stick.

"Benjin Hawk," he said, extending a hand to the monk, who shook it with obvious reluctance. "It was a good thing Gwen--Sister Gwendolin-- was here. She patched me up, and I'll be just dandy with a little more time to heal."

Brother Vaughn frowned at Benjin and cast a disapproving glance at Gwen.

"We were out gathering herbs for Sister Brunhilda. Benjin has an interest in plants too."

The monk's expression didn't change.

"I still haven't found the trees Brother Bastian asked me to bring back for him. Benjin said he saw some fruit-bearing trees west of here about two days' walk."

"If *Benjin*," he said, venom in the tone he used to pronounce the name, "will draw us a map, we can get the saplings on our way to Vasterberg."

"Sure thing," said Benjin, his tone as challenging as Brother Vaughn's.

That evening after they'd eaten a meal in tense silence, Benjin went out to the barn. Gwen followed shortly thereafter. She found him scratching out something he'd written on a parchment.

"I'm sorry Brother Vaughn was so unwelcoming."

Benjin shrugged. "No matter. He's just being protective. Can't fault him for that."

"No, I suppose not, but that's no excuse for acting so rudely."

He shrugged again. "I can take it. I'll be heading out of here in a day or two anyway, and it sounds like you will be too."

"That's what I came to talk with you about, Benjin." She bit her lip.

"He wants me to leave now?"

Gwen laughed. "Probably, but he didn't say so, and that's not what I came to talk with you about." She sat down on the straw bed next to him and glanced over at the parchment. She saw a semiaccurate drawing of mother's root and some crude notes about the plant.

"What is it, then?"

"It's about Vasterberg. I was thinking maybe you could come with me. Brother Vaughn needs to get back to Ohmahold before the snows begin. I can't see why he should make such a long journey to the Westland and risk not making it back to the monastery if I have someone else who can travel with me."

Benjin looked at her and spoke with resolve. "Vasterberg is west, and I'm headed east, Gwen. I've been thinking a lot about what you said. It's true Wendel and I fought over Elsa, and it's true she loves him, not me. I don't think I'll ever get over her, but I need to leave her behind . . . here in the Greatland. I need to go home."

Gwen almost screamed when Brother Vaughn's voice drifted in through the barn door.

"Shall I send a messenger to your father to let him know when we'll be arriving?" he asked, his tone a reprimand.

In that second, Gwen looked at Benjin and knew what he'd said was true. He was in love with Elsa, and his love for her would never change. And Gwen was as foolish as he. He would forever love someone who loved another, and so would she. It was their shared destiny.

Gwen took a deep breath. "No. But I'd like to send him a message and let him know I am well and will be returning to Ohmahold to take my final vows."

Brother Vaughn left, and Benjin turned to Gwen. "What's going on? You said you wanted to go to Vasterberg."

"I changed my mind." She glanced at the parchment. "That drawing's all wrong, and you have the details all wrong too." Her words were sharp and uncaring, and she hoped they hurt his feelings.

"I can't remember what you said about it." He held out the parchment and the quill to her. "I'd appreciate it if you could help me get it right."

"Oh, for heaven's sake," she said, taking the parchment and quill. She scratched out what he'd drawn and quickly drew another image, albeit sloppier than her usual drawings. Then she wrote down the plant's properties, made notes about handling the plant to prevent accidental overdose, and listed the preparation instructions in the same order the monk in Sutherhold had given her. While she wrote, she could feel Benjin's gaze on the parchment. She cast a sideways glance at him and saw the keen interest in his expression, which stung all the more. If only he'd looked at her that way.

Angry, hurt, and resentful, she shoved the parchment to the side and stood up. "I'm sure we'll leave by dawn. Safe travels, Benjin Hawk."

"But--"

Gwen didn't give him a chance to finish. He could tell it to Elsa Mangst and the stupid parchment.

Chapter 26

Never pick a fight you can't win.
--Arbuckle Kyte, Lord of Ravenhold

* * *

Aside from the time spent collecting fallen fruit and digging up the saplings she'd promised to bring back for Brother Bastian, the return trip to Ohmahold was a blur. Brother Vaughn seemed to sense Gwendolin's need for isolation because he kept the sailors away from her while they were aboard the ship that took them around the southern tip of the Greatland and up the Endland coastline to the Northern Wastes. He brought hot food to the small cabin they shared and respected her unspoken request for privacy, remaining outside the cabin except for when they slept. Gwen's thoughts ran at full speed, and the visions she'd had played over and again in her dreams, and she'd awaken covered in perspiration and breathless. She tried to still her mind by meditating, but she couldn't focus on quieting the voices in her head--hers, Benjin's, Wendel's, and Elsa's. Cursed Elsa. The beautiful woman who had no appreciation for the heart she'd captured, the heart of the only man Gwen could ever love.

She tolerated the mule ride from the coastal port to Ohmahold, but once she saw the eastern mountain range, the end of which they'd skirt to access the great crevice protecting the entrance to Ohmahold, she longed to reach the serenity of the Inner Sanctuary. Impatience stamped every step the mules took, and by the time they arrived at the entrance to the Outer Sanctuary, emotional exhaustion had left her spent.

Sister Brunhilda was among the monks who greeted them, and Gwen handed her the baskets and bags of herbs and roots she'd collected. The monk wasted no time in peeking into the containers.

"What fine specimens, Sister Gwendolin! You've exceeded all expectations."

"Be careful with the double-bagged one, Sister Brunhilda. Wear gloves when you handle it. It's mother's root."

The old monk gasped and clapped her hands in delight. "I've read about it, but I never in my wildest dreams hoped to have a sample."

"It's more than a sample. I collected the entire plant." Sister Brunhilda's eyes sparkled with excitement, and it warmed Gwen's heart to see the old woman express such joy. "I'll transcribe my notes about it for you. But first, I need rest. Have you anything to help me sleep . . . without dreaming?"

Sister Brunhilda nodded. "You do realize you'll be sleeping in the Outer Sanctuary until you've undergone purification again, right?"

"No. I hadn't realized that."

"Not to worry. I'll have the guard lead you to one of the guest chambers. If you need any of your belongings, just let him know, and I'll arrange to have them collected and brought to you." Then the woman did something Gwen hadn't expected. She wrapped her arms around her and hugged her as if she'd missed her. "I'll send over some of my special tea. You'll sleep as peacefully as the dead."

Gwen thought the analogy should disturb her and felt odd that it didn't.

"Welcome home, Sister Gwendolin."

A guard waited patiently nearby while she arranged to have Brother Bastian's saplings and fruit specimens delivered to him. Then the guard led her to a sleeping chamber. Soon thereafter, the tea arrived, and Gwen drank it quickly while it was still warm. Lying on the bed, she remembered Sister Brunhilda's welcoming hug and her final words before they parted. Home, she thought. Yes. This was home, the home she'd chosen.

As the old monk had promised, Gwen slept the sleep of the dead. She awoke without any memory of dreaming and felt refreshed. She'd have to ask which sedative Sister Brunhilda had used.

Once she'd washed up and put on another blue robe, which someone had placed in the washroom while she slept, the door to the hallway opened. Mother Seema peered around the edge of the door and smiled. "I hope you rested well, Sister Gwendolin."

"I did, thank you."

Mother Seema slipped into the room and closed the door. "Brother Vaughn tells me you had quite the fright while he was in Drascha Stone."

"It was a little scary, yes, but more for the outpost's visitor than for myself." She felt a pang of guilt because she knew she'd omitted Benjin's name to save herself the pain of saying it aloud.

"The Zjhon know the Cathuran remain neutral in government affairs. That is likely the main reason they don't harass us more than they do."

"Is neutrality the wisest course with the Zjhon? They strike me as dangerous and increasingly intolerant."

Mother Seema's expression showed approval, and Gwen appreciated the support for her questions and opinions.

"Indeed. They are both. Neutrality is not the equivalent of ignorance, however, and we have maintained the position that knowledge is power when it comes to the Zjhon. Beyond that, we protect ourselves by not meddling in their affairs and staying within the hold."

She thought of Benjin. "But how will you protect those who are not Cathuran?"

The monk smiled. "That is a dilemma yet to be resolved, Sister Gwendolin, a question for another day. Tomorrow you begin the purification ritual that will end a month from now with your final vows and acceptance into the Cathuran order--if you're still of a mind to join us, that is."

"More than ever," Gwen replied with utter confidence in the truth of her words.

Mother Seema smiled widely. "I couldn't be happier for you and for us. I must leave to finalize the preparations. I'll see you when you have completed the ritual, dear sister." With that, she turned and left the room, her robes flowing behind her like a bride's train.

Gwen chose to spend the day and night alone. In her chamber, she penned a letter to her father, carefully thinking through each word and phrase to reassure him of her safety, comfort, and happiness. She also asked him to tell Gilly, Thomlin, and Mignon how she fared and to congratulate the couple on her behalf. She asked the guard who stood outside her door to tell Sister Brunhilda she'd like to have Mignon's shawl from her tiny apartment in the Inner Sanctuary. By midday, he delivered it, and in the early afternoon, she wrapped the shawl around her and took a stroll through the narrow, winding streets of the city. She wondered at the intricate carvings and statues of animals and the natural world, and by dusk, she'd had her fill of exploring. She'd have the rest of her life to get to know every nook and cranny of Ohmahold. For now, she settled on the peaceful feeling it provided, despite the hubbub of daily comings and goings, purchasing and selling, idle chatter and intense debates not unlike those she'd witnessed in Sutherhold. She returned to her sleeping chamber, and a guard brought her evening meal, along with more of the tea Sister Brunhilda brewed. Gwen drank it with gratitude.

At dawn, someone rapped on her door, and she opened it to find a hooded monk whose head tilted downward at such an angle she couldn't see a face. She followed the robed figure through corridors she thought she'd seen previously but couldn't pinpoint her exact location or even vaguely identify the route they'd taken. Being completely lost in the maze of corridors and stairwells didn't disturb her, though. Gwen knew she would end up in the purification chambers, and eventually, that was precisely where the monk led and left her.

For what she knew subconsciously to be a month, but which seemed to her conscious mind no more than a few days, Gwen once again underwent the varied rituals of purification--this time each segment more intense than she remembered, each period of rest producing a deeper sleep, her thirst more strongly quenched each time the monks brought her water. Or maybe this time, she simply immersed herself more fully in the rituals? She had considered that a possibility as well, but in the end, knowing the reason didn't matter, and she let the thought go. She did the same with invading thoughts of Benjin and of life outside of the monastery. When she did focus, she centered her thoughts only on the beauty and serenity of the natural world, of plants and animals and the arcane mysteries of seasonal changes, of earth, of sea, and of sky. She allowed her body to remember its place as the tiniest of specks in a vast universe. Yes. That was it. Her body remembered its place.

And when the rituals ended, Gwen dressed in the dark tan robe left for her. She sat alone in the final purification room, soaking in the feeling of a freed spirit and mind.

Mother Seema entered the room and greeted Gwen with a cup of fresh, cool water. "I am so very proud of you, child. You've completed the purification with grace and a humble spirit. Your caretakers have reported your progress to me. Indeed, they claimed your transformation so fierce as to show a visible difference daily. I would argue that point," she said, leaning over and lowering her voice to a whisper, "I would call your glow not fierce but exquisite."

Gwen smiled. "Brother Vaughn was right about you."

"Oh? He tattled that I don't always let others know when I disagree?"

Gwen laughed. "No. He said I would come to love you and cherish your wisdom. He was right."

Mother Seema wrapped her arms around Gwen. "I can only hope you know how much I love and cherish you too, my dear sister. You mean more to me and to this order than you yet know." Stepping back and releasing her, the monk took her by the hand. "Come. It is time for you to stand before the Cathurans and exchange pledges."

The exchange of vows surprised Gwen. She'd assumed only she would agree to the conditions and requirements of the order. But Mother Seema had instructed her to repeat what each monk said and did, and when she heard the first monk--Brother Vaughn, as it happened--speak the Cathuran oath, she understood why the order thrived. Each monk pledged three things to her: to assist her in gaining the knowledge she thirsted after and needed, to feed her spirit and mind with truth and the sharing of their own knowledge and expertise, and to protect and defend her life and spirit with their very own if need be. Each monk embraced her and whispered the Cathuran promise in her ear, "By all that is sacred and true, I swear it to you, Sister." And after each did so, Gwen pledged the same three things, embraced her new Brother or Sister, and whispered the promise in return. The ceremony took a full day, and Gwen stood throughout it. When Mother Seema gave the formal induction speech and the ceremony officially ended, Gwen welcomed the celebration feast with heaps of fresh-baked cakes and jugs of summerberry wine, but most of all, she welcomed a chair on which to sit.

That night she lay in the Inner Sanctuary apartment with the view of the Tree of Plenty within sight from her bed. While contemplating the bounty of the tree and the bounty in her life, she drifted into a peaceful, wine-aided sleep.

She awoke to mournful news: Sister Brunhilda had died during the night.

The potting shed duties fell to Gwen by default, as nobody else had ever worked with Sister Brunhilda. After paying her respects to the deceased monk, who looked angelic as she lay on the pyre awaiting cremation, Gwen left the mourning service and went to the potting shed to assess and prioritize tasks requiring her attention. She entered and closed the door, as she always had, and noticed the window panes in the door didn't rattle. Gwen melted into tears, and although she'd known the monk for only a short time, her passing brought a deep, unexpected sorrow.

Mother Seema's soothing voice interrupted her sobs. "Why are you crying, Sister Gwendolin?"

"I'm sad she's no longer with us. She was like a grandmother to me. She spent her life caring for others, and I suppose I feel sad because nobody seemed to care for her in return."

"Whatever do you mean?" asked Mother Seema, concern contorting her usually calm expression.

Gwen pointed to the panes in the door. "That glass was almost falling out. Nobody bothered to repair it for her. Before I went to the Southland, I asked Sister Lucinda to arrange for someone to do it while I was away."

Mother Seema chuckled.

"How can you be so cruel to laugh at neglect? She deserved more than that."

"I'm sorry, Sister. Let me explain. Sister Brunhilda was well aware of the loose panes. Before you came to Ohmahold, when Brother Martyn came around to make repairs during his yearly rounds, she told him to leave the panes alone because she wanted to be able to hear when someone entered the shed. She was hard of hearing, you see."

Gwen's hands flew to her mouth, covering it. "I didn't know. I meant only to--"

Mother Seema stepped forward and wrapped her arms around Gwen, who buried her face in the woman's shoulder and wept without restraint. When her tears slowed, Mother Seema released her and turned to the potting bench. "That's the special plant you brought her, isn't it?"

Gwen recognized it as the mother's root she'd given Sister Brunhilda. "Yes."

"When you were undergoing purification, she spoke about it during our evening meal one night. It thrilled her to have it, and it meant so very much to her that you'd thought to bring it to her. Did she ever tell you she believed you have a special gift for recognizing the energy in plants?"

"No," Gwen replied, shaking her head.

"Well, she did. She said someday you might master sensing disturbances in plant life from a great distance."

"Really?" Gwen couldn't imagine what benefit such an ability might have. What could be gained from sensing a blade of grass stepped on or a pussy willow bent by the wind?

Mother Seema chuckled and nodded. "*If,* and she stressed this part," the monk said, hesitating before continuing, as if to pile her own emphasis atop Sister Brunhilda's, "'*if* you could master clearing away questions from your overly busy mind.' Yes. I do believe those were her exact words."

Gwen was taken aback.

The monk smiled as if amused by Gwen's expression. "I should add she believed you would be successful in doing so."

Tears welled in Gwen's eyes, and she choked out the words, "I promise I'll try my best to justify her faith in me, Mother."

"I know you will," said Mother Seema, "And you will have everything you need, my dear, dear Gwendolin. I promise you."

Chapter 27
The greatest barriers are within.
--Mother Seema, Cathuran monk

* * *

Gwen worked daily to hold true to her promise and vows. Seeking knowledge from her peers, she pored over tomes and scrolls in the monastery's vast collections and looked for ways to help others, whether in the city or the monastery. During the winter, she read and meditated and met with other monks, questioning them about ancient beliefs. She explored chambers filled with relics and studied philosophy, spiritual practices, and history. From spring until the first snow of winter, she took short trips out of Ohmahold to survey the plants on the mountains surrounding the valley and brought back specimens to cultivate in a greenhouse Mother Seema had ordered Brother Martyn to build for her. Though she never admitted it and showed nothing but gratitude for having such a perfect space to grow herbs and other medicinal plants, Gwen never stopped preferring to work in Sister Brunhilda's rickety old potting shed, and she did as much of her work there as she could.

Such was the routine Gwen established for her life among the Cathurans until well into mid life. She was happy and fulfilled, surrounded by Brothers and Sisters she loved. Although she corresponded regularly with her father until she received news that he, like her grandmother, had died peacefully in his sleep, she still carried folded in her pocket all these many years later his first letter to her. It had become a reminder that her life as a Cathuran was a life of choice. Mostly the life she'd chosen--a life of studying, service to others, hard physical labor, and long hours--kept her dreams and visions at bay, but occasionally one would still haunt her. When the one about Rolf with the bloody arrow returned and persisted, Gwen turned to Mother Seema for advice.

"I don't know how to interpret the dream, Mother. I'd like to know what it means, if anything. This time, it feels more . . . urgent."

"There is a way you might gain clarity: the viewing ceremony."

Gwen had heard of it, but one hadn't been conducted in all the years since she'd entered the monastery. "That's the ceremony in which the monks chant to raise power while the seeker expands consciousness through a portal?"

"Yes. The ceremony funnels the combined energy of the monks who participate from behind walls into the viewing chamber, and the viewer's consciousness rides the vibrations out into the world. Some have found the answers to their questions in that manner. If you'd like, I can arrange a viewing ceremony for you."

"I'd like to try," said Gwen.

"Then so shall you."

Gwen underwent a brief purification before the viewing ceremony and was led into a small chamber with a magnificent throne-like chair of umber sitting in the middle of the room. The walls on either side had holes leading into other rooms, and a porthole-shaped window devoid of glass pierced the outer wall of the chamber, which looked out over the western mountains. Gwen took a seat in the chair, and the monk who had accompanied her to the room exited. As soon as he closed the door, the sound of chanting filtered into the room from the holes on either side wall. Gwen closed her eyes and meditated. After a few minutes, she could feel the vibrations. She tried to grasp the energy and send it out through the porthole, but it kept slipping out of her mind. After repeatedly trying, she gave up, and the chanting waned into silence.

"I couldn't do it," she told Mother Seema afterward when the order's leader entered the chamber, followed by a monk who handed each of the women a mug of water.

"There's no shame in that, Sister Gwendolin. Few can, and truthfully, most give up much sooner than you did." Her voice was raspy, and she took a drink of water.

"An hour of trying isn't all that much."

"An hour?" The monk laughed. "You were there for two days."

"What? It seemed no time at all."

Mother Seema nodded. "Time is relative and, though we cannot prove it, it would seem the energy of our consciousness has no respect for time at all. But remember, nothing forbids you from trying again, though I would counsel you not to try too often."

"Why not? Is it dangerous?"

Mother Seema chuckled. "I doubt it's dangerous if you're unable to achieve the result you seek. It is, however, terribly wearing on the vocal cords of the monks who are chanting."

Gwen gasped. "How thoughtless of me!"

"We aid each other in any way we can, Sister. We are happy to do so if you need us."

"You were chanting too?"

Mother Seema nodded. "Indeed. I've not the stamina I once had, though. But you must try again and again. The chanters need the practice from time to time." She winked mischievously, and Gwen laughed.

The leader's words turned out to be an understatement. Within a year, she became frail and made public appearances with waning frequency. One winter evening, Gwen was called to Mother Seema's apartments. The old woman, whose hair had grown long and as white as the ice caps on the highest peak, lay in her bed, around which monks stood with bowed, hooded heads chanting in barely more than a whisper yet in a sound so full it seemed to envelop the entirety of the space.

"Mother," whispered Gwen as she knelt beside the bed and kissed the old woman's forehead. "How may I serve you?"

"You must not give up your attempts in the viewing chamber," she replied in a weak, airy whisper. "And you must find an apprentice to help you in the greenhouse."

"I am happy to do the work, Mother. I don't wish to burden another."

"You won't be doing the work anymore, dear, dear Gwendolin."

Gwen's heart thudded in her chest. "Have I done something wrong?"

"No," Mother Seema whispered. "You've done much right, but I cannot ask you to work at two specialties. I leave this world tonight, and I wish you to take my place."

"Surely there are others more wise and better suited."

"Oh, yes, there are," said the monk, who then chuckled and gave her mischievous wink again. "But it is your shoulders upon which I place the fate of Ohmahold. The fate of the Greatland rests with you, Gwendolin, and only by love can you save her."

The words, first spoken by the gypsy in Vasterberg, echoed as if Mother Seema had screamed them, though Gwen knew she had only the strength to have whispered. She opened her mouth to speak, but Mother Seema placed a finger first on her own lips then on Gwen's before whispering, "You will have everything you need, my dear, dear Gwendolin. I promise you." Then the monk lowered her hand to her chest, closed her eyes, and sighed her last breath with a tender, peaceful smile.

The sobbing that rushed out of her came without warning, and Gwen lay with her head on the dead woman's chest until Brother Vaughn came and lifted her up. He scooped her into his arms and carried her to her apartment, where he gently lowered her onto her bed and tucked the covers around her before extinguishing the lantern and leaving. She watched the shadows of the Tree of Plenty quiver through her tears in the cloud-obscured moonlight, and she fell asleep weeping.

Mother Seema's mourning began the next day, and none of the monks mourned more fiercely than did Gwen. She had lost her mother not once but for a second time, and her heart ached pitifully.

When the mourning ended and Mother Seema's ashes were buried beneath the giant tree in the center of the Inner Sanctuary courtyard, the monks convened for an Ascension council. There was much bickering and arguing about Mother Seema's choice for a successor, and Gwen found no energy to participate in it. She sat silently and grief stricken while some of her peers pointed out her failings and insisted monks much older and wiser would make better leaders than she. It was Brother Vaughn who ended the conflict.

"Whether we see the wisdom of Mother Seema's choice matters not. Is there one among you who did not trust her?"

No one responded.

"Then trust her now, and follow her final orders, for that is the way of the Cathuran. If any doubts the choice, then I say he or she has an obligation to aid Sister Gwendolin in becoming as wise as our dear, departed Mother. Rejoice in your service to the order, and honor the pledges we've given to each other."

Though some monks grumbled under their breaths, none spoke out.

"Good. Then let the Ascension begin tomorrow," he said.

When all but Gwen and Brother Vaughan had left the meeting room, Gwen gave him a hug. "I know you mean well. I'm just not sure I'm up to this, Brother."

For the first time since she'd met him in Sutherhold, she saw his temper flare. His face reddened and he set his jaw so hard Gwen could hear him grinding his teeth. "Then get up to it, Sister. She chose you for a reason. Figure it out." He turned and left her standing alone in the meeting room.

Those words became for Gwendolin a driving force. Following the ten-day Ascension ceremony, she set to running the order with fervor. She had gained a valuable insight from Mother Seema and from her own time at the monastery: the best way to get anything done was to seek and rely on the superior expertise of her peers. All the order needed was general guidance and someone to settle disputes, but even then, Gwen found most disagreements about policy could be converted into agreement once everyone had shared their unique perspectives on a matter.

She found she did have some ideas about the direction the order should take when it came to the problems of the Greatland, and particularly as they related to the Zjhon. Brother Vaughn proved instrumental in convincing the others that Ohmahold needed fortification and that the Cathuran needed a more reliable means of obtaining information about what was going on in the world outside the hold. He relayed to them the experience he'd had in Sutherhold, and Gwen told them about the way the Zjhon had tricked the people of Vasterberg into sending their sons to Sutherhold, as well as the way they'd barged into the little outpost in the Southland. There had, in addition, been word delivered sporadically but consistent in its message that the Zjhon had taken over areas with resources as needed and had, as Gwen's father had written, conscripted the population when it suited them. No news they'd received had given them any reason to believe the Zjhon had become less of a threat, and the news of late had been less frequent and informative.

Under Gwen's direction, the monks of Ohmahold maintained neutrality in government affairs, but they secretly fortified and prepared an emergency shelter deep below the monastery. They built an army from among the loyal citizens of the city outside the monastery walls and contributed to the commerce and education of the families living in the city. They continued to gain knowledge, and Gwen, much more lenient than previous leaders, encouraged them to travel to collect more knowledge while retaining the mysteries of the Cathurans and the closeness of the order. She encouraged them to share what they learned with each other in an effort to more thoroughly understand the world around them. Ohmahold prospered. Brother Vaughn established a communications network using birds trained to fly from one monastery or outpost to another with messages and news.

Throughout the years that followed, Gwen tried time and again to ride the vibrations in the viewing ceremony, but she never managed to achieve more than brief glimpses of men in Zjhon uniforms marching eastward. That information added nothing to her knowledge about the visions, and it only reinforced what Brother Vaughn's communication network had already confirmed: the Zjhon were depleting the resources of the Greatland, and it would be only a matter of time until they marched on Ohmahold.

Mother Gwendolin intended to be ready for that day.

Chapter 28
The wicked live within us alongside the righteous.
--Brother Ramirez, Cathuran monk

* * *

Mother Gwendolin oversaw Ohmahold with concern as the comets, which the ancient tomes predicted would appear in the night skies, indeed took their places high above. Only a year before, Brother Vaughn's communication network had brought news that the Zjhon had sailed with the largest armada ever assembled. With each passing day, Gwen could feel the land on the verge of a dangerous transition.

The first snow had fallen when Gustad and Milo, two monks who had requested permission to journey in search of items needed for an experiment, returned to Ohmahold with unexpected visitors in tow.

Captain Longarm had brought word to Gwen that one of the visitors, a man named Benjin Hawk, had requested an audience with her.

Gwen caught her breath when she heard the name.

"He didn't know you're the leader of the order. I'm not sure we can even trust this fellow. You should've seen the amount of weapons he and the others were carrying. I can send him away."

"No. Please bring him to me first thing tomorrow. Escort him to one of the side chambers in the outer temple. I'll meet him there."

"As you wish, Mother."

After Captain Longarm left her apartments, Gwen felt short of breath. Why would he want to see her now after so many years? She had left thoughts of him behind. The pain she'd once felt had faded when she took her vows. What could be so important that fate would so cruelly bring him back into her life? She had worked herself into a frenzy of questions by the time Brother Vaughn arrived at her apartments.

He wasted no time in getting to the point. "I heard Benjin is in the city and wants to see you."

"It's true. But I can't imagine what he wants."

"Mother . . ." His face flushed with agony.

"What is it, Brother Vaughn?"

"Forgive me for what I'm about to say, but please hear me out. I know how you once felt about Benjin. I saw it when you were in the barn with him that night. This must be very painful for you, I'm sure. But you are Cathuran, and you must remember and honor that above all else. I'm here, Gwendolin. I'm here to support you. I and the others, we cherish you. You've supported and guided us these many years, but please, just this once, let us do the same for you. Let me silence the questions in your busy mind. For your own good. For the good of Ohmahold. For the good of the Greatland."

She hadn't heard her name spoken without "Sister" or "Mother" before it for so many years she'd forgotten what it sounded like. Her eyes filled with tears, and she held out her arms to the monk. Brother Vaughn stepped forward and gave her a comforting hug, and when he released her, she thanked him for his kindness and honesty.

"The past is in the past, and if Benjin Hawk was ever my destiny, he was but a driving force to confirm my path among the Cathuran. I'll always love Benjin, but not in the same way I once did."

"And you'll stop questioning yourself?"

She laughed. "Yes. I'll clear away the questions in my busy mind." She made a face and muttered, "Why does everyone know that?"

Brother Vaughn chuckled then left her alone in her apartments.

What little sleep she got that night was restful only because she'd meditated and reassured herself everything happened for a reason. If Benjin had come all the way from the Godfist to see her, it must be for something important, something only she could help him with.

In the morning, she bathed, dressed, and had her breakfast alone. Shortly after she'd finished eating, her guard rapped on the door and called out, "Mother Gwendolin. Your guests have arrived."

She took a deep breath and refocused her energy on moving with grace. She'd always enjoyed the feeling of gliding, as the Cathurans called the resulting effect, and she'd become more than adept. That was the posture she struck when she entered the temple and first laid eyes on the man who had stolen her youthful heart.

After a brief incident in which the girl with Benjin slipped and bumped her head, Gwen settled everyone into a sitting room. Benjin introduced what seemed a slew of young men, and when he got to the girl, his introduction was unnecessary, though he gave it anyway. Gwen recognized Catrin Volker as the daughter of Wendel and Elsa because the girl looked just like the young woman she had seen in the vision of Benjin and Wendel fighting. In short order, it became clear they needed more privacy to discuss the matter that had brought them all to Ohmahold, so Gwen led them to a room deeper in the temple.

"I apologize, Mother, but our tale must be kept in confidence. I fear anyone who learns of it will be in danger. I'm hesitant to place such a burden on you, and I'm prepared to tell you pleasant lies if you decide that is best. I would ask your preference," Benjin said.

She smiled, nodding in acknowledgment of his warning. "First, I must ask you to address me as Gwendolin while we're in a private setting. It will lighten my heart to enjoy your company as equals. Second, I wish to hear your tale, no matter how dangerous the information may be. I sense this is no minor matter, and I'll do what I can to assist you."

Benjin then told her about Catrin, referring to her as the Herald of Istra, and he explained they'd come hoping Catrin might learn more about the power she wielded. He added that they knew she was in danger because the Zjhon would like nothing more than to capture and destroy her, as they'd already attempted to do.

Gwen found the tale bewildering, but she didn't doubt its truth. So she stuck to her promise to help them and sent Benjin and the others, all except Catrin, back to the inn in the city so she might learn more about Catrin's power and help the girl learn whatever she needed to know.

Once alone, she questioned the girl about the specifics of events in which Catrin had wielded the power, and she discovered, much to her dismay and Catrin's that the girl had accidentally destroyed an ancient relic of power known as Imeteri's Fish. That discovery had sent the poor child into fitful crying, and she'd fallen asleep in Gwen's arms.

When the girl was deep in sleep, Gwen got up and asked the guard outside the door to send word to Benjin that Catrin would be staying the night. "There's no need to worry him, so please tell him she's just very tired after all my questions. I'll send word to him again once I know what course we'll take."

Gwen lay down again on a cushion not far from Catrin, thoughts swirling in her head as she watched the girl sleep. Catrin Volker, the Herald of Istra, had come to Ohmahold seeking refuge. Gwendolin hadn't been able to stop the thought from forming when she'd first learned who and what Catrin was. How ironic that the child of Elsa Mangst, the beautiful girl who'd stolen Benjin Hawk's heart and broken Gwen's, had grown up to need Gwendolin's guidance and protection. But Gwen had let the thought go, had sent its negativity back into the darkness of a past she'd let go of when she had taken her vows. She had forgiven Benjin and Wendel for falling in love with Elsa, and she had forgiven Elsa for being so lovely and lovable. She'd even forgiven herself for the petty jealousy and bitterness that had sent her to Ohmahold to live a life so very different from the one she'd imagined as the wife of Benjin, the mother of a brood of children who would have looked like him.

And now Catrin, so very like her mother in so many ways, had pierced Gwen's heart as deeply as Elsa had. The child, clearly loved deeply by Benjin, had suffered because she didn't understand the power she came by so naturally, and she had inadvertently destroyed something precious and sacred. That the girl felt deeply sorrowful and regretted having done so spoke to the courage and honor she held inside. Gwen felt determined to soften the blow the girl had delivered because of her ignorance. She'd find a way to help her overcome it.

When morning came, Gwen slipped from the room before the girl woke up and arranged to have breakfast delivered to her. Then she went in search of Brother Vaughn.

"Good morning, Mother," he said when he saw her.

"Good morning, Brother Vaughn. I'm sure to be busy with my guest. It's a very long story but one I know you'll want to hear, and I promise to share it, but I need to ask you to retrieve something from the archives for me."

"Of course, Mother."

"There's a little box, a wooden one with filigree corners and a serpent-shaped clasp. It's in the collection of artifacts Brother Ramirez left us, may his spirit feed the earth. Do you know it?"

Brother Vaughn rubbed his chin. "Hmm. I think so. I'm sure I can find it."

"It contains two small noonstones. I'd like to give them to Catrin, the girl who is with Benjin. If you could find them for me, I'd appreciate it."

"Yes, Mother. I'm happy to do it." He gave her a questioning look.

"I'm fine, Brother Vaughn. I promise." She kissed his cheek and returned to the chamber where she'd left Catrin.

Gwen found Catrin awake and disturbed because Benjin had expected her to return and she'd fallen asleep, so Gwen let her know she'd sent word about Catrin's staying for the night and had invited Benjin and her friends to join them for dinner that evening. With the girl more at ease, the two walked in the gardens and chatted. She'd thought about Catrin's situation, and she'd concluded the girl needed more clarity before the monks could help her most effectively, so she suggested Catrin undergo the month-long purification ritual. To her delight, Catrin agreed, and after a long evening meal, during which Gwen listened to Benjin and his companions and made mental notes about details of their journey to later parse with the information she and the other monks had about the Zjhon, she helped the girl settle in for the night then excused herself.

Realizing the situation Catrin faced was dire, Gwen called together her most experienced and diversely knowledgeable monks. After hearing her explanation, they agreed Catrin's case was special, and it called for extreme measures. All of them would undergo the purification ritual along with the girl so they, too, would have clarity when the time came to answer her questions and assist her in moving forward in whatever direction her quest might go.

Gwen had forgotten how the ritual challenged perceptions, and several times during the experience, she found herself pondering uncertainties she'd long thought set aside, such as what had become of Brother Jacques and the other Varic monks and whether any of the Vasterberg boys in Sutherhold had made it home. By the end of the month's activities, however, she had once again gained control of her thoughts and had attained a state of fresh clarity. The other monks expressed the same effect when they convened under the great tree in the courtyard of the Inner Sanctuary, where they waited until Catrin's escort brought her to them.

Their conversation was enlightening. Gwen discovered Catrin had a bright mind full of curiosity and a genuine desire not just to gain knowledge, but also to apply it in dispelling dangerous and deadly misinformation. After hearing more of her story, Gwen and the others concluded the Zjhon had targeted Catrin because their narrow-mindedness prevented them from seeing the truth about her: she, like many others under the influence of the Istran comet cycle, experienced an elevated affinity for energy. The girl seemed relieved to separate fact from fairy tales, and her willingness to consider truths given in answer to her questions gave Gwen hope the girl might survive an almost guaranteed attack by the Zjhon.

Hoping to give Catrin some respite from the depressing and overwhelming options the monks' answers opened up for her, Gwen proposed a change in subject, a focus on the potential of an inherited ability to control energy. "Perhaps this would be a good time for you to tell us a bit more of your story. It may answer some of our questions and raise new ones in your mind. I know it may be painful, but would you tell us of your mother and the circumstances of her death?" Apprehension tugged at Gwen when she asked for the details of something so painful for Catrin. Opening old wounds was not her intent.

As Catrin described the meal her mother had eaten and the symptoms she suffered afterward, symptoms leading to her death, Gwendolin felt ill. She forced herself to sit with her hand covering her mouth while mentally checking off each of the characteristics of the only substance she knew that could have caused such a death and still remained undetected: mother's root. She recoiled in horror as she remembered the night in the barn in the Southland and pictured the transcribed notes she'd made for Benjin.

"Oh, Catrin," she sobbed, pounding the soil with her fists. "I'm sorry. I'm so very sorry. I could have saved them; I should have. How could I have been so selfish and blind?"

The girl's face bore total confusion, but she went to Gwen and tried to console her.

After a long moment and some water brought by a young monk, Gwen managed to pull herself together. With deep shame, she explained what had happened on the night she and Benjin had sat in the barn, how she had fallen in love with him but he had been so in love with Catrin's mother that he hadn't even seen it. She'd felt jealous and hurt by his indifference toward her, and she'd angrily scribbled down only the most basic details about mother's root when he'd asked for her help. "I remember omitting the information on the effects of an overdose simply because I didn't feel like doing it."

Chapter 29

Perception is a poor measure of reality.
--Mignon, hedge witch

* * *

She deserved whatever hatred and anger Catrin might express for the woman who had robbed her of a mother. Gwen prepared herself for it. When the girl merely folded into Gwen's arms, however, it shook her to her core, and she openly wept along with Catrin.

When they'd cried all the tears they could, she said, "I will send Benjin an invitation to meet with us this evening. There is nothing we can do about it now, but he deserves to know the truth."

Gwen had thought the day's news could not be worse, but she was wrong when a monk interrupted them to deliver an urgent message that had arrived via one of Brother Vaughn's pigeons. She read it then said to Brother Vaughn, "I think this will be of most interest to you. It would appear a landslide in southern Faulk has uncovered the skeletal remains of a giant winged beast. The message indicates the beast would have been larger than a warship--incredible." She handed him the note and continued to the group, "There is also word of Zjhon troop movements. Several large detachments are converging near the northern tip of the Inland Sea in Lankland. I suspect they will be bound for Ohmahold by the spring melt. It would appear the Zjhon have reason to believe Catrin is here." She looked at Catrin with concern and compassion.

The girl became almost apoplectic, and Gwen could see the guilt she felt at drawing the Zjhon toward the peaceful monastery and its inhabitants. Gwen reassured her that she had nothing to feel guilty about and went so far as to tell her about some of the preparations they'd made for just such an event. "Do not be overly concerned. Ohmahold is well defended and well provisioned."

Sensing everyone needed a mental break from all the information they'd passed between them and all they'd learned, Gwen dismissed the monks and took Catrin to meet with Benjin in the Outer Sanctuary. While Benjin filled Catrin in on the antics of their companions, Gwen retrieved the mother's root page from her own plant journal. She returned to the room where they waited for her and took a deep breath before stepping inside. She didn't know where to begin, so she started with an earnest apology.

"Benjin, I have wronged you, and I am very sorry. I'll put this as kindly as I can, but there is no easy way to tell you. When we first met, I fell in love with you, and I was envious of your feelings for Elsa. You pined after her when I was right there for the taking." She stopped a moment when she saw the look of shock on Benjin's face, which slowly turned to one of comprehension and shame.

"How could I have been so blind?" he said softly.

She couldn't bear to let him feel guilty, and she interrupted him. "Do you remember when you asked me to help you transcribe my notes?" she asked, and he nodded mutely. "I was angry and my feelings were hurt, and I did a poor job on the pages I transcribed. I copied what I considered the most important things and left out some of the cursory details. My omission cost you dearly, and again, I'm very sorry. I would change it if I could," she said, and she handed him the page she'd retrieved.

As she watched the gravity of what had happened sink in, Gwen couldn't hold back her tears, though she fought to maintain some composure.

He paced angrily, his hands curled and twitching. Then it seemed all his rage was spent. "You must not blame yourself for this, Mother, nor should I be allowed to blame myself," he said in a voice thick with emotion. "We are not responsible for their deaths. We did not murder them. If circumstances had been different, perhaps I would have been able to save them, perhaps not. We would have saved them if we could, but we could not."

Gwen couldn't maintain her composure any longer, and she rushed to him and wrapped her arms around him, whispering through soft sobs, "I'm so sorry."

"I'm sorry as well, Gwen. I never meant to hurt you. I just didn't realize."

Gwen silenced him by putting a finger to his lips, and she knew instantly it was a touch she would remember for as long as she lived. "You need not explain. You are already forgiven. Now that we better understand the past, let us deal with the present," she said.

That night she allowed herself to weep in solitude for Catrin's loss, for Benjin's, and for her own. Her questions about Elsa had exposed her greatest failure--that her bitterness toward Elsa had led her to be negligent in the passing on of herbal lore Benjin had requested of her. Without the knowledge Gwen had been entrusted to share, Benjin was unable to save the mother of the Herald of Istra, Wendel Volker's wife, Catrin's mother, and the woman Gwen knew Benjin had loved from first glimpse and would love for all his days. She'd caused Benjin to feel inadequate and responsible for Elsa's death. The stab of guilt over Elsa's unnecessary death brought pain, but Benjin's forgiveness pierced her, heart and soul.

She awoke with a renewed conviction to help Catrin figure out how to survive the Zjhon initiative, and it dawned on her there was something that could give Catrin and Catrin alone the insight she needed. She explained that time was short, and the situation called for something more intense than purification when they met after breakfast.

"Please go on," the girl said.

"It's called a viewing ceremony, and I find it helps me focus when I'm unable to resolve a debate or conflict. Would you like to try?"

Catrin agreed to undergo the ceremony, and preparations were made by the monks who would participate. Once the ceremony was under way, however, it became clear that more monks would be needed. Three days into the ceremony, Gwen began to worry about Catrin's well-being. The girl sat in a trance and twitched now and again, as if dodging an object coming at her. By the end of the fifth day, Benjin had begun to insist on seeing Catrin.

"You cannot disturb her, Benjin. It is dangerous to bring someone back once their consciousness has left the body. She must return of her own accord," Gwen had told him.

"Then at least let me go in and be with her."

How could she refuse him? He'd lost Elsa. He feared losing Catrin. And Gwen, for her part, could not bear the thought of being responsible for breaking Benjin's heart again. "Very well, but you must undergo purification. We cannot risk your negative energy influencing her at this time of great vulnerability."

For Catrin's sake, Benjin agreed to undergo a simplified purification ritual, and two days later, when he'd completed the ritual and had been escorted to the viewing chamber, he sat on the floor at Catrin's feet. Gwen turned her attention to the ceremony. She ordered more monks to prepare for chanting, even if it meant pulling cooks and temple guardians from their posts. Then despite protests from her most senior advisers, she relieved one of the younger monks whose voice had gone mute from chanting.

A week later, Catrin awoke but remained in a stupor. Benjin appeared near death himself, and Gwen could hardly speak. But everyone had survived, and the ceremony had been successful. Catrin had discovered the information she sought plus more. She knew what she needed to do.

Though Catrin's mind was so stimulated she wanted to get up and start working on her plan right away, Benjin convinced her to rest a bit and put some sedative in her tea to make certain she did. Wanting to stay beside her, he refused to sleep. Gwen knew arguing with him would do no good, so she acquiesced and, after ordering him some tea, slipped a difficult-to-detect sedative into his mug as well, masking it with chamomile. Then she went to her own apartment and fell onto her bed, grateful for its softness but knowing she'd have been equally grateful if it had been hard and lumpy.

When she awoke, she bathed and dressed and immediately went to check on Benjin and Catrin. She found Benjin still sleeping, but Catrin had awakened and wanted to stretch her legs, so Gwen strolled with her through the corridors of the Inner Sanctuary. As they walked, Catrin abruptly stopped, as if struck by sudden recollection.

"I don't mean to pry, but are you aware of a large hall, within Ohmahold, that is filled with books, swords, and a variety of oddities covered in dust?" she asked.

Gwen thought perhaps the girl had merely dreamed about it because it didn't sound like any room she'd seen. But Catrin insisted. Gwen thought it wise to accommodate her until they reached a four-way intersection, beyond which the rooms had been designated as death passages, areas set with traps by the inhabitants of the monastery so ancient no records existed of them.

"All these corridors are death chambers. We can go no farther this way," she told Catrin, and she gasped when the girl stepped fearlessly forward. No traps sprung. But Gwen couldn't let the girl go into the passages alone, despite the danger. Something tugged at her to stay with the girl, so she took a deep breath and caught up with her.

Hand in hand, they walked around the corner. Gwen's mouth fell open, and she held her palms to her cheeks when she saw the chamber, exactly as Catrin had described it. It brimmed with items Gwen knew were priceless, some perhaps as ancient as the original inhabitants themselves.

Shouting interrupted their silent survey of the room's contents, and the two of them rushed back down the corridor. When they gained the mighty stair, Gwen shouted to those above, "What is it?"

"Men down in the pastures," someone called back. "Enemy in the hold!"

Catrin bolted for the stairs, and Gwen followed. She could see Benjin ahead of them among a throng of armed monks and guards. When they reached the plateau, the group sprawled outward, and Gwen stopped near Benjin to survey the situation. She could see two young horses in the field below and two men lying at their hooves.

The Zjhon were coming. Gwendolin had no doubt of that, but she also didn't doubt that this was her dominion. She had sat in the viewing room so many times she'd lost count. There was no inch of soil in all the hold she had not trod, yet she'd failed to project her mind across the land the way her visitor had so easily done. Gwen closed her eyes and prayed in a whisper, "Please, just this once. Let me feel it. Take me to the threat."

A bright light flashed, and she was tempted to open her eyes, but she exhaled slowly and remained focused on the land--the seed pods of herbs she'd collected, loose rocks she'd avoided when climbing the hillside, the trees under which she'd sat and read the journals of her predecessors. For the first time, she felt the connection she'd tried to tap into for so many years. Gwen set her mind free to scour the landscape surrounding Ohmahold. Then she saw them.

Behind rocks at the edge of the cliff crouched two assassins. She opened her eyes, blinking away the vision, and turned to tell Benjin what she'd seen. He stood frozen, his eyes already widened and filled with fear, his mouth gaping in a silent scream of terror. What horrified him? Had she missed another threat? Her gaze followed the trajectory of his. It stopped on Catrin Volker, the daughter of the woman who had stolen Benjin's heart and broken Gwen's.

Gwen looked toward the cliffs again and saw an assassin had stood up and revealed himself. He was nocking an arrow and drawing back his string arm. She shoved her mind toward the cliff and could feel the snow pressing down on top of the dormant grass beneath the man. Boots. A Zjhon uniform. A man with a scar on his forehead. An arrow painted with red. Rolf!

Gwen's consciousness slammed back into her when Catrin screamed the names of her fallen companions who had already been killed. She saw the girl bolt toward them, too far away for Benjin to stop her. The daughter of Elsa Mangst, whom Benjin loved as much as he had loved Elsa, ran straight into the sight line of the assassin's arrow, an assassin Gwen knew never missed his target. In a split second, she was struck by the pain she thought she'd let go of until Brothers Gustad and Milo had led Benjin and Catrin into Ohmahold. On the whetted tip of an assassin's arrow, Destiny offered her a mirror with which to bounce back onto Benjin and Elsa all the anguish they had caused her.

And Gwendolin knew what she had to do.

Chapter 30

Destiny rules us all--inescapable and immutable, it is often unkind.
--Madame Verona, soothsayer

* * *

Gwen ran at an angle toward Catrin, who stopped just short of the two dead bodies lying in the pasture. The color in the girl's face had drained, and Gwen knew she would faint. Limp, she'd be easy to shove out of the way. Rolf wouldn't anticipate a stationary target suddenly moving. He could not have seen her knees buckling. Gwen had time to make amends with the only man she'd ever loved, to save the girl Benjin loved more than his own life. Just as she reached Catrin, she felt the fabric of her robe parting with a ripping sound, and Gwen didn't need to look down to see the blood staining her smock. Using a technique she'd hoped never to need, she numbed her body, except for the one finger she'd pressed to Benjin's lips. That she let herself feel, and it warmed her very soul.

Daylight dimmed quickly, which surprised her, and the last thing she saw in the fading light was Catrin's shocked expression. She wanted to reach out and hold her, to comfort her and tell her everything would be fine, but her arms wouldn't move. Then everything turned dark.

* * *

In the distance, Gwen saw a pinpoint of light, and it seemed to reenergize her limbs. She stood and walked toward it, and it grew brighter and larger with each step. Just before she reached it, she heard the crunch of boots on snow behind her. She turned around, expecting to see Benjin. Instead, Rolf stood there, his face that of his boyhood.

"I'm sorry, Gwen. I swear I didn't see you."

"But why, Rolf? Why would you try to kill Catrin? She's just a young girl, not the monster the Zjhon have made her out to be."

"I'm not proud of what I done, but I didn't do it out of hatred. The Zjhon have my daughter, Bonita. They threatened to kill her if I failed, and now I suppose that's exactly what they'll do. I messed it all up, Gwen, and I'm sorry. I didn't mean to hurt you. Please forgive me."

Her heart ached for him. She knew what it was like to hurt someone without meaning to. She'd done the same with Benjin and, by extension, Elsa, Wendel, and Catrin. "I forgive you," she whispered.

"Not necessarily." A voice Gwen knew but couldn't name came from the light. She turned to see who was there, and the white robe Mother Seema wore rippled in a breeze. "There's still a chance we can gather enough energy to help Bonita save herself. We'll need an archer and a monk, though, and a few more helpers. And then we'll have everything we need." She motioned behind her, and more figures stepped out of the light hand in hand--Sister Brunhilda, Gwen's grandmother, and finally, Margaretta, her mother.

Mother Seema gave Gwen the same warm and affirming smile that had driven away grief. "Welcome home, my dear, dear Gwendolin."

Epliogue

Death teaches what it is to be alive.
--Mother Gwendolin, Cathuran monk

* * *

Gilly shook the braided rug just outside the doorway, sending dust particles fluttering into the crisp winter air. From just beyond the kitchen garden outside their front door, she heard the uneven thuds of Thomlin's boots on the frozen soil as he limped from the millhouse toward the wagon with a grain sack slung over one shoulder. When she'd set his leg, Mignon had told Thomlin he would suffer dull pains in cold weather, for the slivers of shinbone would knit together imperfectly. His shattered leg would always be slightly shorter than the other. Gilly remembered Mignon questioning Thomlin repeatedly while examining the leg and had found it hard to believe Gwen could have done it alone. According to her mother, the force it had taken to break the leg was like that of more than one full-grown man, and large ones at that. Gwen, whom Thomlin had said swung the plank then threw it away from her as if it were a twig, was just a wisp of a thing. But Thomlin stuck to his story and insisted Gwen had acted alone. How she had mustered the strength to do it remained a mystery.

On cold days such as this, Gilly imagined the once crushed bone in Thomlin's shorter leg must have ached miserably. She could only imagine what he felt because her husband had never once complained about it, not even when asked. Nor had he let it stop him from doing anything that needed doing, including chasing after their children when they'd been young and full of the spritely mischief of their namesakes, Rolf and Gwen.

A cold chill blew past her at the thought of Gwen, and Gilly felt overwhelmed with sadness and a bone-chilling fear. She looked past the wagon in search of her children, who now were young adults.

Thomlin closed the wagon gate and came over to her, kissing her atop her head. "You look worried."

"I don't see the children."

"They're in the woods. Rolf was on about an elusive hare while he was slopping the pigs, and Gwen said she wanted to go with him so that maybe she could talk him out of shooting it."

"I had the strangest feeling, Thomlin."

"About what?" he asked, turning her toward him and cupping her face in his meaty hands. It was what he'd done all their years together to allay her worries.

Despite the wrinkles that had begun to expose his age, Gilly still saw in Thomlin's face the sweet kindness of his youth. "Gwen."

"She's with her brother. You know she's safe."

"Not our Gwen."

"Gwen Ahlgren?"

"Yes," whispered Gilly, "she's gone, Thomlin. I can feel it." Thomlin pulled her close to him and held her. She took comfort in his embrace, but she wept silently.

The silence of her grief was broken by her daughter's voice calling from the edge of the woods. "Mother! You won't believe what we found!"

Gilly wiped her tears and stepped away from Thomlin as her daughter skidded to a stop in front of them, out of breath and followed by her younger but much larger brother.

"What did you see?"

Gwen grinned and uncupped her hands to reveal an uprooted plant, its roots intact in moist soil and at the tip of its stalk a frail violet. "It was the will o' the wisps. They led us to it."

"In daylight? Will o' the wisps?" asked Thomlin.

"Yeah, Pa. That's what I said." Rolf chimed in. "But I tracked 'em all the way outta the woods and to the tree by the road at the old Ahlgren place, and that's when Gwen saw it."

Gilly looked at the violet and smiled, her heart mended by the message from her dearest friend: Gwendolin Ahlgren had finally come home.

Morgen Rich is author of Incorrigible and editor of the Incorrigible prequels Tempest and Nicked.

For more about the authors, please visit MorgenRich.com and BrianRathbone.com.

We hope you enjoy the stories!